Arcanium

CONTORTION

AURELIA T. EVANS

Contortion
ISBN # 978-1-78430-936-7
©Copyright Aurelia T. Evans 2015
Cover Art by Posh Gosh ©Copyright December 2015
Interior text design by Claire Siemaszkiewicz
Totally Bound Publishing

Published in 2015 by Totally Bound Publishing, Newland House, The Point, Weaver Road, Lincoln, LN6 3QN, United Kingdom.

Totally Bound Publishing is a subsidiary of Totally Entwined Group Limited.

CONTORTION

Dedication

For James, with thanks to Amy

Chapter One

Lately, Valorie had been feeling more solo.

Most evenings these last few years, she'd done her act with fellow tumbler Lennon. Victor, the Man Made of Stone, had been thrown into the mix a few weeks ago to add some dimension to the routine, more as a launch pad than anything. The group act made a nice change from the six to eight hours or so of contortion she did on Oddity Row before the evening performances.

But she and Lennon were old hat at their routines, even with Victor added in. It had been a while since she'd made something up for herself and herself alone. Seth and Lars choreographed most of their own performances now, and she did her Oddity Row routine on autopilot these days — graceful but more sculptural than dance, demonstrations of flexibility rather than real skilled artistry.

Still, almost twenty years at Arcanium and she still got clammy hands before going out on her own before an audience.

You can't fall. You can't fall. She knew that. Twenty years, not a single fall. Plenty of jumps, but no falls, no broken bones from any of her acts—not a one. She couldn't make a fool of herself if she tried, and her solo performances numbered in the thousands. But her nerves didn't care what she knew for a fact.

Lennon came up behind her where she leaned against the ladder to the catwalk and whispered in her ear, "Nervous? Your hand is clammy."

"That's just you," Valorie replied. "It's a wonder you don't mold."

"You always did know how to cut a man's heart to ribbons."

"Thanks," she said absentmindedly, staring at the red curtain that separated backstage from the evening's fare.

Lennon kissed her neck. He couldn't kiss her lips when she was painted up like this. Arcanium loved its Halloween season, the performers taking on their creepier and more fantastic personas from October to February, although the color palettes shifted to more wintery than autumnal in December.

She'd taken a cue from the clowns, who weren't the only scary monsters in Arcanium during the Halloween run. Her lips had been painted a rich dark red, smeared along a thick fake scars running along the hollows under her cheekbones. She'd painted over her eyelids and lower-lid line in the same bloody red, her inch-long false eyelashes emerging from black Harlequin markings that stretched from both eyes. Blood-like paint dripped from the scars down over her chin. She planned to go back to her original color eventually, perhaps in the spring, but for now her hair and her eyebrows were a dark purple.

Lennon had taken his Halloween cue from Troy, the Tattooed Man—though he'd kept his shoulder-length black hair untouched while Troy regularly shaved his head to show off the full extent of his body art.

Lennon's eyes glowed electric blue in his darkened sockets, almost as though with contacts, and his teeth were demon sharp, framed by black and white paint that transformed his face into an eerily realistic grinning skull.

If Valorie hadn't known him, he would have been quite frightening. But there were more frightening things than a painted tumbler in the world—hell, even just in Arcanium.

"You'll do fine. Just imagine them all naked. After Lord Mikhail and Lady Sasha finish, that should be enough to take the jitters right out of you, don't you think?" Lennon murmured against her shoulder, his lips brushing the scrolled filigree of tattoos she'd commissioned from Troy, one section of her body at a time. That had been a painful but exhilarating series of weeks. Troy hadn't had Christina yet, so she'd thanked him the usual way a person thanked another in this peculiar circus. His small trailer had rocked almost every night until all the tattoos had healed.

"Or you'll fall in front of everyone, and they'll laugh at your grisly injuries," Lennon added.

"Very helpful," Valorie said drily.

"How's this, love? You get through your performance, and we can have a night of it—just you and me."

Valorie gave him the side-eye.

He'd been living with her for a couple of years—ever since Bell had moved in with Maya, leaving Valorie to her own devices in her expansive RV and no man to warm her bed. Lennon had his own trailer, but it was significantly smaller, and only a stupid person said no to extra accommodations in exchange for regular sex just the way they liked it—fast, rough and without strings. Lennon wasn't stupid.

He'd just been distracted lately, but Valorie's sex drive hadn't waned in the meantime.

"I'll put you through your paces," Valorie said, not quite managing to hide her intrigue. "You've been very neglectful."

"I'll apologize several times over. Cross my heart and hope someone else dies tonight."

"Deal," she said. She reached behind her, searching before stroking the front of his black leather trousers. Oh, he was as attentive as a soldier, this one. Lady Sasha must be doing her snake dance out in the ring right now. Lord Mikhail hadn't performed yet, or else the slow simmer low between her hips would have become a rolling boil by now.

"Not so fast, love," Lennon said, although he certainly didn't try to get away as she rubbed along his length— prodigious, considering his shorter stature. "That'll be one less apology if you keep at it."

"No, it won't," Valorie murmured, her lips less than an inch from his as he panted over her shoulder. "You can't fool me. Besides, we all know what the chicks want from you, don't we? A nice, thick piece of meat they wish they could tear into. But they can't. Because you've promised yourself to me, Lennon. All of this... This is mine tonight. Which means I don't care what Lady Sasha's doing out there, whether she's gone all the way and done a striptease and plans to take Lord Mikhail right in the middle of the ring. You're not going to come. You're going to go out there and do flips and handsprings and splits with a raging hard-on, and you'll do it gladly."

"Gotta give the customers what they want," Lennon breathed, swaggering British bravado gone as he tightened his painful grip on the slight flesh of her strong but thin arm. She had to stay thin. She was too tall to fit into a box that would impress, but she needed to fit into one of those hard vintage suitcases in her exhibition tent on Oddity Row — and sometimes during an evening performance, depending on the night.

His hand on her skin made him look especially pale — white like the underbelly of a fish, although not as sickly. And it made her look especially dark, although she had more than a handful of creams in her coffee and sometimes looked more Latina than black to other people, especially when she dyed her hair blonde.

They couldn't touch lips, but he met her tongue with his, the tip strangely pointed. She licked his tongue with a playful flick before sidling away. In the low light, his erection was nevertheless apparent. Those leather pants Lady Sasha made never hid anything, especially if it varied at all from the norm. That's what they'd been made for.

"You're a bitch," Lennon said, shifting from one foot to the other as he adjusted to his new state and the new fit of his trousers. "Thanks."

"Any time," she replied.

Then she shimmied up the ladder, but not before he gave her latex-covered ass a good smack.

He wasn't really mad. Lennon had gone out and performed with worse. Most of the men had. At least for the women, arousal was easier to conceal from the view of the audience.

In most cases, the audience wouldn't blame them, being surrounded by foxy women and crazy fit men — with a few exceptions, of course. Arcanium was first and foremost a freak show, but not all of them were visibly freakish, and even the freaks had their charms.

As a contortionist, Valorie straddled the line between oddity and performer. She could twist her body into shapes that made people hurt just watching her, but it wasn't conceited to admit she was more conventional than the average oddity, attractive and slim enough for outsider approval — not as slim as Sandra, of course, but no one expected Valorie to be slimmer than the circus' Human Skeleton.

Her confidence began to return up on the catwalk, and not just because her dark purple and black harlequin latex costume made her imagine herself as some kind of superhero scaling city heights. Up here she felt like she was already in her performance — the long walk to its start, her feet bare and sawdusty but graceful as she made her way.

She wished her costume matched the red of her makeup, but she had to distinguish herself from Maya's year-long palette of black and red. The girl rocked it better than any other variation, so Valorie let her have it, but that eliminated a sartorial favorite if Valorie wanted to stand out at all. Arcanium went default black leather when the Halloween season came up, but late spring, summer and early fall was the fantasy faire circuit, and they'd go more into subdued browns and creams. Valorie could rock white, cream and gold so much better than Maya, so she had that going for her during the hotter part of the year.

Valorie had lost all her jealousy for Maya's relationship with Bell, which had arisen after Bell had spent seventeen years with Valorie and discarded her practically the minute Maya was cursed into Arcanium. But that didn't mean she couldn't be petty and jealous of Maya for other reasons — the kinds of things that a woman was often jealous of in another woman. Two of them were quite prominent on Maya's chest.

But Maya couldn't lick her own pussy if such a thing struck her fancy, so that was another point in Valorie's favor.

The latex molded itself to her body. It was an unforgiving fabric, even more so than leather, but Valorie prided herself on there being nothing to forgive. With a little help from Bell and Lady Sasha, it became supple enough for her needs but didn't stretch itself out after only one or two wearings.

God bless dark magic.

Valorie smoothed her hands over her abdomen, up over her breasts. The suit had built-in support and some shaping, but there was something to being able to wear a plunging neckline without having to deal with boobs falling out. It meant that the audience couldn't fantasize about it the way they did with Maya or Lady Sasha. But she didn't have to be psychic to know that, with her, the audience fantasized about other things.

She stroked down to her hips. She sensed the second Lord Mikhail stepped out into the ring, because her hands were drawn to her pussy almost against her own volition. Valorie groaned. That feeling never got old, and it was early enough in the spike of lust that it wasn't frustrating. It helped knowing she'd be taken care of when the performance was over.

Seth and Lars were already on the platform right above the ring, but their hands were in places on each other that told her she should pretend she wasn't there yet. Valorie still didn't understand why they didn't come out of the closet about their singular relationship. Everybody knew about it. They literally couldn't keep their hands off each other—they'd been cursed that way. It wouldn't be the most scandalous thing to happen in Arcanium. Hell, these days it was almost normal. It wasn't like the cast would needle the boys about it.

Okay, a little needling. Friendly mocking. They'd been here five years now. They were family, as weird as family could be in Arcanium, and family earned some grief.

Still, since the two young men kept their relationship quiet, there had been a kind of understanding among the cast—even with Joanne and Jane, the conjoined twins whom they clearly loved as well—that no one would call them on their denial. No one asked whether they'd been wrestling the night before because their RV had been rocking so hard. No one mentioned that the way they touched each other's bare torsos all the time was in no way one-hundred-percent straight, no matter how bro they tried to be about it.

Valorie shook her head, but she stayed on the backstage side of the catwalk, cocooned in its darkness while the men gleamed from the bright ring lights beneath them. She'd had both men. It wasn't like it would hurt their reputation if they came out as bisexual. They were excellent fuck partners with women, and she guessed they'd be just as good with men.

Nevertheless, the illusion of their secrecy had to be maintained, because in Arcanium, people rarely talked about who was hooking up with whom—at least to their faces. In a circus, there was precious little privacy, and everyone guarded what privacy they were allowed.

It was rare anyone managed to actually keep their relationship a secret, though—not impossible, just exceptionally difficult. Kitty, the Bearded Lady, had done it for hell knew how long. Covered with reddish brown hair from head to toe, not to mention a full and lovely beard that often hung down to her navel, she wasn't exactly inconspicuous. Neither was her man, the barrel-chested, devilishly handsome Ringmaster who now announced Seth and Lars' aerial act. Yet they'd done it. No one except Bell had known about them until they'd made themselves known — and Bell didn't count.

Then Valorie was alone on the catwalk. Maya would join her after Seth and Lars were finished, but for now, she was high and horny, and that was enough to dispel the rest of her nerves, especially when she settled on her round swing like a canary in a cage.

Through Seth and Lars' formidable aerial acrobatics act below, Arcanium started to show its stripes as the circus of the impossible — of illusions that the most cynical and skeptical audience members could never crack, even the ones who were magicians themselves. Of shock and awe and spectacle and magic, of childlike and not-so-childlike wonder. There was absolutely no way anyone could look at the way that Lord Mikhail and Lady Sasha displayed themselves in their strength and balance routine — or the way that Seth's and Lars' bodies slid over each other, like erotic artists oiled with sweat and desire — and think that any wonder it incited was childlike.

There was a reason that Arcanium was closed to anyone under eighteen after eight o'clock at night.

In purple latex, bloody wicked face paint and thick gold thread that held the separate Frankensteined pieces of the costume together — exposing that she wore no bra or underwear and calling attention her tits and ass without shame — Valorie was just another reason, and she knew it.

The boys came back up into the heavens and dismounted their trapeze bars, body language similar to Lennon's when she'd left him. She met their eyes, glanced down at their prominent bulges then returned her gaze up with a small smile on her lips. Seth blushed easily, pale in a different way than Lennon. If Lars blushed, she wouldn't be able to see it, dark as he was. They were a tasty pair. If only they knew how tasty they'd be together for all to see, how the twins would love to see them love each other, how Valorie wouldn't mind watching them make out for an hour so.

Misha, the sword swallower, and Carlo, one of the Human Torsos, were quiet but not secretive about their relationship—mostly because Carlo was a randy little fucker, and while he had a special place in his heart for Misha, he'd screw anything that stood still and parted their legs. He was as shameless in his desires as Seth and Lars were ashamed, although not quite so shameless as to snog Misha in front of everyone.

It wouldn't be the same, though. Carlo was an attractive man. As half a man, he was still twice the man that most were. Misha, not so much. It wouldn't be the same as seeing two hot young things like Seth and Lars.

Alas, that was something she still had to keep in her fantasies.

One of these days. And she'd be there to see it. She'd been their sexual introduction to Arcanium. They owed her that much. Just a kiss on each other's lips. She didn't think it was much to ask.

The spotlight, blue for Seth and Lars' act, went white again. Victor ran out, his stone-gray and pitted skin rippling. He was a treasure to look at—not quite as alarming as Bale, the Lizard Man. It was as though he'd been carved from boulder stone and would grow moss at any minute, but his skin was supple as skin could be. The places where Lennon stood on his shoulders pushed in like normal flesh. It looked like he was wearing a particularly convincing body suit and had a genius of a makeup artist. Circus-goers often discreetly looked for zippers, seams and brushstrokes on the stranger of Arcanium's oddities. There weren't any to be found.

Victor held Lennon by his calves as he ran, straight-backed. Lennon took over the brunt of his balance, but it still had to be like standing on a running horse without a saddle or reins.

Lennon was good at what he did. He'd been performing much longer than Valorie, and he'd been the one to teach her tumbling and acrobatics in her early years. He was steady, as though standing on solid ground.

When Victor reached the center of the ring, he abruptly stopped and released Lennon's legs. Lennon leaped from Victor's shoulders, flipping what seemed an impossible number of rotations before landing on the ground and continuing in a summersault to the wooden partition of the ring.

He hit it with his feet then, like a swimmer, somersaulted backward to return to Victor, who lifted him from under his arms and tossed him into the air. When Lennon came back down, still tucked like a pill bug and spinning, Victor caught him by his back and threw him up as though he were a basketball, over and over again to the rhythm of the industrial orchestra playing through the speakers.

As soon as the audience would be getting dizzy, Lennon popped open and landed on his hands on Victor's shoulders. Then, stiff as a board, he fell back until he touched down on his feet in the sawdust.

Introduction concluded.

What followed was a series of higher jumps and more elaborate twists, like watching a diver in the Olympics attempt to do his routine above the ground instead of water. Victor gave him additional height, but Lennon still impressed the audience. They'd been greased by many of the prior performances and were easy to please, but that didn't mean that their pleasure was undeserved.

Valorie was so often a part of the routine that she quite enjoyed just being able to watch them, even if it was from an unenviable position above. She knew what it *would* look like from a better vantage point, though. She'd always been good at seeing potential.

She thought that was one of the reasons Bell had taken her into his bed and into his confidence way back then. She couldn't see into the future to save her ass, but she was usually good at guessing. In another circus, she might have been the fortune teller instead of Bell — another circus and another temperament. She preferred dealing with the public from a distance. She had to display herself for hours on end, but at least they had to stay out of reach and she didn't have to acknowledge the fourth wall.

When Lennon and Victor retreated behind the curtain once again to thunderous applause, the white light shifted to gold that would turn her skin to honey.

The catwalk crew member, silent and dressed in black, lowered her swing down the center of the ring. The spotlight, gentler than when the whole ring was being used, caught her as she descended past the canvas that separated the catwalk in the heavens from the ring. She kept herself perfectly still, her legs tucked and crossed like a secretary's, although she didn't know of many secretaries who wore latex catsuits to their jobs. There were probably a few bosses who wished they did.

"In one of the most anticipated acts of the night," the Ringmaster intoned from his platform, his voice low, sensual, mysterious and resonant through her bones, "our world-renowned contortionist returns to the spotlight, bringing her singular, sexy, spine-aching skill to the air. Give a warm hand, mere mortals, to the darling of the broken dolls, Miss Valorie."

The Ringmaster loved his job way too much, as much as a man like the Ringmaster could love anything. Which, as it turned out, was quite a lot—although a person would never be able to tell when he wasn't in the ring.

Still, once they got used to it, Valorie was pretty sure almost everyone in Arcanium liked their job way too much. Things could be worse—much worse.

Valorie had chosen an electric violin piece to perform to, but first she had to milk the silence that followed the applause.

After a single extended note, Valorie came to life.

She leaned back, swinging down. Her knees, still crossed, kept her on the swing as she cascaded her hands down in elegant twists. She kept going, though, once she stretched as far down as she could reach, arching her spine backward until she could grab her ankles, uncross her legs and climb up her legs to her knees. Her body made an almost perfect circle, a nonviolent ouroboros. She held her position as the swing began to turn, displaying her from all angles like a piece of crystal in an auction house.

The applause was sincere but polite.

It was okay. The show was just getting started.

She let go of one leg and extended it straight behind her to show off its length, swinging on the circle by one knee as she counted the click of the ticking sound like a clock hand on the music track.

Then she took hold of the swing with her hands and unfurled her body, turning it into a pendulum. Back and forth. Back and forth. More force each time. She used the built momentum to kick her legs forward and push herself back up before spreading her legs and catching the upper part of the circular swing with her ankles.

Valorie released her hands from the swing again, holding herself upside down by her ankles alone, her back against the bar as she spread her arms and accepted the audience's applause. She didn't linger too long this time. She slid her ankles along the edges of the circle until she was hanging just by the juncture of her bridges at the swing's widest point.

She was flexible, not immune to pain, and it did hurt holding herself up like that, but it was worth it for the image. Her ability was all about the pictures she could make. This was no different.

She climbed her upper half up her legs again, keeping the tendon tension all along the line of her body to keep herself aloft by her feet. She breathed a sigh of relief when she grabbed the bar and let her ankles off before swinging back up into the circle.

For the next minute and a half of the song, she took a short break from the acrobatic element and focused on her contortion. The swing was roughly between half and three-quarters of her height in circumference, so it wasn't easy to fit herself in it without making angles of herself within the frame.

The angles themselves, though, were easy. The jerky, minor-key eeriness of the music coupled with her face paint meant that she could go as bizarre as she wanted, twitching her limbs and even her neck into painful, broken angles. She rotated her arms and legs and spine at least one twist beyond what the usual contortionist could do, her tendons stretching but not screaming, all to the mingled delight and disgust of the audience. She moved about in the swing like a spider in her web. With the right grasp and strength, gravity and orientation meant very little to her. It made no difference whether she was upside-down, sideways or right-side-up — or some variation of the three, depending on where her legs happened to be in relation to her head at any given time.

She ended that section of the act in a handstand, her legs straight up on either side of the top of the circle.

The violin became more frantic, and her moves more graceless, like she was going to lose her balance at any point from the harshness of her movements. Valorie brought her legs down along the curved line of the circle again, but this time not holding on to it with her ankles. She could lean her legs against the bar, but her only hold was still her hands. Like a clock with its hands out of sync, she brought her legs down, beat by beat, into the splits. Then farther…and farther…and farther, until they both pointed straight down. She jerked her feet to the side, locking them together.

And let go.

She swung down on nothing more than the locked arches of her feet. That's when the applause thundered in her ears like sea in a shell, making the scream of the violin less shrill as she spread her arms again and extended them down. Her body became a human iris hanging from the swing.

Following the climax of the song, Valorie drew herself back up with an upside-down plié, climbed into the circle, raised one long leg then tucked it behind her head, the ankle around the top of the swing. The swing ascended into the heavens once again as she waved goodbye with her arm twisted behind her back.

Piece of cake. Her nerves could kiss her ass.

* * * *

Contortion involved being in tune with her body and what it was capable of. It involved knowing where her center settled, how long she could accept a little bit of pain without injury, knowing how far she could go, trusting skin, sinew and bone. It involved complete awareness.

And awareness and arousal — like arousal and fear — were not so far apart. She could practically hear the men and some of the women in the audience wonder what it would be like to have sex with her when she spread her legs or arched her back and her neck as though in ecstasy — and always just a little farther, like she could do one better than anyone else, including pleasure. It was no wonder that she started her performance turned on and ended it nearly in a frenzy, although she appeared composed. It didn't matter how many performances she'd done. She'd be the first to say that, like the Ringmaster, like Seth and Lars, like Lord Mikhail and Lady Sasha, like Maya, like Bell, like Lennon, like most of the rest of the cast...

Valorie loved her job just a little too much.

Latex wasn't the best material to get wet, but there was no helping it by the end of a performance. The ring was kept cool with a series of fans this time of year rather than their usual air conditioners, because of how cold it was outside and how warm it could become inside the big top tent. So her temples felt damp and the latex stuck to her skin in a few places, but it was between her legs that she was most uncomfortable, like her pussy was wearing a patent leather shoe.

She hurried down the ladder as Misha broke up the acrobatic acts with his sword-swallowing, sacrificing grace completely in favor of the sometimes humorous, sometimes gut-wrenching gross-out. The audience would never know just how gross it really was.

However, no matter how much Misha looked like he was going to kick the bucket any day now, he somehow managed to make his act engaging and more disgusting than outright alarming.

The cast didn't do curtain calls. Valorie didn't have to stay for Maya and Bell's closing. In fact, during the performance was usually the best time to leave, when there were no adoring fans trying to weasel themselves in where they weren't wanted, on edge and hard and not always in the mood to hear no from a professional tease.

Fuck that noise. Valorie wasn't interested in looking outside the circus for her pleasure. The isolation of the circus could be suffocating, but she also didn't feel comfortable walking among the normals anymore. Though she wasn't as extreme as Joanne and Jane or Kitty in appearance, she'd stopped feeling normal early in her tenure at Arcanium.

The truth was, she'd lost her patience with the outside. Arcanium was a world of illusion, but not anywhere near what the rest of the world was. When the curtain closed and the lights went out, the illusions ended. Valorie respected—needed—that honesty, even when it could be cruel, like she could sometimes be. She hardly distinguished herself in that way, in good company within the circus.

Some wouldn't be proud of it, and she wasn't. That's simply the way her life was these days, and it mostly worked for her, although life at Arcanium had soured a little after Bell had moved out. Lennon was *a* man to fuck. Just like Victor. Or Ciàran and Moss, the circus' Tall Man and Short Man. Or Seth and Lars. They were there, and it was fun, but she didn't even just fuck Bell anymore. *That* had meant more to her. Lennon and Valorie had their own chemistry, but it wasn't anything that could last. And she had miles to go before she slept, a long time before she left the circus for a normal life again.

A normal life.

Even if she wanted to, Valorie didn't know if she *could* leave anymore.

She left through the backstage exit, passing by the lion and tiger sitting placidly outside their cages. They'd finished their act with the Ringmaster, Carlo and Christina and were relaxing before they had to be put back in.

Fleet of foot and nearly silent without shoes on, she ran to the part of the circus grounds where they kept their cavalcade of trailers and RVs.

The light wasn't on inside her RV, but Lennon didn't need light to see or feel his way through. It was big for an RV, small for an apartment. There wasn't much to get lost in.

She was about to open the door to step in so that she could finally peel the latex off for Lennon's private viewing pleasure. He didn't like taking clothes off her, because there was almost always a trick to it. He liked watching her do it for him.

But she stopped when she glanced over at Lennon's RV, with the metal trailer attached — like a horse trailer but with smaller windows, temperature control and a few additional custom amenities. Her sinking-stomach hunch paid off in the worst way when she noticed that, though there weren't lights on in his tiny wreck of an RV, the light was on in the trailer. The light was blue, dim. Too much light hurt Melanie's eyes.

Valorie stepped lightly toward the trailer. Quietly as she could, she opened the door and peered inside.

The tank was about the size and volume of six large, full bathtubs. It was clear, framed with steel, utterly empty except for the woman who lived in it. There were buttons on the outside, shielded by plastic covering that allowed the woman to push them without getting water on the board. They controlled filtration, temperature, jets, salinity, like a large, clear fish tank combined with a spa tub.

The setup wasn't as luxurious as it sounded. It lacked the hominess of aquariums. Instead, the tank had the clinical cast of a magician's escape prop.

This was Melanie's home for the foreseeable future. Unless they stopped somewhere with a lake or a pond that wasn't dormant or filthy with algae, Melanie stayed here or in the smaller tank in her exhibition tent, where she was transferred every Friday, Saturday and Sunday. She wasn't getting out of her restrictive body any time soon, so she wasn't getting out of the water either. Bell was too mad at her.

It didn't make a difference, really, that Melanie and her friends had threatened Maya in particular, as well as Christina and Troy. If there was something to say for Bell, it was that he took deep, personal offense to outsiders threatening *any* of his people, not just his favorites. Melanie was stuck with her tail for the foreseeable. She should be grateful that Bell even allowed her, John and Shawn to talk now that he trusted them not to scream for help.

Valorie brought her eye to the crack, keeping her lips pressed tightly together to remind her not to make a sound.

Melanie swam up to the surface of the water, her long bluish-green mermaid tail curling like a sea serpent behind her. She propped her elbows on the edge of the tank to watch Lennon by the smaller tanks in the back of the trailer as he caught fish and put them into a small container. Melanie could stomach human food, but her cravings ran wilder. The end of her tail lashed like a cat's, and she vocalized her hunger through a gill-slashed throat. The slits were closed, her lungs taking precedence above water.

"There's a good girl," Lennon crooned as he came around to the bench next to the tank. He stood on it, too short to reach the edge without the boost. "Who wants a nibble?"

"Stop teasing," Melanie said. Her voice wasn't what it used to be. It seemed to double back in on itself and echo, as though she used both sets of vocal cords at once. Her sharp, conical, snaggled teeth clicked together. She stared down at Lennon with her too-large, frustrated eyes. The limpid eyelid that covered them in the water had retracted. Her long brown hair plastered itself to her face, neck and shoulders like seaweed.

Melanie curled her bluish lips in revulsion as Lennon held the wriggling sardine up to her mouth, but that didn't stop her from snapping hungrily forward like a seal. She gnashed her teeth as she held the tail, ripping pieces off the living fish and swallowing them whole with a backward toss of her head. Finally, she threw the tail in. Her webbed, clawed fingers were coated with remnants of fish scales, but she didn't clean herself off, because Lennon had more.

He watched, utterly entranced, as Melanie ate fish after fish, although after a while the ones he gave her no longer wriggled.

As soon as he took a few for himself, Valorie realized he really wasn't coming back to her RV tonight. Valorie wasn't partial to the smell and taste of raw fish. He'd completely forgotten about his promise. She wanted to slam the door shut and take care of herself as best as she could for the night, preferably by imagining how she was going to get him back for bailing.

In spite of that, she remained. Neither Melanie nor Lennon were going to notice, engaged in their fishy feast as they were. If they did notice, Valorie didn't particularly care. Lennon was the one who had something to apologize for. Valorie was part of the contingent in Arcanium who still shunned Melanie and her original companions—all part of the process when new cast members were brought in under…inauspicious circumstances.

Not that Melanie, John and Shawn were companions much anymore. Melanie's limitations meant that she spent most of her time isolated. Shawn might have been her boyfriend before they'd become a part of the circus, but he was dealing with his own shit, as was John. They suffered alone, the way Bell had intended.

Except for Melanie, who apparently got Lennon, which could be considered either a blessing or a curse. With that short, arrogant bastard, it was kind of hard to tell.

Once the container of fish was empty, Lennon set it on the bench. Then Melanie submerged herself, lanky, wet hair becoming lustrous underwater. She clasped her hands between her breasts, bare in privacy and bobbing up and down independently from the rest of her body as she curled into the corner. She watched Lennon through the glass, not trying to run away from him but waiting.

Afterbirth from a perforated asshole, Valorie swore to herself as Lennon brought his hands to the front of his black, skintight leather trousers. His erection hadn't waned in the slightest since Valorie had stroked him to hardness. If it had, it had reared back up with a vengeance as he'd fed Melanie fish one by one, like an ordinary man feeding his lover strawberries.

But Lennon wasn't an ordinary man—not in the same way that Melanie was no longer an ordinary woman. Lennon had never been a normal man.

His teeth, like Melanie's, were often thought to be prosthetics by circus-goers. His eyes could be special contacts. But there was no way for someone to explain Lennon's skin changing from near white to a sickly chartreuse, nor his black hair dreading and writhing into suckerless tentacles, black anemones that moved over his shoulders like Melanie's hair in the water.

It was little effort for a tumbler like Lennon to vault from the metal edge of the tank into the water without splashing. He sank to the bottom, able to breathe through his mouth and nose underwater as easily as above. The dark red flush of his cock contrasted with his greenish skin, which didn't appear so sickly against Melanie's cyanotic cast.

They seemed made for each other. Melanie might not have been thrilled about the attentions of a demon, but she didn't resist anymore.

If she'd once denied him, she now actively welcomed his ability to rub the itch that the incubus and succubus, Lord Mikhail and Lady Sasha, gave the circus. The desire grew even more intense during performance nights, when the sex demons actively sent their magic out. It sometimes turned excruciating if they also fed on afterhours trespassers, as the guard dogs of Arcanium— like the clowns, except not quite so gruesome in their killing.

Lennon stroked Melanie's wild seaweed hair. His trill rippled and bubbled the water as Melanie leaned into his touch then pushed herself up to kiss him. They cupped each other's faces with their long fingers, the webbing between more pronounced than in the average human being. Lennon had been predator longer than

Melanie. It was he who seemed to devour her, pushing her against the side of the tank as her tail lashed around his legs like ribbon.

Valorie couldn't hear much beyond the lapping of the water against the top of the tank from their movements inside. Lennon was a rough-and-tumble kind of man who screwed a woman the same way he did his routines. He didn't mind getting dirty, and he was still incredibly skilled. It didn't hurt that he was demon and, by virtue of his heritage, could seduce a businesswoman to part with every hard-earned cent of her salary in a heartbeat if greed struck his fancy.

Valorie felt very strongly that a girl never really lived until she had a demon cock inside her. Ciàran and Bell in his true form had been impossibly, frighteningly big. As humans, they'd cause damage, and Valorie knew they *could* cause damage if that was ever their intention. But most of the time in Arcanium, pleasure was the aim — and even when pain and torture were a part of it, the subject of the attention didn't always complain.

Valorie wasn't quite as depraved as that. She'd never been much for masochism, and she didn't like obedience. If a demon was going to tell her what to do, she'd better get something better than just pleasure out of it. And if she told them what to do — if they'd earned that honor — they needed to give her the same courtesy that she showed them.

The demons couldn't take the humans in Arcanium against their will. And the incubus and succubus couldn't have them at all, for obvious reasons — Bell liked keeping his cast around, even the ones he wanted to suffer. They were his alone to curse, the Ringmaster's to punish if they broke the circus rules, and not for any of the other demons to play with, at least not without the human's enthusiastic permission.

So Valorie didn't *like* Lennon, but she'd respected him and liked him inside her. She'd thought he respected her too, respected the honor she'd given him—at least enough to keep his promises.

He made his way down from Melanie's mouth to her breasts. His teeth had left behind flushed marks where he hadn't broken the skin. Melanie's face twisted as though in pain, her mouth gaping open, but it was her gills that flapped with gasps of air.

Lennon gripped the frill on her hips that ran down to just below her abdomen. Her tail showed signs of the thighs that had once been, but with her legs forever closed in her new form, alterations had had to be made.

Valorie didn't know whether mermaids really existed or if Bell had just made Melanie into what people thought a mermaid could look like. If they did exist, Valorie couldn't speak to the accuracy of Melanie's mermaid anatomy, but it seemed logical to her. A flap of thicker scales acted like a kind of loincloth where the apex of her thighs would have been. As Lennon moved his hands in toward it, the scales retracted and parted like a curtain to reveal Melanie's pussy, the delicate clam of folds leading up to her pretty pink clitoris.

Valorie wouldn't have been surprised if Melanie had played with her new self in her early days plenty despite her terror and disorientation, especially with the incubus influencing her from afar, able to see her own bits for the first time. Valorie remembered doing the same. It was quite different touching oneself when one could see the equipment. No wonder men liked playing with themselves all the time and didn't understand why women didn't.

While Valorie had literally been homicidal when Maya had taken Bell away, Valorie wasn't mad at Melanie for letting Lennon at her, shunned or not. He was as relentless as he was generous when he wanted something. It was no wonder she'd eventually caved. But Valorie was fucking *furious* at Lennon. There was no reason his attention span should have been so short, even with the lure of a water woman.

Unless he really *was* finished with Valorie. She wasn't heartbroken. Bell had broken the heart she hadn't known she had, not Lennon. But that didn't mean she didn't have feelings and that they weren't hurt. The demons couldn't physically harm humans, but damn, they could still offer a girl the world and stab her in the back with a shattered globe.

Now he slithered his inhumanly long tongue through Melanie's furrow and into her pussy as he rubbed frantically at her clit, making her arch, arch, arch almost horizontal in the water, her cry bubbling from her gills in a torrent. Lennon didn't give her any relief, his tentacles caressing her tail and her stomach and his tongue sliding farther into her, twisting, licking, probing until Melanie thrashed with both sets of her eyelids closed.

Lennon climbed up her body and bit the cord of her neck as he thrust his dark cock into her pussy, the folds stretching around him, clinging to the shaft as though grasping and pulling him in the aftershocks. With the novel angle of the mermaid's anatomy, Valorie could see everything, every thrust. Nothing was hidden.

Valorie had to watch as Lennon took the woman, thrusting into her at a furious, frantic, forceful pace that Valorie wanted for herself. Her latex clung to her like a second skin, warm from arousal, wet between her legs, and she wanted cock so badly. If frigging herself would do any good against incubus magic, she would have sworn everyone else off entirely after being ousted from Bell's bed, but a girl still had needs when the sex demons spread their magic like a constant pulsating mist over the circus. Dealing with it herself only worked for a little while.

She'd never had to go very long without sex. She didn't know how some of the others did it, waiting days, weeks or even years between sexual encounters. While Melanie regularly got some, Valorie was pretty sure that John and Shawn didn't, and until last year the two men on the carousel had gone years to decades without so much as a touch. It was a wonder they hadn't gone batshit nuts, the way she felt right now.

Valorie slammed the door shut, not bothering to pretend she hadn't been there. Let Lennon know why she locked her door against him. He could stay in his shack of a trailer or sleep with his pretty fish if that's what he really wanted.

The evening performance concluded, the audience was leaving out the gates in bulk. People, her people, were returning or had already returned in broken groups, usually couples. Any of the ones she'd accept in her bed were already paired off, sometimes twice. She wouldn't want any of the ones left over.

She wondered if she was allowed to deputize a golem, the mindless drones that made up the circus crew. They were technically zombies, but they were well-preserved and obedient to Bell. A few of them were even attractive. She was sure she could convince Bell to let her have one as a toy for a while.

But that made her feel even cheaper. She was no slouch in the bedroom. She knew it. Everyone else knew it. It was difficult to be *bad* in bed in Arcanium. Part of it was just another side effect of the sex demons' influence, but she'd also had enough experience and variety in her life to please any man with a taste for women, even outside the circus' boundaries and influence.

Valorie wasn't looking for a husband or a life of domesticity. She'd already had that. She wasn't looking for forever when nothing but a demon could promise that with a straight face. She wasn't looking for true love. She was only looking for consistent sex and a man to make her feel good, like a queen instead of just another fucking princess.

So why was she going home alone yet again?

John abruptly stopped to avoid running into her on the way to his trailer.

"What are you looking at, Freddy?" Valorie snapped.

A good portion of his face gleamed with mostly healed burns. The circus often received comments about how strange it was to have a fire-eater with such a severely wounded face. When he performed in the ring, the Ringmaster introduced him as the victim of a terrible fire accident in his youth that had led to his new obsession. His features weren't melted together like in some other burn cases, but the skin on about three-fourths of his face had the appearance of dark, partially melted candle wax. His eyes were bright and too beautiful to be allowed. One eye even still had its eyelashes.

However, she hadn't forgotten the reason he got to have his pretty face burned and healed over and over again. John, like the other two, had seemed to learn his lesson and his place in Arcanium within a year. Separate from his friends and under the knuckles of his curse, he'd become far more placid. But that didn't let him off the fucking hook, and he should have known better than to stare at her like she was still a freak in her exhibition tent.

John shrugged, flinching from the bite of her tongue. He could speak now without burning his throat, tongue and lips every time, but he turned his head away from her to continue past Lennon's trailer and out of Valorie's line of sight.

Again, she didn't bother holding back as she slammed her RV door and jerked the locks closed.

She peeled the latex off and left it on the floor like a serpent's shed skin. She grabbed the bar that Bell had mounted into the ceiling and slipped her legs over it, hanging naked, upside-down like a vampire, blood rushing to her head. It was supposed to calm her down, but it just made the roaring in her ears worse.

If she'd had any of her wishes left, she'd visit Bell in a bare second to wish for a man to exorcise this need, someone she could have on the regular instead of jumping from man to man, bed to bed. Kitty might be equipped for that kind of life. Caroline, the carousel engineer and a mostly normal girl, might be equipped for handling two men at once. But Valorie just wished she could *feel* loved again, even if she hadn't really been loved by Bell the first time. She just needed *something*.

As long as she didn't get to the point where she'd take anything.

That's what scared her.

Chapter Two

It didn't matter that she was hornier than a teenage boy when she woke up. She still had to get her makeup back on, her purple and black catsuit pieced together and zipped up, and her hair smoothed down in time to climb into her suitcase for the beginning of the exhibition on Oddity Row — the area of the circus that formed a crescent around one half of the big top tent. It was exhibition tent after exhibition tent of freaks on display, and from opening to evening performance, she was one of those freaks.

From opening to evening performance — with breaks for a snack and a drink and to walk around the circus, showing off her skills up close and personal if the mood struck her. That had comprised her Fridays and weekends for almost twenty years.

Oddly enough, those moments in the closed suitcase before the gates opened and the customers found their way to the Row were her most peaceful, limbs folded and wrapped and her head against her foot, mouth close to some of the air holes that lined the side so she wouldn't suffocate.

If someone had told Valorie twenty years ago she was going to be a contortionist in a circus full of demons and trapped souls that was run by a wish-fulfilling jinni—and that she'd be mostly okay with that—she would have never believed it. For one thing, it sounded like a mash-up of fairy tales and horror stories gone wrong. For another, before being brought into Arcanium, Valorie hadn't been able to touch her own toes, much less bring her head all the way between her knees and climb out the other side.

Arcanium consisted of three types of beings. There were the demons. Then there were the humans who had signed on voluntarily—although they might not have known at the time that roughly half the cast were actually monsters, and not always the ones they would have expected. Then there were humans who had been brought in against their will.

Among the involuntaries, some had been brought in because of a wish they'd made that Bell had twisted for the express purpose of adding another oddity or act to his line-up. Not all of the people he cursed became a part of Arcanium—which could be a good or terrible thing, depending on the wish. The other subset of involuntaries were the ones harshly cursed into Arcanium as punishment for some sin they'd committed against the circus and its people.

Valorie had been cursed in by a casual wish. She'd since transitioned into a voluntary cast member, which meant she could step outside the wrought-iron fence without excruciating pain followed by a few lashes of the Ringmaster's whip. It also meant that she could leave permanently if she chose. She could terminate her unwritten contract, return to the world of normal.

She wasn't sure if she'd be able to take her ability with her, but she felt Bell owed her that much. He wasn't human, and though he was telepathic, that didn't mean he always understood the emotional aftermath of his actions. He could see into the past, present and future, which was the reason he was Arcanium's fortune teller. But a being that could see out in both directions didn't always understand that the space between present and future could be littered with shrapnel. Kitty and Maya tried to help him understand, with little success. Valorie hadn't had as much of a problem with it until she'd become the collateral damage in his foresight games.

That probably made her a bitch, but Valorie didn't have a problem with that either. Most of the newbies hadn't been here more than a few years. Valorie had done her time. She was the human who'd been here the longest, even longer than Kitty. She'd had to claw from struggling against the inevitable to accepting her fate to actively embracing it, and she didn't think it was Stockholm syndrome that kept her here, the way it was for some.

She didn't see the demons as anything more or less than they were. No one liked where they were, what they did and who they had to do it with *all* the time. A person learned to handle their life or change it, and she liked hers enough now not to change it, even though Bell wouldn't deny her if she tried.

The key was to not resist it for a few years. The more a person resisted, the tighter Bell held them in with the reins of their wishes. A human being needed to give their service to the circus long enough to enrich it, like an indentured servant paying a debt. And those cursed in for punishment needed to wait like prisoners through the full length of their sentence, which was usually longer than just a few years. Jinn were immortal. In addition to having a long memory, Bell knew how to bear a grudge and had a profound sense of retribution.

It was best not to piss jinn off. A demon was just a jinni who had gone all dark, who sought destruction in all its forms, especially against humanity. Jinn were less one-sided. But with all their power, especially Bell, they were still dangerous as hell and capable of evil things. Just like humans with missile silos

In her early days, Valorie had felt the vengeful lash of the Ringmaster's whip, although not as often as Maya. No one got lashed more than Maya, but that was because she asked for it, crazy woman that she was. In time, though, Valorie had become acquainted with and accepted Bell's colder side, and she'd accepted the terrible things the demons did as long as they didn't do them to her. Demons could be whipped too if they stepped out of line, and it hurt them just as much.

After her third session with the Ringmaster and hearing too many badly worded wishes, Valorie had learned to be more careful and color within the — albeit unconventional — lines. It had been over ten years since her last whipping session, but that was only because Maya's second wish had stopped her from incurring the worst of Bell's wrath. Valorie probably wouldn't have had a back to speak of for months, and she would have lost Bell anyway. Even now, she probably wouldn't have completely healed. Bell was powerful enough that he could keep a wound around for a long time.

That was his power — the power not just of wishes but of his whim, within the framework of a wish. He could make one wish last centuries if the logic was sound.

Valorie could still remember the day Bell had granted her first wish.

She hadn't been in Bell's fortune teller tent like most of them. She'd been walking past it, wearing jeans she wouldn't be caught dead in now.

Valorie had been enjoying one of the days off she'd jumped through all the right hoops to get, and she'd arranged for co-workers to cover for her if anything came up. Because, damn it, she'd wanted her week-long vacation. She hadn't used all of her vacation days since getting the job, and this had been her third year in. She'd sacrificed her plans the last two years. She wasn't sacrificing this time.

So when her boss had called her right before she'd decided to get a turkey leg for lunch — fuck her diet — Valorie had silently fumed. She'd been about ready to throw away her bulky nineties mobile phone and live off the land by the time her boss had told her he wanted her to come back in. She had been three hours away from work and four hours away from home, but her boss had told her it didn't matter if she had to return in her casual clothes for the afternoon. She just needed to come in. It had been an emergency, sure, but it had been an emergency that other people in her part of the office could have handled.

She'd realized at that point how much of a prick her boss was, but she couldn't tell him that.

What she'd said within Bell's hearing was, "Look, sir, I wish you'd give me a little flexibility on this."

After that, she hadn't had to go back to work anymore.

As far as everyone knew, Valorie Cain was a missing person, presumed dead after seven years. Valorie didn't know what her boss or her co-workers had thought happened to her. Probably nothing flattering. It wasn't them or the work she missed. It had been a job, something to give her income and benefits until she found something better, and damn straight she'd been looking.

But being kidnapped into Arcanium hadn't exactly been the escape route she'd had in mind.

She'd started out doing standard and not-so-standard contortion in her tent. That had been all Bell had required of her as she'd adjusted to her new life and the fact that she couldn't run away from it, no matter what she tried. Craft and cunning couldn't measure up to magic.

After a month, Bell had given her a circular platform in the middle of the ring during the weekly rehearsals and told her she had to perform the following weekend. In the early days, he'd given her direction, shown her how far her body could go—which was farther than it ever should have gone.

Valorie had no medical training, but she was pretty sure some of the shit she did wasn't supposed to be possible without grievous bodily injury, even for the most flexible contortionist. She wouldn't know. The only training she had was from Bell, not from dancers or kinesiologists or people familiar with the limits of human anatomy. Bell didn't know limits. If he could have reasonably pushed her body further and not had people think it was a trick rather than a feat, he would have done that to her. Fortunately, it never hurt.

In some ways, she had to thank him. There were monks in Tibet who hadn't contemplated their own navel as much as she had. She could spend a week focusing on all the things she could do with one toe. That was how attuned she was. Most people—her old self included—went through their lives as though their bodies were merely vehicles. Or enemies. Because of all the time Bell had spent with her in those early days, coaxing her, molding her, Valorie had a much better grasp of how she *was* her body as much as her brain.

A virile man like Bell didn't put his hands on a lovely, flexible young woman every day while a pair of sex demons made the joint sexy without the woman finally putting her hands on him.

A few years later, Valorie had wished for a bigger, more luxurious trailer than Bell's, which had been shockingly modest and dated for the real man in charge. Bell had yielded his old trailer to the pool to be modified for someone else and joined her bed on a permanent but open basis. She hadn't been jealous of his one-offs any more than he'd been jealous of hers. They tended to happen in Arcanium. Sparks flew, people got naked, marvelous shit happened.

Maya had been different because it hadn't been a one-off, and everyone else around them had known it.

The other thing she'd wished for soon after getting the RV — and the fact that she'd used all her wishes was the only reason Maya was still alive today — was to make her hair more manageable to dye, straighten and style, either by Kitty or by an outsider. Part of it was practical for the circus — a way to distinguish herself from normals and make herself more a part of the circus as an oddity rather than just a performer like Seth and Lars or Maya.

But after some years had passed, she'd pulled a brush through her hair and wondered whether that had been the right wish to make. She wasn't sure she'd have the hair her mother gave her ever again. And when she looked in the mirror and didn't recognize the woman she saw there as either herself or part of her family's history, Valorie mourned what she had lost.

Bell's magic kept them from aging. It didn't keep them from changing.

When Valorie was packed in a suitcase like this, the past always seemed to creep up on her. It didn't help that she could probably lock herself in, drink smoothies brought to her by golems by using a straw through the air holes, and no one would miss her.

She could be abrasive, caustic, ball-busting and snide, but she wasn't evil, and most of her worst qualities weren't intended badly. She had her defense mechanisms, same as everyone else. She'd brought a knife to the Maya fight, sure, but that was an anomaly — an anomaly that had been taken care of.

However, for the first time since a year or so after becoming a part of Arcanium, her future had gone blank. Not in the 'blank canvas', 'look at all my options', 'I could do anything' sense.

In the 'I have no idea what's left for me here, but I don't know what's left for me out there' sense.

At the first murmur of customers milling outside her tent, Valorie pushed the suitcase open with her elbow and waved to the crowd. Already she heard the clink of change in the tip box.

How generous.

Maybe it was time for her to leave Arcanium. If she retained her abilities, she could take a job as a contortionist with a regular circus or freak show. She could do erotic performance art. She could strip.

But she'd still be alone. She wouldn't be able to return to her family and friends, twenty years older than the last time she saw them. Valorie didn't even know which of them might have died. Maya, Caroline and Kitty all had ties to the outside world and reasons to keep in touch with them through their electronic devices. But there was no explanation for the fact that Valorie hadn't aged and no explanation for having run off and joined the circus without telling anyone. After twenty years, Valorie had run out of excuses. She couldn't go back to where Bell had taken her from. That Valorie might as well be dead.

So this Valorie was, for all intents and purposes, alone. Leaving wouldn't solve her problem.

But it didn't matter how big the bills that men stuffed in the tip box were when she lay on the floor, spread her legs into the vertical splits over her curled-up body, and touched both toes of both feet onto the wooden platform. It didn't matter that she liked contortion or that she didn't mind being gawked at. Art didn't exist in a vacuum. It liked an audience, and Valorie functioned better with public acknowledgment.

However, working here had lost its luster. Staying wouldn't solve her problem either.

She needed a change. Taking on solo work again was a change, but it wasn't *progressive* change. It was just going back to how things used to be, as though she'd hoped to reclaim the old glory, the old love and loyalty for Arcanium — for Bell. Wonder of wonders, the adrenaline high of the performance was nice and all, but there were only so many times she could walk like a pretzel before it became mundane.

Maybe it really *was* time for her to leave. She hadn't thought it was Bell keeping her here, but there was no denying that she'd expected to last here a lot longer — fifty years, seventy-five, always looking twenty-three, distancing herself year by year from the rest of her old world until she could step back into it and never be recognized, caught.

But once she'd had to strike out on her own, Lennon was a poor substitute for what she'd once had, and he didn't even want her enough to keep a thirty-minute-old promise instead of visiting his underwater partner. Nothing made a girl feel rejected like a demon passing her over for an imprisoned mermaid, no matter how pretty her curves—a woman who couldn't wrap her legs around his neck, a woman as slimy in the tail as the fish that he enjoyed eating.

But Valorie wasn't bitter or anything.

She crawled over her stage armchair like a woman possessed, her back bent as far as it could go and her head twisted around like an owl. She snapped her head over to look at a group of three girls. They squealed and laughed.

There was a reason why Bell had invited her to join the haunted funhouse when he eventually set it up— and with a horde of slaves he wasn't using trapped in the carousel, he had the means to follow through on his plans soon. Nothing said unsettling like body parts in all the wrong places. That would be a change too. Not the kind of change she needed, but it was something.

The truth was, she'd done everything she thought she could do. And that was also considering Bell had been incredibly generous in his granting of her spell over the years—giving her all kinds of flexible skills, from contortion, dance and gymnastics to the more complicated aerial acrobatics and tightrope walking. Basically, short of dislocation, Valorie wasn't sure where to go from here—on so many levels.

When Valorie decided it was time to take a break for the afternoon, Bell was waiting for her in the back of her exhibition tent with a glass of sparkling white.

The back of Kitty's tent was practically a small apartment, because that was where she preferred to live. It was bigger on the inside, perfect for the dressing and makeup room that it had also become. But the backs of everyone else's tents were fairly spartan, with a cushioned ottoman and a small table in case they wanted to eat. Her display platform was more comfy than her private backstage, but here she could get away from the eyes.

"You've been thinking traitorous thoughts very loudly, my dear," Bell said. He held his hand out to her, and she accepted. He guided her into his lap like an impish Santa and gave her the wine.

He'd always known just what she needed.

He was a touch shorter than she was—when he was wearing his human form, that was, and he'd only shrugged out of that for her once. Not as ripped as Victor or Lord Mikhail, but his strength was substantial in his more compact form, his skin golden tan, his hair coarse, dense, cinnamon shot with honey, a touch of curl in spite of how short he kept it. He had the perfect combination of undeniable masculinity tempered by a touch of fae in his grace and the prettiness of his cheekbones. His was an unaggressive strength, his voice like Scotch, his skin warm to the touch.

It was no wonder that he was so successful as a fortune teller, even though he didn't always tell happy fortunes. He appealed to men and women alike, putting them at ease with his very presence—or if they were ill at ease, it was the kind that came from such an enticing, satisfying enigma.

Looking at him, interacting with him, one would never guess what he was and what he was capable of.

Short of Maya and perhaps Kitty, not a human in the world knew him better than Valorie—his worst and his best, the terrible and wonderful things that he had done and would do, those amber eyes calm and the fire in his head burning slow and long, caged from laying waste to everything around him. Bell was a man in control. If he wasn't omnipotent and omniscient, it was only because he chose his own limitations. He could shed them at any time.

Just being near him, held against him, was like dispensation from a prince. He kissed her neck as she drank, but although his touch was familiar, comforting, it wasn't like it used to be. He kept his lust at a distance—not of his own volition but because Valorie had been the one to let him go.

Bell would have been happy to satisfy both her and Maya. But Valorie needed to be the center. She couldn't share the spotlight the way that Colm and Riley shared Caroline. If Bell missed her as much as Valorie missed what they'd had, he didn't indicate those feelings to her. His affection now was affection alone. He was as demonstrative in some ways as he was aloof in others. Touch had never been one of his more aloof traits.

"I'm not a traitor. What a melodramatic thing to say," Valorie replied after downing half the glass, sip by sip. It flushed her cheeks and made her mellow.

"I? Melodramatic?" Bell said.

"Say it ain't so," she agreed. "They were just idle thoughts."

"They're not idle when I can hear you thinking all the way from my tent," Bell said.

"So I have strong idle feelings. So what?"

"Do you want to leave, Valorie?" he asked, his countenance shifting ever so slightly from playful to serious. His expressions were almost always subtle like that, but anyone could discern what they meant—transparent yet obscure. Bell was paradox made flesh, and that was the way he liked it. "Is there not enough here to satisfy you?"

"I'm between satisfactions," Valorie said. "Don't suppose you could peek into the future and tell me when I can stop being frustrated?"

"Where's the fun in that?"

"Or tell me whether I'm going to leave?"

"That's for you to decide, Valorie."

"You're sometimes an infuriating douche. You know that?"

"It has crossed a few minds," Bell said, unaffected by the insult.

"Then let me make this simple," Valorie said. "I told you I'd stay unless I got bored. I'm not bored yet, but I might be getting there if there's nothing but my job to stay for."

Bell stroked her lower lip with his thumb, gazing at her as though, for a few seconds, he would gladly devour her. The moment passed. "Lennon is a jackass."

"Not so much of a jackass," Valorie said grudgingly. She took more than a sip of wine this time. "Well, okay, he's a jackass of the first order, but not for dumping me for a mermaid. It was a temporary deal between us. I'd totally poison his coffee, but I wouldn't do it because I hated him. He just needs a stomachache now and then."

"I like it when you're diabolical," Bell said.

"Only because you think you rubbed off on me, you narcissist," Valorie replied. She grinned as she climbed off his lap and stretched her legs. "I'll have you know I was already this bitchy before you got to me."

"I know," Bell said. "Your solo performance last night was inspired. You've lost none of your touch. It pleased me to see you return to center stage, and I don't want to see you go."

"Then grab me a man, tie him up and stuff him in my RV tonight," Valorie said.

"Is that your wish?" Bell asked.

"I don't have another wish, Bell. You know that," Valorie said. She finished her wine. Bell accepted the empty glass and set it on the table next to him. She still planned on stretching her legs the normal way, walking through the circus, occasionally doing a routine on a booth counter or picnic table to please the customers.

"That doesn't mean I can't still grant some of them," he said, crossing his arms. "In other ways."

"No, that's not my wish. Don't abduct someone on my account. I'd rather you abduct them on yours. Keeps my conscience clean."

Bell raised an eyebrow. He could host an international race with that eyebrow.

She may have been watching more TV on the small screen in her living room after Bell had left.

"Cleaner," she amended with a grin.

"Poor woman," Bell said, stroking her face, his fingers trailing into her hair.

He slowly turned her around and undid the twist of braids that lined her head until her hair hung free over her shoulders. Valorie wanted to pinch the bridge of her nose at the thought of Kitty having to put them back in again tomorrow.

But if Bell was undoing her hair, it was because he wanted to see how it looked that way for the rest of the day and the evening performance. Ever since she'd had it changed, she hadn't liked it loose. It made her look young, as young as her body was, which felt too young for her mind. Immortality was all well and good to keep the wrinkles at bay, but Valorie sometimes wished she could age the good ways at least. It was strange to be pursued by people in their late teens and early twenties when they seemed entirely too young for her now. Valorie wouldn't call herself mature, but when she spent time around her usual outsider prospects, she felt like a wise woman in comparison.

"You know I don't like performing with my hair loose," Valorie said quietly. "It gets in my face. It's all a little too nineties music video for me."

"Try it for a while," Bell said. "Give the follicles and your forehead a rest. It won't run off if you don't tie it down."

"Are you being metaphorical again?" Valorie asked.

He didn't let her know one way or another, which meant he was. "You think that if you look soft, they won't take you seriously. You have all the hard edges you need, Valorie. You're the knife trap at the bottom of the pit, and I love you for it. Having some softness doesn't make you weak, and it doesn't detract from the hardness. It merely provides a basis for comparison."

"I think I'm close to enough sweet people to sand down the rough places," Valorie replied. After all, her tent was between Kitty's and Troy's. But she tucked her hair behind her shoulders, and it did feel better on her temples. She'd gotten used to the pull of it on her skin. "I don't need to be sweet."

"Who said anything about sweet?" Bell said with a crooked, catlike smile. "I'm merely saying that a knife must have a handle."

"God, did I use to have a daily diet of that much metaphor, or are you just feeling poetic today?" Valorie asked.

"That's my contortionist," Bell said, stroking the small of her back. His palm ghosted just over the curve of her ass, but not quite there. "Go cut some throats. Just not mine, my dear. Not today."

"I won't wait forever, Bell," Valorie said before she ducked out. "I've got things I could be doing, and I think I've waited long enough." She wasn't talking about how horny she was.

"Who said anything about forever?"

Ooooh, he's in rare form today. A girl could pull her purple hair out in patches when he was like this. Scheming, secretive son of a bitch. If he wasn't the boss and she didn't still have a soft spot for him, she'd slap his smug face and hope some sense got in. However, he'd probably like it. And a man like him didn't learn.

* * * *

She'd been right. Having her hair down meant that it got in her way, but it was mostly a nuisance when she was doing contortion in her tent or among the patrons, when it could get caught under her while she was trying to shift from one position to another. She'd had to ask more than one customer to move her hair for her. Sure, it got her more tips, but Valorie wasn't keen on strangers touching the goods. If Bell wanted her to keep her hair down instead of in Heidi braids, she'd have to compromise and find a rubber band in Kitty's stash to keep the color within at least a few lines.

Up in the air, however, Valorie understood the change he'd intended to make. It didn't get in the way up there because there was nothing for her to lean against. Instead, she simply had an violet curtain of hair hanging over her, making her more human in the audience's eyes, less otherworldly...which deepened the creepiness of her face and created a contrast to the edge of the leather and latex.

As usual, Bell had his vision. He respected Valorie's in most cases, but she respected his whenever he offered it. Arcanium was his baby, his magnum opus, his purpose. He never steered his people wrong when it came to the circus.

She was also a little less headachy when the evening performance was over, so that was a plus.

This time she had nothing to hurry home to, so she stayed until the end with most of the rest of the cast.

"Whose idea was it to let it loose?" Kitty asked, finally getting a chance to breathe after double-checking everyone's hair and makeup for each act. She knew Valorie preferred her hair braided and well contained.

"Didn't have the time to put it back up after the gang bang," Valorie said.

"I don't believe a word out of your mouth about gang bangs. You're not Maya," Kitty said.

Valorie sucked on the inside of her cheek to keep from laughing. "Bell. Picture it. A romantic moment alone where he slowly...lovingly...painstakingly unbraids my hair...and that's it."

"I heard Lennon's back in his own trailer," Kitty said. "I take it you're in a dry patch?"

"Is it that obvious?"

"You're not usually *this* sarcastic."

"Shame," Valorie said. "Because I'm so good at it."

Kitty rolled her eyes like a mother. "You damaged women and the walls you put up. You're lucky some people like the challenge."

"Not lately," Valorie muttered.

"Ciàran and Moss never say no. They still talk about you," Kitty said.

"Those two are a glutton's appetizer. I'm looking for a meal I can eat all the way through. Thanks, but no thanks," Valorie said. But acknowledging reality over her pride, she added, "Not yet."

"You and Victor seem to get along," Kitty suggested. "He's without a woman to call his own."

"Your old sweetie is a sweetie," Valorie said. "He prefers outsiders, like you. He's a good beer. Not a meal."

"Are you hungry, by the way?"

"A little."

"There's always Marcus," Kitty said.

This time, Valorie had to cover her mouth to keep her laughter from making it past the curtain. Bell *could* muffle the noise backstage, but he'd never had to, and Valorie didn't want to be the one to break unspoken tradition.

Marcus was a relatively new acquisition, and not under very good terms, given that he'd tried to break into Lord Mikhail's trailer. From what the rest of the cast knew about him, he'd been something of a dull petty thief with a mean streak who also happened to be gay and exceptionally susceptible to Lord Mikhail's magic. He'd gotten the drop on Lord Mikhail with a Taser, which had deeply shamed the strongman incubus, like a high-school jock who'd been pantsed. It had also earned Marcus one of Bell's famous second chances— Die by clown or serve Bell in a manner of his choosing through an open-ended wish.

Most of them usually wished for what Bell wanted, when given the chance. Marcus was no exception. No matter how bad things got, people chose life over death.

And that was around the time Arcanium had introduced the Rotting Man. There were some unusual and unlikely pairings in Arcanium, but *no one* went near Marcus. Valorie doubted anyone would for at least a century. He tended to slough, and he was a bit…moist. In Arcanium, weird wasn't a deterrent. Not even gross was, otherwise Misha probably wouldn't get as much as he was getting. Turned out decay was the line freaks drew. Even Carlo wouldn't tap that.

"Have I really reached that point? Have I sunk that low?" Valorie asked, once her laughter had worked itself out without disturbing the audience.

"Yes," Kitty replied. "You're untouchable now. No one is ever going to want you again."

"Ouch. Can I get some salve to go with that dose of truth?"

"I was kidding, Valorie."

"I'm pretty sure I recognize sarcasm, pussycat," Valorie said. "But if you tell me it'll happen when I stop looking or someone's out there for me because there's someone for everyone, I'll slug you right in your furry face."

"I was going to suggest you take out the big dildos, but okay."

"Now you're talking my language." Toys didn't work much better than masturbation against sex demon magic, but it took some of the edge off.

Valorie leaned back until she was resting the wrong away across the foot of the chaise longue she and Kitty shared while Bell and Maya continued their act out in the ring. Another evening concluded.

"It's because I'm mean, isn't it?" Valorie said.

"You're not mean. Well, you *are* mean, but you *mean* to be mean, and most of the time, it only seems mean if a person doesn't know any better. We all know better, Valorie," Kitty said.

"Is it because I'm too normal?" Valorie asked. "Is that it?"

"*Now* I'm going to tell you to give it time," Kitty said.

"Bitch."

"Hear me out. You spent most of your years in Arcanium with Bell. For all that time, you were Bell's. You didn't really look beyond him, and because you were his, no one pursued you either. They weren't foolish enough to go after Bell's girl. You've only been away from him for a short time in comparison, and you had Lennon for most of it. Now you've been a free agent for all of a day. I suggest you get used to beer and appetizers and toys and take a breather. It's hard to be alone in Arcanium, but it can be done," Kitty said.

Valorie was about to say something snide to Kitty, but she caught herself. She only would have been snide because Kitty had actually said something smart that Valorie didn't want to hear. And Kitty had her own issues, so the woman knew her shit. When she'd joined Arcanium voluntarily, Bell hadn't needed to do anything to change her. She'd been born the Bearded Lady, with hair all over her body. Valorie didn't pity her for it—Kitty never demanded pity. But Valorie did sympathize, because it couldn't have always been as carefree as Kitty had pretended to be while banging the Ringmaster on the side. The woman had demons of her own.

Basically, though, Kitty was speaking the credo of the single lady—*Take a breath and learn to love you for you. Figure out who you are without a man.*

Worthy advice, except it had never really been about not being single for Valorie. She knew what she was like on her own. She was mostly fine with herself. Who was a hundred percent fine with all of themselves if they had an ounce of self-awareness? And she had well more than an ounce. She'd never been owned by her men. Kitty had inadvertently called Valorie Bell's, but that wasn't how it had been. It hadn't been one-sided like that. She hadn't belonged to the boss, and she hadn't belonged to Lennon. With Bell, she'd been in love. With Lennon, she'd just needed a fuck. Now, she wanted something *real*. And Valorie wasn't sure Kitty understood that, nor did she know how to explain it without sounding like a hopeless romantic and ruining her reputation.

"Sure. Thanks. I'll put it under advisement," Valorie said, running her fingers through her hair.

"You do that. And please, for the love of God, eat something," Kitty said.

Valorie hit Kitty's hip with the back of her hand, but the gesture was halfhearted and limp. She could definitely go for something greasy right the hell now.

After waiting for the audience to clear out of the circus, Valorie headed for the food booth and asked for fried things that she'd need lots of napkins for. They always stayed open for requests after Arcanium closed, since not all the cast liked to eat and feel heavy before a performance. After Caroline came around, the food booths had started staying open all night. Her carousel men only came to life after the audience left, like the opposite of Cinderella's pumpkin, and they sometimes got fed at odd hours.

Valorie noticed Caroline and her men eating at one of the picnic tables with Joanne and Jane and Seth and Lars. A threesome and a weird-ass foursome. She didn't join them. Everyone was set up together like a pre-planned orgy. Valorie had no interest in being the eighth wheel in their hippie love fest. That, and she was eating like a caveman with no regrets. It was easier to have no regrets when other people couldn't see her.

Except the clowns. She didn't have any problem with the clowns seeing her eat, because they had worse table manners than she did. She gave them a nod of acknowledgment as Tragedy, the female of the group, and Comedy and Murphy did their rounds near Oddity Row, searching for stragglers and felons, anyone who didn't belong, fair game. Valorie found it was best not to interfere with the doings of killer demon clowns.

She dumped the paper, cardboard basket and dirty napkins from her meal into one of the trashcans in their little trailer park. Eating comfort food hadn't made the high-tension hum of arousal inside her any better, but it had made her a little less cranky.

She didn't like being around herself when she was cranky either.

Valorie opened her RV door and turned on the light. She nearly tripped over the legs of the man who took up half her living room.

John, the fire-eater, had been bound in rough sisal rope on his ankles and wrists—easy knots to untie when one wasn't the person tied up—and he hung from the bar she used for practice during travel days. He'd been gagged with something Valorie assumed was fireproof, or else she wouldn't have an RV anymore.

He looked massively pissed.

Tucked into the front pocket of his pants, in Bell's spiky, somewhat old-fashioned cursive, was a note.

Why not play with this one for a while? Wish granted, absolutely free.

Chapter Three

"He doesn't always mean well," Valorie said, glancing up at John before considering the note again. "But this time he really does, the endearing jerk. If I take that gag off you, you gonna be nice? Because I did *not* put him up to this."

John nodded, some of his annoyance dissipating — slowly, but dissipating nonetheless.

Over a year of quiet reflection had done wonders with this one. His bullying felon compatriot, Shawn, still hadn't recovered from the shock and trauma of his transformation, which was why he was confined to his exhibition tent when the circus was open and didn't perform in the ring, although sometimes the Cyclops was trotted out under the spotlight to show him off.

John's eyes were bright and aware as she untied his gag. He had a tent on Oddity Row too, but he didn't use it much. Bell wouldn't let the canvas or anything else within the boundaries of the tent catch fire, but for both the man's and the audience's peace of mind, it was much better to have lots of open space around him when John's fire act got more elaborate. The clowns had a makeshift ring of driftwood planks and sawdust. When the clowns weren't cavorting, John would often do his act there, for the protection of the customers. It never went wrong when people were watching, but better safe than sorry — whatever John needed in order to do the things that Bell wanted of him.

"How long have you been here?" Valorie asked.

He performed during the day, but he hadn't been assigned an evening act yet. He could have been here for just fifteen minutes or the last few hours.

"Since everyone started gathering in the big top," he replied.

She hoped he'd used a toilet before Bell had abducted him.

"Anything hurt?"

"Does my pride and dignity count?"

"No," she said.

"Then no. Wrists, a little." John leaned his head back and stared at his wrists bound to the bar. He was a tall boy, and with his ankles bound and deliberately stretched out in front of him so that it was difficult to get his footing, most of the weight was on his wrists. The flesh had been chafed by the unpleasant rope.

She thought of him as 'boy'. He was about Seth's and Lars' age, the age that she appeared. Still young for her as she actually was. He had a football player's broad shoulders and physique, though not as meaty as Shawn. His skin was darker than hers, but not as dark as Lars'. It took on a pinkish cast where his scars boiled over his hands and face.

"You know why you're here, fire-eater?" she asked. He hadn't earned his name yet, this relative stranger in her home. Calling him Freddy before, however, had been unkind. She didn't usually jibe about freakishness with her fellow oddities. And she didn't know him well enough for her insults to be considered affectionate.

"The genie didn't elaborate," John answered.

The common English pronunciation for jinni was close enough for Western purposes that Valorie wouldn't slap his knuckles with a ruler.

"He just grabbed me, poofed me over here, tied me up and told me to wait like a good boy." John sneered. With the scars, it was a good sneer. Valorie approved.

She jumped back to sit on the small kitchenette counter.

"Aren't you going to let me down?" John asked. She gave him a point for trying to conceal the petulant demand in his question.

"Not yet," she said, crossing her ankles. "You know, I've been whining with my people about how awful it is that I have to go without sex for a while. I'm used to a lot of it, and I'm not pleased that my access has been cut off for the last few days. Actually, I'm the one who cut it off, but that doesn't mean I'm happy about it."

"Gee, just a few—"

"Don't finish that sentence, or I'll leave you up there all night," Valorie said.

She'd do it too. There were potions for healing something like rope burn—superficial wounds were a cinch. There weren't potions for insolence. Or if there were, Bell didn't supply them.

Valorie leaned forward with her elbows on her thighs, looking him over.

"It occurs to me that you must have had it quite…hard these long, long months. All the same impulses that the rest of us have, plus your healthy young male libido, finally liberated from the more depraved impulses that brought you here in the first place… All the magic and none of the release. Your hand doesn't cut it anymore, does it? What do you use these days? Do the golems bring you fruit that you warm up in the microwave? Or pie? Do you use pie?"

John opened his mouth, whether to protest or stammer she'd never know, because he shut it again. His expression had twisted from annoyance to comical bewilderment—and discomfort, like any boy who had been caught in his desire. She deliberately avoided looking at his trousers, but she didn't have to in order to know what she'd see. Poor boy was probably on a hair trigger after all this time.

"It doesn't matter what you use," Valorie said. "I'd been planning on using a slew of toys tonight to keep myself satisfied. Probably wouldn't have worked very well, if the tingling in my nethers tells me anything. Lord Mikhail is feeding. Would you say Lady Sasha's doing the same?"

John nodded. He swallowed thickly, his prominent Adam's apple bobbing like an arrow trapped in his throat.

"Now, Bell made a big gesture in giving you to me. But it was all show," Valorie said, sliding off the counter and stepping closer. Her feet didn't make a sound. She wanted to disturb nothing but him. "I can't *make* you want me. I can't *make* you have sex with me. But now that you're here, I see potential, boy. I really do. You're nice to look at."

"I don't like it when people make fun of me," John snapped.

She pinched his chest then slipped behind him. "In this business, you get used to it. But I'm not making fun of you, fire-eater. I like what I see. Us veterans don't really *see* the ones who come in as punishment. You've been cold-shouldered enough that you know what I mean. But you must have made Bell happy enough over the last year if he's handed you over to me. Now that I see what I've been missing, I think I could definitely do worse."

"Thanks," John said. He hadn't been in the sarcasm game with her long enough. His venom didn't even faze her.

"Good body," she murmured. Now she ran her nails along the line of his shoulder. The unscarred skin pebbled with goosebumps. "Lovely eyes. Hot mouth. Are you going to hurt me with that mouth if I let it please me, pet?"

"Is that what I'm going to be? Your pet?" John asked. He swayed in his bonds.

"It's not such a bad thing to be. A girl needs to take care of her pet. Feed it, stroke it, make sure its needs are met, sometimes even before her own—but not most of the time," Valorie replied. "Most of the time, the Queen's demands are to be obeyed." She stroked the line of his jaw, almost brushed the scars on his lips but pulled back at the last second. "It won't be an even balance. Understand?"

"I get it. Slavery and servitude. I guess you learned from the best."

"That's very hurtful," Valorie said. "I already told you I can't make you have sex with me. I can't make you stay. If I untie you and you want to leave, I'm not allowed to stop you."

She stepped around in front of him again, still determined not to look down at his trousers lest her mouth start to water, ruining the tone she'd set.

"Bell wrapped you up into a nice little gift for me. He's a showman. He's good at presentation," Valorie said. "He's not the only one."

She reached behind her and unzipped the catsuit from where it started between her shoulder blades, down to her ass. That was another plus to flexibility. She never had to ask anyone to do her zippers or her corset ties. She could always reach.

Valorie peeled the leather away from the top half of her body.

"Oh God, that is so not fair," John groaned as Valorie exposed her breasts and her abdomen, all the way to the crease where her mound began.

"It's important for you to know what your options are, boy," Valorie said. She pushed the rest down her legs without having to bend them. "And what you're getting if you choose the way I want you to choose."

She stepped out of the catsuit and smoothed her palms over her body all the way back to upright. Arcanium got rid of modesty and body shame pretty quickly. Most people and demons didn't wear much of anything. They were all shapes, sizes and colors. And they all kept getting naked with one another.

"In order to have me, you have to do for me. I'll make sure you're satisfied after I'm satisfied that you've done well," she said.

Valorie stepped to either side of his bound legs stretched out before him, gradually drawing closer and closer to his hips. The way he was hanging, she was taller than him. It made her powerful, him looking up at her with blatant need shining through his half-obscured face.

"Now, I don't know how good you are yet or how much instruction is going to be involved. But if you don't want a woman telling you what to do, even if it gets you what you want, you can waddle right on out that door like you've been riding a horse for a month. You got your ways, I got mine and this is *my* home. You're not going to get me into bed and take over. I can kick you out if you try to play the fool with me. I've been here a long time, boy. Bell would be very displeased if you were to do something I didn't want. *Comprende, chico?*"

"You're really serious? You're not just playing me? Because it feels like *decades* since I've had sex, with all that damn magic flying around," John said.

Valorie took his face between her hands. He exhaled an involuntary sigh like a moan.

"Does it look like I'm playing around?" Valorie asked.

She didn't know how much feeling he had in his lips with the build-up of scar tissue there as well as some places inside his mouth. But when she licked his upper lip then caught it between hers in a kiss, he twitched violently, swaying in his bonds. Any time he tried to take the lead, she changed the angle, and he couldn't do anything to stop her.

Finally the boy figured things out. He sagged from the bar and let her strip him of control one magically fueled moment at a time. She rocked her hips against his in slow undulations, almost like a dance. Her cunt dampened the front of his leather trousers. But she didn't give him any pressure. Any time he tried to lift his hips up by pushing at the floor with his heels, she shifted back, away from his cock. At best, he'd be able to feel that she was *there*, the brush of her, perhaps the heat. But he couldn't rub himself against her, couldn't relieve the tension straining up from under the placket.

From what she could feel of him, he certainly wouldn't be Arcanium regulation during the day.

The only thing that kept Bell from criminal lewdness charges all over the place was magic. Just enough to entice, not enough to shock. Kids were allowed in before eight o'clock, after all, although Arcanium made no secret that it was not a family circus. In its advertising and on the information boards at the ticket entrance — either at Arcanium's gates when they were solo or at the gates of the faire or park that they'd attached themselves to — Arcanium warned that the circus wasn't recommended for children under the age of thirteen. They left the discretion — and the risk — to the parents. They weren't quite the lewd, crude, rude freak sideshow that some of the other circuses were — which wasn't a bad thing, just not what Bell had been going for. But they had a little bit of everything.

John had a lot of something. It felt good. And he wasn't even a demon.

"What do you say, fire-eater?" Valorie asked against his mouth. When he tried to taste her again, she met him with her tongue but didn't let him in. "You ready to play according to my rules, or are you going to forfeit the game?"

"I thought girls hated sports metaphors," John said.

"I wasn't talking sports." Her nipples brushed his chest.

"I'll do whatever you want," he said, practically leaping up. "Please don't make me leave. I think I'm going to explode if I don't…"

"You won't explode," Valorie said, stepping back. He groaned at her absence. "You might go a little crazy."

"I'm already a little crazy," John replied. "Because of your boss."

"Who did this to you because…?" Valorie prompted.

He sighed. Not a moan. "I'd blame Cameron, but his death was bad enough without me damning him more. The genie did this to me because of me. Because of what I did."

"The pup can be taught."

"What are you in for, then?" he asked as she worked on the knot that tied him to the bar.

"Stupidity and random chance," Valorie said, "which is better than you, pizza oven. There."

John dropped onto his ass, grunting and wincing because he hadn't been able to prepare himself for it.

"Now…" she continued, stepping back and sitting on the coffee table. The golems would clean any mess she or they made, like elves in the night. They always did.

She sat back and spread her legs. Not to an inhuman degree, but enough to make the boy salivate. He wet his lips.

"Come over here and lick me, pet," she ordered.

"Aren't you going to untie me?" John asked, holding up his wrists.

"I already did. Oh, you mean unbind you? Nope. Not until you make this pussy purr," Valorie said.

"Oh, come on."

"Do you want me or not, fire-eater? It's as simple as that. If you do, you crawl over here like a caterpillar and make me come. Once I've had what I need, I'll give you what you need. If you'd rather get it from warm pastries, be my guest."

With Bell, she'd been an equal in the bedroom, even though Bell had really had all the power. With Lennon, they'd been equals, more or less.

John was not her equal. John was still in the penalty box, if she had to go with a sports metaphor. He wasn't on probation, despite Bell bringing him to her. He was in prison. If he got a conjugal visit, that was one of the few perks a prisoner could have, but it didn't make him free and it didn't make him her equal. He had to earn his way up—with Arcanium as a whole and with her. It had taken Misha over ten years before Bell had given him some reprieve. Colm, one of Caroline's carousel men, was still a prisoner after over fifty years, although allowances had to be made for the fact that Colm used to be a demon himself. Bell adjusted the sentences accordingly between mortals and immortals.

Those pretty eyes, almost as black as a demon's, glared at her, but he couldn't keep them away from her tits and her pussy for very long after such an extended period of self-denial. Valorie knew he wouldn't say no. He'd take what he was offered and take it gladly.

Was it flattering that she was a condemned man's only option, something he couldn't afford to say no to after about a year and a half of celibacy? Not really. But it wasn't flattering to him either that he was only there because she didn't have anyone else to play with. So she guessed they were even on that, if not equal. Beggars couldn't be choosers, and they could both do much worse.

John rolled onto his side to push himself up by his elbows and knees. He couldn't crawl like a normal person with his arms and legs bound the way they were. The ropes weren't just on the wrists and ankles, but twisted up his legs and forearms in crude mimicry of Japanese bondage. He couldn't part his elbows and knees very far.

Valorie licked her lips pointedly as he shuffled toward her. He clenched his teeth, well aware of how undignified he must look. She'd never had a bound man crawl to her like this. But now that it was happening, she wondered why she hadn't demanded it in the past. His ass wriggled from side to side, and he just looked so humiliated by it. She wished she'd opened his trousers for his cock to beckon her the same way.

As unflattering as it was that he wouldn't want her if he had anyone else clamoring for his bed, the fact that he was willing to do this for her made up for it.

When he reached the coffee table, she lifted his chin with one black-painted fingernail.

"Very good boy," she murmured. "You want your treat?"

"Am I allowed to talk?" John asked.

"Depends what you want to say," she said.

"That's a no, then."

"Pets are allowed to talk if they can. Some you can't get to shut up. Try me."

"I don't like licking pussy," John said. "I never have."

Valorie smiled, her tongue pressed to one of her canine teeth. "I think you should try it again. People change. Go on, pet. Have a taste."

She drew him in by the sharpness of her curved nail on his chin, all the way to her folds, but he gazed at her face as though captivated. His eyebrows were furrowed, curious, perhaps wondering what secret she wasn't sharing as he finally lowered his gaze and parted his lips.

With just the tip, John ran his tongue along her slit. He slipped in, spreading her taste over his tongue and swallowing.

Then, groaning, he darted forward again to plunge his tongue inside her. He drew out more of her juices, smearing them over her folds and her clit. He sucked her like candy, grunting and humming like a man feasting to his heart's desire, a gourmand presented with his favorite meal, the waiter putting more and more in front of him with no end in sight.

So maybe she was still a little hungry, but she didn't think it was for food anymore.

Once he got started, his enthusiasm helped hide some of his novice errors. So did the sex magic thick as smoke and fog in the RV and probably all over the circus. He was new, but he had good instincts, and her clit had low standards when she was this turned on. Besides, he was her pet now. She could instruct him, and given the way he buried himself between her legs, coating her juices all over his face without a care in the world, he'd be amenable to learning a thing or two.

As much as he was enjoying it, though, Valorie guessed that eating a woman out was still something he probably wouldn't be caught doing on the outside or if anyone else was watching—though he'd gladly accept and expect a woman's mouth around his cock, she was sure.

She considered this part of his reconditioning. Every touch was new, every taste, every smell. Everything was so fucking good when incubus and succubus spells went through a body like fever. A person developed a whole new appreciation for sex—all kinds of sex with all kinds of people.

It was truly a shame there weren't more female demons in Arcanium. The human women had all the demon cock they could stand, but men didn't have demon pussy to sink themselves into, with Lady Sasha off limits. There was also Comedy, the female of the clown trio. But no one but Caroline was stupid enough to even try to get near the clowns without Bell around, and no one could figure out why the clowns liked her when she kept saving children from them and getting whipped for it.

Valorie had sampled the available male demon pool—which was totally worth the sampling and how—but John really didn't have anyone to lose his mind and his dick in unless he was a little gay, which she doubted.

Looked like he was stuck with her, but he didn't seem to be too unhappy about that turn of events at the present moment.

Neither was she. She petted his smooth head, the nerves in her palm seeming to startle when they passed from scalp to scar. But she got used to it quickly, because now she was guiding his head, and he could take direction, and *oh God, keep licking right there, and suck it a little…*

Valorie had been able to go telepathic with Bell with her needs when her mouth had stopped being able to form words. She didn't have the same malady with John. Words spilled from her lips and he obeyed as though it was second nature, as though everything that made her croon, moan, gasp, or cry made him feel just as good.

She taught him how to vary his tongue on her clit, little flicks, around it rather than on it, firm strokes, broad, soft laps, humming as he sucked on her. She directed him between her folds until he finally moved with just her hand, even though he had no hair to pull.

Valorie whimpered when he plunged his tongue into her as far as he could. It wasn't as good as Lennon, who had real length to his tongue, not to mention dexterity. But while she couldn't help but compare, she didn't begrudge him for the fact he was human, and the way he fucked her with his tongue only intensified her anticipation of other things he was going to fuck her with.

"Back up here, pet," Valorie said. She guided him to her clit once again, her orgasm bubbling under the surface. She was ready to boil.

John rubbed his bound hands against the front of his trousers, the best he could without full use of his hands. His moans vibrated through her every time he applied pressure to her clit.

"Lick it, pet. Lick it hard and *suck* it," Valorie snapped. She mashed his mouth against her, but it wasn't enough, even though he looked like he might come just from eating her out and the awkward strokes through his leather.

His eyes rolled back as she pushed herself standing. She still didn't let him take his mouth off her, practically smothering him.

Valorie pushed John up and back, back, bowling him over. He shouted, muffled in her flesh, as she pinned him to the floor and sat on his face, frantically rocking her pussy over him as he writhed underneath her.

"Faster, faster, faster," she gasped.

Her skin broke out in pleasure like gooseflesh as the orgasm galloped through her. She didn't care if she was causing his tongue to cramp. He wasn't going to let up until she was finished.

Valorie cried out as she came. When a man did a good job, she had always believed he deserved to know his work was appreciated.

It had been a long time since Valorie had climaxed outside Arcanium. She was pretty sure the world outside was going to royally disappoint her after twenty years of consistently amazing orgasms. They weren't all the *same*, of course, otherwise she would have started taking them for granted a long time ago. But every single one of them was good, no matter how bad she was feeling, and she hadn't gotten tired of it yet. Tired of constantly needing sex? Sometimes. Tired of the earth-shattering sex she was having? Not at all. If she had to have sex this much, it damn well better be good.

"Oh..." she sighed, sliding back over his chin and smearing her juices, her scent, along his neck and chest before lying back over his bound arms. The rope scratched the valley of her spine, but she didn't care.

She rested her head on his thigh, inches away from his cock.

Now she could get a look at him to her heart's content. No, definitely not demon big, but that wasn't as important as what he could do with it. If he could use his cock half as well as his tongue, Valorie thought they'd get along splendidly.

Demon cocks should hurt like hell, and the largest should perforate organs, but they didn't. The stretch of her pussy around them ached with terrible pleasure instead of pain. Her body always seemed to accommodate the obscene lengths and widths without strain or organ bruising. Some kind of magic on their side, no question.

Human cock, though? She hadn't had a man who wasn't masquerading since Troy, and that had been damn fine. Just because John couldn't measure up physically with her usual fare didn't mean he couldn't use what his mama gave him just as well.

"You learn quickly, pet," Valorie said, stretching with feline luxury.

His cock moved in his trousers. He must have been terribly uncomfortable, pants that tight, cock probably leaking and needing room to grow.

"You like that?" she asked.

"Yeah," he replied hoarsely.

"Now what do you tell me?"

"Thank you?" John asked. He was too stunned to add sarcasm.

"Well, yes. And you're welcome. I was thinking more along the lines of 'Mistress knows best', but that works."

He turned his head and bit her thigh above her knee, where she was still kneeling on either side of his head as she reclined. She jumped then laughed a little.

"What about your side of the bargain?" he asked. He lifted his hips involuntarily as she shifted her head closer to the place where the leather seemed molded to his scrotum with the tightness from his erection.

"What bargain is that?" she asked. She nuzzled his balls, turned her neck more so that she could mouth them, one side then the other.

You know what they say – more than a mouthful's wasted, she thought with amusement. Tight, close balls, but thick cock. She brushed it with her cheek a few times as she lavished her attention, one layer removed, on his testicles.

"The one where...if I give you...what you need...you'll...give me...what I need," John said. What she was doing to him kept taking his breath away, as though it was sucked right out of his mouth every few words. It was cute.

"But what do you *need*, fire-eater? What do you really need? What do we all really need?" Valorie murmured up the ridge of his cock. Then she pulled herself up until she was sitting on his chest.

"Come *on*," he begged. What sounded like annoyance was really just desperation. "Are you shitting me?"

Valorie laughed again, a little wickedly. She let him wonder whether she was going to do for him as she stood. His face was shiny. She could smell herself on him. He brushed some of it away with his rope, but rope wasn't made for absorption or cleaning. He winced at the roughness against his skin. She thought he might actually cry in anger if she were to deny him. With his history, she almost wanted to see that. But she had mercy on him — mercy he didn't deserve, but she decided to give it anyway.

"Oh, thank God," he breathed when she crouched down and began to undo his trousers.

"No, thank *me*," she said.

She made a small noise of appreciation when she wrapped her fingers around the shaft and pulled him out. He was a satisfactory size, but even better to her was his heft. His cock pulled to the side under its own weight. The purplish head gleamed from pre-cum, and she polished him with her palm. The cords of John's neck stood out as she rubbed the lubrication along the length, like a groom rubbing her horse down, until he shone everywhere.

"One of these days, if you're real nice, I might suck this as well as you sucked me off," Valorie murmured. "But right now, I need a cock inside of me, and I think yours will do nicely."

"Whatever I can do to help." It sounded like his throat had narrowed to the size of a toothpick as he watched her position her cunt above him, the cunt that he'd made so slick with her orgasm and his saliva. She nearly slammed down when he breached the entrance. Valorie forced herself to take it slow, however, to torment him and to get a longer look at his eyes rolling back once more, his teeth clenched, his hands clasped tightly against his chest like a man praying, his whole upper body tense... The man looked possessed, even though he was the one entering her.

Once she'd taken him all in, seated against the base, Valorie groaned, moving her hips in small circles to tug at the tight flesh around his base.

"Yeah, that's what I've been needing. Don't need to be a demon to do it right. God made this one just as special," Valorie muttered. It didn't mean anything, just a moan put into words.

She clamped her knees on his hips, tucking her feet under his thighs so she had some measure of a hold.

She squeezed her cunt around him and slapped his damp cheek lightly when he tried to thrust up into her.

"You. Stay still," she said over his agonized groan. "I'm going to give you what you want. You don't get to take it. I'm not even making you do any work, and you'll get to shoot up all inside me, no rubber, so stop your grousing."

"Fuck, you're a dirty girl," he said.

"You have no idea," Valorie replied.

She didn't squeeze or do anything else with her hips over his cock anymore as she began to untie his wrists.

"I don't care about being tied up," John said, pleading with his eyes. "I just want..."

"It's not about what you want," Valorie said. "It's about what I give you, boy, and I'm giving you a small bit of freedom so you can play with my tits as I take you. Or hold on to my waist. Whatever strikes your fancy, as long as I'm still the one riding you and not the other way around."

It didn't take long. As soon as his wrists were free—there was some blood, but he didn't seem to notice it—he pushed himself sitting only for Valorie to tighten her muscles around his cock again and point him back down.

This could be it. Valorie was devious, more experienced, older, certainly more flexible, not averse to fighting dirty, but he had strength on her. If he decided that he wanted to do it his way, there was nothing she could do to stop him except attempt to bash his head against the coffee table or the floor, which she wasn't going to do. And Bell wouldn't come running, because she'd be enjoying herself. There was no denying that the image in her head of a big, strong, athletic man over her, being the top, pumping powerfully into her, was appealing. It wasn't what she wanted tonight, certainly not from John, but she wouldn't say no if he insisted.

But she wouldn't let there be a second chance if he broke faith now. He could choke his chicken for the next year and a half for all she cared. He'd come into Arcanium with the trust completely obliterated, especially when it came to sex. He could have languished for far more years than this if he hadn't had the good fortune of one of the human women of Arcanium needing to get laid.

He wasn't going to take her against her will either way, but he could make this about power, and that was the same thing that had gotten him here in the first place.

John panted as she tightened herself around him, as much like a vise as a slippery orifice could be. His hips twitched on their own. She could practically see the internal struggle.

Take or accept.

He slowly lowered himself back on his elbows then lay down on the floor again.

"There's my boy," she whispered, leaning down and stroking his chest. It had a few burn marks too, as though he'd been hit with a drop or five of boiling water on his shoulders and chest, but they weren't as extensive as the scars on his face and hands. His skin felt like skin instead of warm, dried wax, and she enjoyed kneading the muscles that he'd cultivated after years of sports training. As soon as he slid his hands up to her waist she began to move over him, lifting her hips even as she kept the rest of her upper half almost steady.

When she was done exploring his chest, her cunt revved up again like a revived motor at the shallow strokes of his cock she gave herself. She propped herself back up, using gravity's help to grind down.

As she bounced, her small breasts jiggled. He brought his hands up her ribs when she really started to ride him so that he could stroke the pert nipples with his thumbs. He didn't cup them, didn't stop her breasts from moving—and when she really started bobbing over him, the jiggling began to ache pleasantly and unpleasantly at the same time. The undersides hit his palms with light slaps, and in the meantime he made her nipples ache pleasantly and unpleasantly too. She was so sensitive there. She'd never known whether it was because they were small or whether it was just her, but she was used to them hurting and practically zinging with arousal that shot straight down between her legs. It meant he was doing something right, her nipples tightening until they were hard little pebbles under his thumbs.

Two could play at that game.

Actually, she doubted playing with his nips and pecs would get her the same kinds of reactions, but she could still squeeze her cunt muscles around him off-rhythm to her pace and the natural contractions like flutters on his cock. It wasn't right that she was the one who wanted to scream when he was the one who'd been without sex for so much longer.

His hands started grasping. His breath became ragged, and he pounded his heels on the floor. His teeth were gritted against any sound, almost as though he didn't want to give her that, didn't want her to reduce him anymore. But she wouldn't have it.

Valorie leaned back, grabbing his still leather-clad thighs, and rode him at an angle that was tighter on him and pulled her folds back from her clit. That was where she brought one hand now, stroking herself furiously above and around but never directly on. Sometimes her fingers slid down to where he split her, which he had to see even better than her, given the way he was unable to tear his gaze away.

The ends of her hair tickled her shoulders and arms as she let her head fall back, focusing all her power, strength and speed on the movement of her hips and her hand.

"Oh God." Each word wrenched out of him. "Oh God. Oh God. *Fuck!*"

His hips snapped up, but she could forgive him the lapse, because he slickened her further as his cock jerked. It seemed to go on forever. He'd probably expelled more than his share of seed into his hand all this time, but *something* had been held back. That something let loose now, over and over until he practically screamed with each pulse of it inside her.

It was messy, wet and exhilarating, knowing that she was the one who had cut the thread that finally let him come, really come, freeing him for a time from the cumulative effect of the sex demons' magic.

And it kept him hard and hot for her while she drove herself to her second climax, using his cock while he cried out and bucked on the floor, holding on to her hips like a life raft.

When he'd released her and gone limp, she was almost concerned that he'd screwed himself into unconsciousness. He probably hadn't even known how sexually tense he was after a while.

But John stared up at her, his eyes hooded as she brought herself down from her own high.

"Was it worth it?" she asked, crossing her arms on his chest and resting her chin on her forearms to stare down at him.

"Did I melt inside you?" John asked. "I'm pretty sure I actually started turning into a liquid."

"We'll figure that out when I let your cock out of me," she said, grinning. "But you seem solid enough to me — more or less. Want a drink?" She could reach the fridge from where they lay, but she eased him out of her and stood, heedless of the wetness trickling down her thigh.

He sat up and accepted the open bottle of beer that she gave him.

As she knelt at his feet to undo the ropes there, Valorie started giggling madly.

"What?" John asked, cautiously insolent.

"Now it looks like you've been fucking a cinnamon bun instead of pie."

He took in the sight of his cock, softening and covered with her juices and a considerable amount of his own semen.

His embarrassed, crooked grin was made more appealing by straight, white teeth. All-American, this one, in many ways — bad as well as good — but no denying the charm when he wasn't being a grade A enema. There might be hope for him yet.

"I'll let you have the shower first," she said. "I'm dripping, but you've got a little…me on your face. And a lot of me and you on your dick."

"I'm damn sure I had a lot of you on my face," John said.

She slapped his bare ass before he could pull up his trousers.

"Once I'm out, though, I expect to see you gone," Valorie said, taking a swig of her own beer. "I don't keep pets in my bed, and I need my beauty sleep."

"Pretty sure you don't," he muttered.

But he didn't protest as he ducked into the small but manageably sized bathroom and closed the door.

Chapter Four

Lennon sat down next to her and popped a raw egg into his mouth. It bulged his throat as he swallowed.

"What are you doing?" Valorie asked. She had her own breakfast in front of her on the fold-up picnic table backstage where the cast took their morning meals. On circus days, the golems made breakfast burritos. Sometimes Lennon had them and sometimes he preferred his eggs uncooked.

"I'm sitting," Lennon replied.

"But why are you sitting *here*?" Valorie asked.

"Because there was a seat. What? You need regular access to my prick for me to sit next to you? Is that how this works, love?" Lennon asked.

Valorie glared at him, but while annoyance wasn't a difficult emotion for her to access, she couldn't manage to stay mad. He'd sat next to her before they'd started having sex. There was no reason why he couldn't sit next to her after they'd stopped. She could ignore him just as well now as she'd used to.

"Whatever," she said.

He popped another egg into his mouth in response. He didn't force her into conversation. Talking wasn't really their thing. Besides, he'd won the argument.

"Yeah. Could you imagine only eating breakfast with those you'd slept with?" Maya asked with a smile.

"The question wouldn't be who you'd sit with, it would be who you couldn't sit with," Valorie replied.

"There aren't many people I've been with that you haven't been with first."

"Calm down, girls," Kitty said, not looking up from her paperback. "You're not competing for circus slut. Besides, I'm pretty sure I have both of you beat on overall quantity." She raised her fist, still focused on her book. "I win."

"It makes a black heart so proud," Lennon said, "knowing how our women have grown."

"You're just proud you corrupted us," Maya said.

Bell continued eating his breakfast in silence, wearing one of his subtler smirks. He ate his breakfast burrito with a fork and a knife. He was clearly not human.

"Who said *they* corrupted us?" Valorie asked. "Who said we weren't already like this before we were pulled into here?"

"I'm pretty sure I was never this slutty," Maya muttered with her mouth full. "I don't know about you and Kitty."

"What're you doing there, champ?" Lennon asked. "Catching flies or misfiring brain cells?"

Valorie glanced over her shoulder. John stood by their table, holding his plate and staring down like a loser in a school lunch room.

"What?" she said, with not a small touch of acid. One night of good sex—not even great sex when it came to Arcanium, but good—didn't absolve him from his sins. At least that was the way Maya would say it, in her incessant and frankly insane need to continue being a good Catholic girl while boning a jinni whom some would call a demon, regardless of how he identified.

"I—" John began. He swallowed then looked away. "Throat was burning. Had to take a moment."

"Move along," Lennon said with a grand flourish.

John continued past their table to the one where Shawn and Marcus sat. They each took opposite ends of the same bench, effectively eating alone. John sat in the middle on the other side. Melanie had been put in her transfer tank away from the tables, closer to the animal cages. They were all isolated. Even Jason and Lily, the lion and tiger, had each other.

Valorie felt nothing as John walked away. She continued eating her breakfast burrito. Not a single shred of guilt.

Bell caught her eye after she'd returned to her meal. He raised an eyebrow in query.

As though he didn't already know.

Valorie nodded slightly, running her finger over her lip and licking it.

"Glad to be of service. Feel free to avail yourself of the gift whenever you like."

But no. Valorie wasn't interested in settling again. She didn't want a consolation prize, even if that prize was a decent pet. She wasn't the fire-eater's handler, and she wasn't interested in being his partner, his buddy or his lover. Once was fun, but enough as far as she was concerned.

* * * *

She tapped her forehead with her toes. Her stomach was on the carpet on her platform, her legs bent over her from either side until her feet rested comfortably on the curve of her head. Some of the members of the audience giggled, especially when Valorie opened her eyes wide and looked up, as though to see who was knocking.

Valorie stepped forward with her feet in front of her face. She unwound until she was in a backbend then lifted herself to standing.

She bowed to applause, but her acknowledgment of the fourth wall didn't last long when she was in her tent. Valorie had music instead of conversation to keep her entertained. She couldn't knit like Kitty or watch TV like Arnie. Even Sandra, the twins, Victor and Christina could mostly just sit around looking weird. Lady Sasha, Lord Mikhail and Valorie's oddities, however, required constant demonstration.

Valorie counted herself lucky that she could choose her own music, as long as it fit with the atmosphere of the circus and she kept it low enough that it didn't interfere with anyone else's tent. The placement of the speakers kept the sound limited to her platform and the area right outside it. Caroline was stuck listening to carousel music all day, even when no one was on the carousel.

Valorie was pretty sure she'd have become homicidal a lot sooner if she had to listen to that stuff for hours on end.

She turned around and spread her legs into an A-frame. The boys, who tended to stay around her tent more often than the women, whistled as she bent down to place her hands on the ground, her ass high in the air. The leather would shine and accentuate it like a comic book heroine's. But she couldn't think of a single comic book heroine—with her admittedly limited knowledge of the more obscure corners of the graphic novel world—who could walk her hands on the ground as she twisted her spine so that she could grab her knees and appear right-side-up between her thighs. Some of the whistles turned into winces of sympathetic pain, but one guy howled his approval and clapped. In appreciation of her skill, no doubt.

If there was one thing the cast of Arcanium got used to, it was being viewed as an object, often a sexual one. Arcanium did nothing to discourage it. It was usually the point. Not all of the members of Arcanium were intended to be viewed sexually, of course—although Kitty had often pointed out that *everyone* appealed to *someone*, and Kitty should know. Sex appeal and curiosity. That's what paid the bills around here.

People didn't need an incubus and succubus to be oversexed assholes. Having Lady Sasha and Lord Mikhail around didn't always help either. However, it had been a long time since Valorie had had to call for Bell because of a belligerent customer. By and large the visitors to Arcanium were as respectful as normals could be. Ignorant little shits, sometimes, but Valorie had learned to tune out most of the bull.

Kitty had a lot more patience for people's stupidity than Valorie, which was why Valorie was glad she didn't interact with people as much as Kitty did. When Valorie left the tent to do her act among the commoners, she didn't do the talking thing like Kitty, who was Bell's little pusher both inside and outside the circus. Valorie just played human sculpture. As long as someone didn't think that meant she was human furniture, everyone got to keep their face unmarked. Valorie didn't have to be a demon to leave claw marks.

So while in another life she might have gotten in someone's face for catcalls and wolf whistles, here they were just part of the job. The audience could admire her ass and fantasize about her pussy all they wanted, as long as they kept it to themselves or in their little bubble of personal space, which was a good rule of thumb in Arcanium and out.

While Valorie was twisted between her legs, John passed by. Usually she wouldn't bother with a second glance, especially since he wasn't looking at her. But he also had a lit candle on his head, and that caused a double take for more than just her.

The red candle was about the width of a man's fist. It had been partially melted, the wax at the bottom molded to John's head, which was why he was able to walk without painstaking balance, although he still had to keep his back and neck perfectly straight to avoid jostling the candle. The grass was dry and brown. A single candle would go out before it hit the ground — and if not, wasn't likely to cause a fire — but that didn't mean walking with an open flame wasn't without risks. With teenagers around, there was an increased likelihood that someone might try to startle him or trip him up.

Valorie caught a glimpse of Ciàran with Moss on his shoulder, shadowing John on the other side of the Row, with its line of additional souvenir booths, the makeshift ring that the clowns used and Misha's open platform.

She didn't know what was so serious. All John seemed to be doing was walking with a lit candle on his head, his expression intense in its professional blankness. He wasn't even putting anything into his mouth.

Valorie shook her head, unraveled herself and eased into a new position.

With one hand on the arm of the armchair, her body made a C with her legs above her head and her other arm out in front of her when John walked by again.

This time he had the lit candle on his head and one on each of his shoulders. He'd amassed a small group of followers, some of whom were taking video or pictures with their phones.

She'd tucked herself into pretzel mode on the seat of the armchair — as surprisingly comfortable as shutting herself in the suitcase — when John walked by again.

He had his forearms out like a man in meditation. He looked mellow enough, as though the repetition of his routine had sent him into a trance. Two candles had been tucked into his elbows, resting on his forearms to join the other partially melted candles, still going strong.

Valorie stayed in her pretzel mode, which wasn't all that interesting for the audience — or rather, it didn't keep them sticking around in front of her tent instead of moving on like window shoppers. However, a lot of the Oddity Row audience had turned toward the center of the Row, waiting for the fire-eater to return. They wanted to see where this stunt was going.

She was curious too. She didn't want to miss him.

He had candles in his hands this time, seven candles in all, flickering merrily in the light breeze. In a big wind there would be no way he could do this, but today was a perfect day for it, and Oddity Row was in shade to best show the light.

This time John stopped just past Valorie's tent, like a soldier called to attention.

He turned around as though finally aware that he had been followed and was now surrounded by an audience.

He kept on turning, again and again, each rotation getting a little faster. The candles were at risk of blowing out.

Then John pursed his lips and blew, and the flames roared up like flamethrowers. He spun faster and faster. The fire trailed behind the candles and seemed to make burning circles around the dervish that John had become. The crowd cheered him on.

When he'd stopped, Valorie noticed that the wax had melted more with the rise of the flames, which had stuttered back to their original size when John stopped spinning. The red wax must have burned with each drip, but John showed no sign of distress.

To the audience's delight, he dropped into a crouch and jumped back up again. He did that a few times then began to kick out a leg with each drop. They all applauded at his impromptu Russian dance. The whole time he kept the candles on his head, shoulders, arms and hands balanced like in a bottle dance. He popped up and down to the rhythm of the audience's claps. When they realized they could control his speed, they clapped faster. He eventually couldn't keep up, and that was when he couldn't help but grin and stay crouched near the ground, running and kicking at half height.

As soon as his legs probably ached from sustaining that position, he jumped back up and spread his arms for applause, still balancing the candles.

Then he walked up to a young teenage girl and lowered himself to one knee.

"Fair maiden," he said, "would you do me the honor of blowing out the candle?"

The girl giggled with her friends at the melodrama, but her face had gone red at being singled out. It didn't matter how scarred he was, John was still attractive, and the girl was old enough to crush on him.

John closed his eyes as she leaned forward and blew out the candle on his head.

All the other candles puffed out at the same time. The girl jumped at the crackle of their extinguishing, but she smiled and clapped with the rest.

"Take it," John said, nodding his head slightly to indicate the candle she'd personally blown out.

She removed it from his head.

"Bring it here," he instructed, and she cautiously but excitedly did what he said.

He pursed his lips again. When he blew, mostly invisible flame that became blue two inches from his mouth and orange at the very end hit the wick, igniting it once again.

John winked at the girl, who giggled again. He stood and walked to a woman standing with a man who appeared to be her husband. John seemed to wisely hesitate to gauge the atmosphere. Then he handed the woman the candle in his right hand. The woman offered it back to him, and he lit it for her before moving on to another.

He varied his audience participation, although they were all female. He picked the last candle off himself and stepped through the crowd, which parted for him.

John came straight to Valorie and held the candle out to her.

There were a series of awwws and a smattering of applause from the audience, the kind that often accompanied spontaneous proposals in public places.

It kind of put her on the spot. Not only did she have to break the fourth wall, but she slowly had to untwist herself and emerge from the chair to meet him. She wasn't sure how she felt when she sat on the edge of her platform and took the candle. With both their hands still on it, John blew his fire from a distance. She felt the hair-sizzling warmth of it, but he had a good grasp of how to manipulate the fire that came out of him these days, and he focused it on the wick, which burst into a high flame before settling again when he let go of the candle.

His body still had remnants of wax on it. He brushed at those places as he backed away.

She didn't know what to do.

Valorie had never had a moment where she couldn't improvise, but here she was, staring like a fool, not smiling, not contorting, not carrying on the performance as though he'd handed her the baton. Annoyance and anger swelled in her stomach, but no one else seemed to notice her temporary paralysis. They gave their final applause to the stunt, and John bowed before jogging away in the direction of the carousel.

She stared at the candle, which flickered merrily. It didn't care about awkward. It just cared about chemistry and physics.

Valorie made to blow it out, but people were watching, and she instinctively understood that would be a disappointment to them.

She set it on the side table next to the armchair and let it burn.

* * * *

As soon as she felt it would be appropriate to leave for a while, she blew the candle out—safety first—and escaped behind the red mini-curtain to the solitude at the back of her tent.

She sat down on the ottoman and wove her fingers through her hair, restrained today in a simple low ponytail that kept it out of her way.

What the ever-loving hell had he been thinking? They'd had one night of little more than itch-scratching and he'd presented her with the candle as though it had been a date — as though he thought it had been the start of a beautiful romance. Arcanium wasn't a Harlequin novel, despite what the makeup on her eyes and her harlequin catsuits suggested. No one got a traditional happy ending around here, especially not with misogynistic criminals like John.

It had been a sweet gesture, which made it dead suspicious in her eyes. What had he hoped to accomplish? Push all the right buttons and get another gooey reward? Classic Nice Guy move, only for him to blow his top when his fucktoy got taken away. Valorie was going to have to talk with Bell about encouraging him.

John didn't return to Oddity Row again for the rest of the day, as far as she noticed. If he did, he stayed on the other side of the curved Row where she couldn't see him, and he stayed out of her way whenever she left her exhibition tent. If she wanted to tear him a new one, she'd have to wait until after the evening performance.

* * * *

There was a light on in his tiny trailer. John probably had to curl up in order to sleep in his own bed, the trailer was so small.

The door was unlocked.

Valorie burst in, storming up the stairs. She had to hunch to keep her head from hitting the ceiling.

John was reading a science fiction novel, looking like Papa Bear in Baby Bear's bed. He had a blanket over his lap. He looked up when she came in.

She was so incensed after the build-up through the day that she didn't immediately register that the whole wall of the trailer across from him was charred black, like logs burned to a crisp. Nothing had lost its integrity. The cabinets were still cabinets, the drawers still drawers. One of the drawers was open, and Valorie could see unburned clothes inside. So the things around him could be burned, but Bell had put *some* protections up. He wouldn't want the trailer to need to be replaced, and he wouldn't want Kitty and Lady Sasha to have to constantly make John new clothes. Nor would he want his fire-eater to spontaneously combust. Bell couldn't use him if he was dead.

There was no way for her to determine when the burns had occurred or whether they'd happened over the course of multiple accidents. Valorie guessed, though, given his state of calm curiosity, it had been a while since the last accident.

So she ignored the burned walls and turned her attention once more to John.

"What the hell was that little stunt supposed to be?" she shouted, stabbing her finger toward Oddity Row in case he needed reminding which stunt he needed to answer for.

"That?" John said. "It was just supposed to be fun. I cleared it with the Man before doing it. He thought it was a good idea."

"I'm not talking about the candle walk and dancing, stovetop. I'm talking about when you broke away from the audience you were trying to impress—"

"*Trying* to impress?

"And handed *me* a candle. Which, by the way, did *not* impress."

"Sometimes a candle is just a candle," John said. He set his book down. Valorie noticed that he set it down behind him, away from where he was facing.

"Let me make something clear," Valorie said, this time pointing at him. "Last night was a one-time deal. You'll be lucky if you get me once a year."

"You're right," John agreed, infuriatingly calm. It made her think he was mocking her, even though he just looked like a studious college boy who'd lost his Internet and had to make do.

"So you don't get to go around giving me a candle like a normal boy giving his girl a dozen motherfucking roses," Valorie continued. "You give it to another girl — or a guy, for all I care. Just don't put me on the spot like that, when I have no choice but to take what you give me for the sake of the audience. If you'd tried to kiss me, though, I would have had something stronger than profanity for you right now."

"I get it. No more candles," John said. "It was just supposed to be an audience pleaser, that's all. I didn't want you to read anything into it. I know you better than the others is all. You were the one I thought would take it."

"Kitty'll take it," Valorie snapped. "And she doesn't have to unknot herself to do it."

John turned around on the bed, placing his feet on the floor and hunching his shoulders in a shrug as he looked up at her. He kept the blanket wrapped around his waist, which was how she knew he was naked underneath. The blanket bunched in such a way she couldn't tell whether succubus magic had gotten to him. She hadn't felt a surge in her own need, but she doubted one fuck had been enough to eliminate all of it in him, even though she'd been leaking semen the whole time he'd been showering and some in the shower too. One of the unpleasant but inevitable side effects of sex, and like most sexual things in Arcanium, she was used to it by now.

"I'm sorry I made you think I believed there was something more. All I wanted to do was try something new," he said.

Valorie huffed, crossing her arms over her chest. "What are you doing?"

"What do you mean, what am I doing?"

"I mean, why are you acting all nice when we both know you're not, like you care about Arcanium when we both know you'd stick a torched stake through Bell's heart if you thought it would do any good?" Valorie said. "You're not fooling me."

"I'm not trying to fool you," John said. "What makes you think I am?"

"Because people don't change like that, especially here—not this much this fast," Valorie accused. "What's your end game?"

"My end game? I'd ask why you're so suspicious, but I've lived here for the last...you know, I don't even know what month it is."

"November," she answered.

"Over a year," John said. "Seems like longer. The point is, I've been here. I know what I did to get here. I know why you're suspicious, why all of you guys treat us like crap."

"We treat you like kings in comparison to how you *should* be treated for what you would have done," Valorie said.

"I didn't say you shouldn't," John said. "Whether or not it's justified, we're treated like crap on top of Bell turning us into Mengele experiments. Melanie is too inhuman and...occupied for it to get to her like it does to Shawn and me. And Shawn's still too far gone for him to do anything about it."

"But you think *you* can do something about it?" Valorie asked. "Everything you do, Easy-Bake, we'll know none of your motives are pure. They're purely selfish. You want to be treated like a man, when you're here because you were always a monster pretending to be a man. If you're occasionally treated like a man, that's not a courtesy, that's a fucking *gift*. At least when the demons are monsters, that's what they're supposed to be. Scum like you are what's really wrong with the world — the monsters that are us. And you don't get to choose when to stop being a monster."

"Before I was brought here, I was a football player with Shawn and C-Cameron," John said, stammering over his deceased friend's name. "I didn't think I was a bad guy. I didn't think anything I did was bad. That's how all that shit gets to you, you know. People who aren't 'bad guys' do it and don't lose their status. And you think, 'I'm not a bad guy either, therefore this shit isn't bad'. It's all just something you're supposed to do, or if it stays quiet, it's okay."

"Charming." She purposely infused iciness that could freeze saltwater into her reply.

"You come up with all the excuses in the world why you're not the one in the wrong. She was drunk. She came onto me first. She liked me. She said yes then changed her mind. She got in the way. She won't tell anyone. She can't stop me. And it's not just the girls. We didn't take during football season, or at least I didn't, but sometimes we took things from stores or didn't pay at restaurants. Sticking it to the Man, we'd say. Fuck capitalism and fuck the police. The world is full of excuses that it gives you, and when you're surrounded by other people doing it, it's easier to justify. Get it? Because these not-so-bad guys can't all be wrong. It's such a little thing, and they can't touch us. We're too good for that. We're too nice. My future's good, and nothing's going to get in the way of that. If it does, there are ways of getting rid of obstacles."

"Are you getting to a point, or can I just vomit on you now?" Valorie asked.

"When Bell made us wish and I had to watch Melanie change—and Shawn—and when I heard what happened to Cameron, I couldn't talk. None of us could. I couldn't argue my case or try to sway him with logic. And it would have been bad for me to try."

"You think?" Valorie said.

"Look, I know that now, but I didn't then," John said, finally showing signs of exasperation. "I thought for sure that if Bell hadn't silenced me, I would have been able to convince him what we'd been doing wasn't so bad, that nothing bad really happened, that I didn't have to be put into my own personal hell for doing nothing."

"Oh man, you were so *lucky* he had you burning your tongue and face every time you opened your mouth," Valorie said, laughing without humor. "I almost wish you'd argued to Bell that you hadn't done anything to his sweetheart and two other members of his circus."

"It still burns," John said quietly. "Not as bad as it used to. And I can talk and eat things without the fire coming out my mouth. But it still burns too hot inside me sometimes, and if I'm not careful… Every time I use it, it's real fire, real heat. I just heal faster now."

"You're still lucky."

"I know," John said. "Shawn got his tongue back, and he's still not talking. But me…"

"You're talking an awful lot."

"Before I came here, I was committed to football. I might not be a nice guy or too big to fail like I thought I was, but I'm still a team player. I always sacrificed for the team. I didn't try to be a star if it meant leaving the team in the dust. I wanted *us* to win, not *me*. The scholarships I got for college were awesome, but I got them because of the sportsmanship too, not just the skill. See? That was part of why I figured I couldn't be so bad. I got awards for being selfless on the field. I was in my church's youth group and went to church every Sunday in college. Wednesday, if we had a game on Sunday. Every week. I was a team player there too. Sang in the choir and everything."

"I get it," Valorie said. "You were the golden boy on the outside, but it was just foil wrapping."

"I spent the first half year or something thinking wrong had been done to me. No one would talk to me or do anything for me. I had to drink smoothies through a thin straw. I thought I was going to starve without a steak or a hamburger. I lived with Shawn then. We were mute together, and we couldn't look at each other without knowing what kind of shit we were in. His eye... I'm still not over watching his eyes dissolve and the one he has now growing in. I still can't look directly at him, and he can't look at my burns. When I burned his ass one night, Bell separated us, and then I was alone. I was so angry."

"Because of what happened to *you*," Valorie said.

"Yeah. I was such a tragic fucking hero. Then I realized that the reason all y'all were shunning me like a plague victim was because *I* was the plague you were avoiding. You were treating me like a monster, as you called it, because I *was* a monster. I was a golden boy before because people treated me like one, and it finally hit me that I wasn't a golden boy anymore, because I was being treated like a monster. And if I was a monster now, I was a monster back then too, because I hadn't changed. Y'all weren't ignoring me because of my face or because I'd spurt fire at you given half a chance. You were ignoring me because I was an asshole."

"Congratulations on your enlightenment," Valorie said, reaching for the doorknob.

"I'm not telling you this for validation or reward, Valorie," John said.

"Don't you *dare* say my name, pig."

"Sorry." John looked down. The contrition appeared sincere. "I'm telling you this to explain why I did that stunt. I didn't stop being a team player. Arcanium's my team now, and as long as people think I deserve to be here—including me—it's going to be my team for a long time. And now I guess I'll do anything for it. I'll do anything to be more a part of this team. Do you get that? If that means being wrapped in rope from head to toe and licking your feet clean, I'll do it. If it means I treat everyone like they're better than me because they are, I'll do that. If Bell wants me to walk around the circus with flammable jelly on my junk and gives me a match to light it, I'll do it. You said people don't change. Maybe they don't, but I get why I'm here. I get what I did wrong, and I want to make it better however I can. Maybe that's not change, but let's just say I want a chance, even if the pain never goes away and I never get to see my family again. I probably deserve worse. And my family deserves better than a son who got himself stuck in hell."

He shook his head. "Six months. Or was it eight months? Whatever. Too long for me to figure out I was in hell for things I did instead of because demons are evil. Terrible as it is, demons do what they're supposed to do, like you said. I was the one doing evil I wasn't supposed to do. And I can't imagine the hurt I caused to people before Christina and Maya and Troy or what I would have done in the future if Bell hadn't stopped me. It causes real horror in me, man. It changes everything when you realize you thought you were the hero and it turns out you were the villain the whole time. I don't know whether I've changed, but I'm trying."

"Good for you. You get twenty-five cents and a toaster. I'm not interested in your confession, fire-eater. I came here to tell you to leave...me...alone. If I want you for some reason, I'll come to you. You keep changing your life in ten easy steps by yourself and maybe you'll get into heaven. But I'm not heaven," Valorie said. "I'd be fine if you rot in the eternal kind of hell, as long as it doesn't interfere with my life."

"Whatever you say," John said.

Once again, that infuriating sense that he was mocking her behind that honest face, as though his burns masked the real thing behind something that appeared damaged and innocent.

"Just so we're clear," Valorie said. "Because you talked an awful lot, and guys like you don't always hear what other people are saying over the sound of their own voices."

"I guess I had a lot I haven't been able to say," John said, staring down at his bare feet and shrugging. "You kept listening."

"My mistake," she said. "If I'd known walking out would have stopped you, I would have done it a while back."

He held his hand to his heart, not a gesture of false sincerity but of a man with heartburn. With him, that was probably more literal than most.

"Excuse me," he said. He scooted back with his blanket still around him and opened the window next to his bed. Like a dragon with indigestion, he expelled a burst of flame into the air outside the trailer. Valorie smelled smoked meat.

John coughed, wincing. But before he could turn back to her, she said, "Just leave me alone," and slammed the door behind her.

She could still smell the burned flesh outside, of course, but more than that, she started to feel nauseated with every step she took toward her RV. She associated the burned smell in the air with the image of a scolded puppy.

It wasn't like he'd done anything *wrong* this time, just something she hadn't known what to do with. Still, he didn't deserve her pity. He'd earned every healing burn down his slimy throat. What things had John shoved down a girl's throat while still thinking he was a good guy? Guys who did what John had been about to do with his friends that night, they'd usually done stuff like that before, which meant John was lower scum than murderers to her. His victims had to keep living with what he'd done, and not everyone could just shake it off or learn and grow and rise up to be the better person.

He hadn't done anything wrong this time, but he'd done too much wrong in his life. He hadn't deserved last night. He didn't deserve anything else. If he thought he could make amends by giving candles and being a nice guy—for his own benefit—he had another think coming.

She was better than this. She was better than *him*.

As she headed for her RV, she saw Joanne and Jane, with Seth and Lars bookending their crablike gait. Seth's and Lars' hands met behind the conjoined twins, but that wasn't their attempt at subtly acknowledging their relationship. Joanne and Jane couldn't get away from each other because their spines were fused. Seth and Lars couldn't get away from each other because they needed to be in constant contact. They couldn't break away from each other if they tried. On either side of the twins, holding hands was how they kept in touch.

Just another reason why their secret relationship wouldn't have been shameful to admit, but whatever floated their boat. They somehow made it work, though, with the twins. It was so comfortable between all of them, so easy in spite of the twins' and the boys' physical complications. Lars kissed Jane's neck—at least Valorie assumed it was Jane because Lars was usually with Jane.

She had closed her hand around the handle of her RV door when she noticed Bell carrying Maya to their own RV, her legs around his waist and her arms around his shoulders. Maya had buried her face in his neck. She was naked, her back lashed as deeply as the Ringmaster could give it to her without shattering bone. This was the only way Bell could hold her if he was going to tend her wounds in the privacy of the RV, although that wasn't always their Saturday night plan following Maya's voluntary beating. Sometimes they shared it with other members of the cast. Sometimes they didn't make it to the RV.

Bell held her so tenderly, his arms and legs flexing with strength. She could see his love plain as the human mask that he wore, except his feelings were so much less of a lie. He was jinn, and some lumped him in with the other demons, but he could love so much more powerfully than Valorie had ever imagined he was capable of when he'd been with her. So could the other demons, although they avoided it whenever possible. It hurt their cred, and love could be dangerous for both them and the one they had the misfortune to fall in love with. But it happened. Valorie had seen it. And Bell was so fucking in love he could probably stop the Earth's core from rotating if he thought Maya would want it. Any love he'd had for Valorie had been a poor imitation in comparison.

Just in case she needed more salt in the wound, she heard Melanie's trailer door shut behind her. The metal door had a distinctive sound. Lennon was with his little mermaid once again.

And here came Sandra, holding Arnie's hand as the golems rolled him to his custom trailer, which allowed them to open the whole back of the trailer for Arnie to climb in without getting stuck in a door. Arnie, as always, looked suspicious and star-struck at the same time when Sandra followed him in.

Troy's trailer was shaking. Christina would be in there. She guessed that if she stepped back twenty paces, she'd see Carlo's trailer doing the same dance.

Valorie hadn't been horny a minute ago. She still wasn't, if she was being honest with herself. Her body had responded with arousal, but her brain hadn't caught up.

She still slammed her RV door shut.

She also slammed John's door shut behind her hard enough to make the whole tiny trailer tremble and rock as though in an earthquake.

"Not a word, fire-eater," Valorie said through gritted teeth as she climbed over him in bed. "You want this? Push the blanket down."

John blinked, startled by her abrupt entrance and the brazen declaration. He might have also been surprised because his window was open and the blinds only halfway down so that he could lean out without obstruction. Anyone could see in if they wanted to.

Anyone could see her with him.

His gaze flicked over her, more impulse than deliberate, but she felt her nipples harden under the leather at his observation.

He warily pushed the edge of the blanket down from his waist. His cock was heavy and full, leaning against his thigh. It twitched under her scrutiny, as though awakening from a lustful sleep.

"How long have you been like this?" Valorie asked. "You can speak to answer."

"Since I woke up. Worse after the act. Worse more after you came in."

But he hadn't stroked himself or squeezed like some guys did when they thought they were being circumspect in front of a woman. They never were, and it always felt suggestive, even if that wasn't the intention.

"Have you touched yourself since last night?" Valorie asked. "Don't speak."

John paused. Then shook his head no.

She grabbed his chin and opened his mouth. "Good," she murmured, before sinking into him, taking him over with her kiss. She was fierce, making him jerk when she nipped at him every time he thought about meeting her kiss with passion of his own. His passion could only be sated by submitting, and he'd learned his lesson from last night. He leaned back against the wall and let her wrest her pleasure from him.

"Undress me," she said as she wrapped her hand around his cock, stroking the shaft and avoiding the head.

The sound of the zipper was deafening in the small space. Valorie rose up over him to kiss him again and to speed up the process, open-mouthed kisses that made his cock pulse, heat, grow even more in her hand. He shuddered, as though cold or afraid, as he folded the leather down her body. She didn't have to move from her possession of his mouth for him to pull the leather from her legs one at a time. She simply contorted until she could grab the leather from him and throw it away, glad to be rid of it because she couldn't wait anymore to have him inside. Having him in her hand wasn't enough. It only whet the appetite in her cunt, arousal that had emerged as desire under her kisses, under his submission.

He would do anything for Arcanium. He would do anything for her because she was a part of it.

"For your sins," she murmured against his lips as she released his cock. Valorie raised her eyebrows at him, expectant. He quickly understood what she wanted him to do.

John exhaled sharply as he took his cock in his own hand and held the head steady for Valorie to slide down around him. This time she didn't take her time. She ground her pussy against his fist, almost taking it in with his cock when he didn't get out of the way.

"This isn't a romance, dragon," Valorie panted, already bobbing over him so fast and hard, keeping herself tight around him, that he shouted. "You can be my pet, but I'll never be your girl. And I'm not your happy ending."

"Whatever you want," he gasped, arching his back, his neck straining.

When she took his face between her palms, prepared to wrench him back into a near-bruising kiss — maybe prepared to draw blood this time — he suddenly covered his mouth with his hand.

His body became inferno hot around and inside her. The air filled with a fresh draft of burned skin because he couldn't get to the window in time. He threw his head back, and Valorie leaned away just enough that the burst of fire roaring out of him, along with his scream, didn't singe her face or hair.

She grasped his shoulders and dug her nails into the flesh, continuing to ride him because the heat... Oh God, the heat. It spread through her like arousal, like her body couldn't tell the difference. Demons had a different kind of heat that suffused a body, tingling like warm water on cold skin, but this...this was the dry heat of an oven, aggressive as it filled her, as she aggressively filled herself with his cock. She'd taken him so quickly that he pulled her taut, hit places that hadn't been any more ready than he.

John coughed. His fire-free mouth didn't look charred like it had back when he'd been forbidden to open his mouth wider than the circumference of a straw. It was inflamed, but he gave a muffled groan when she dove in, tasting the heat that had been left behind.

Smoke was a good smell to her — not cigarette smoke but real smoke. It was the smell of home, family memories. It didn't matter that it came from his body. She wrapped her arm around his neck, kissing him until tears pricked her eyes and she had to quickly brush them away before the boy realized it. She couldn't let him see that. She couldn't let anyone see that.

He surrounded her with his warmth, his strong arms, arms that could hold themselves out for thirty minutes without wavering, and his strong legs underneath her, legs that could dance for ten. The way she fucked him with her cunt was almost violent, but neither of them were going to complain. Their mouths were occupied and her body sang, the music rising higher and higher. Valorie hurried toward its end.

This didn't need to be drawn out. The sooner she could leave, the sooner she could get her bearings and wonder why she punished herself like this, why she had to let him make her feel good when he was one of the last men she should be with. Being with him, encouraging him like this? It brought her down to his level. His disgusting, unforgivable level. And he got *her* after the things he'd done? Twice?

The rest had rejected her. Was John her consolation prize, or was she his?

John took his arms away to grab fistfuls of his covers as he shouted — this time without the fiery column that had singed the already charred ceiling — and came. It wasn't the eruption of before, but he still had enough heat within for her to feel it. More burning arousal trickled down her spine until she couldn't take it anymore. She clenched her teeth against a cry as she seemed to burst around him.

As soon as she was finished and her heart stopped racing as if she'd run a marathon, Valorie got up from him without another word. His cock left a damp stain against his hip.

She snatched her harlequin leather costume and stalked out of the trailer, slamming the door behind her once again.

Chapter Five

"I have ten dollars. I need a minute with the boss, Maya," Valorie said. She held up her bill.

Bell usually didn't like for his cast to interrupt the flow of customers, but Valorie had found the loophole a long time ago. Customers paid for his time. If the cast wanted to pay for the time, he wouldn't object. Besides, Valorie knew from personal experience that he sometimes took time out of the day for his own pleasures. She was mostly sure that she didn't have to bring the money, not with their history, but it was her way to show she was serious, not just banking on their original relationship.

"Sure," Maya said.

She didn't ask Valorie what she wanted to talk to Bell about, nor did she check with Bell first. She stood up from the armchair she used to flash her legs at male customers while Bell flirted shamelessly with the women and stepped out, looking like an extra from a French bordello. Maya never tried to get in Valorie's way when it came to Bell, even though she didn't need to be afraid of Valorie anymore. Maya had won, but she respected what Valorie had once had with Bell as well as Bell's continued affection for Valorie.

"Sit down," Bell said, gesturing to the chair across from him. "Do you need your fortune told or your tarot read?"

"If you want me to not cut into your customer time, I need for this to go more direct, Bell," Valorie said.

"Very well." Bell shuffled the deck. "I will do my best."

He would. That didn't mean he would succeed.

"Why did you give me the fire-eater?" Valorie asked.

"I don't think that's what you really want to ask me," he said.

"Bell."

"I think what you want to know is why I gave you to the fire-eater," he continued with a patient smile. He set the tarot cards next to the small runner of velvet where he read palms.

Valorie leaned back in her chair and crossed her legs. Black leather pants, painted-on leather halter top. She wasn't even cold yet in spite of the chill outside. If she got cold, she had a duster that ironically made her look like a demon slayer of some kind, like she ought to be striding through the circus with a semiautomatic.

"So what if I am?" Valorie asked. He could see right through her nonchalance, but Valorie had too much pride not to attempt to show it.

"You fear that, by giving the fire-eater to you, I've both elevated him and diminished you," Bell said, "and you feel that I'm being unfair, promoting the boy so quickly when I am not usually so forgiving to those who have threatened what is mine."

"What gives, Bell?" she asked, wrapping her long arms around her abdomen.

"I haven't spared him pain ever since I gave him his voice back and made it so that he wouldn't scream every time he burned," Bell said. "He shall have to bear that for much longer. However, when he came to me, begging for a chance to show his loyalty, I recognized his sincerity. I gave him this small oasis because he proved far earlier than many of my lost souls that he could learn. What's more, I thought he could be of use to you, a man compatible to your needs that are no longer being serviced. Was I wrong, Valorie? Is he inadequate?"

"It's not his physical attributes. It's his character…and his status," she said.

"Just being accepted into your presence elevates him, true," Bell said. "It was an unfortunate side effect. However, accepting him into your presence does not diminish you, my dear. I had hoped you might merely find him a pleasant toy, and you have already proved that his reward can also be his punishment."

"Seems awfully cushy for a punishment," Valorie said.

"Only because you've limited yourself by your own insecurity. Perhaps I can help broaden your mind on the matter," Bell said.

"Are you calling me insecure and small-minded?"

"I'm calling you insecure," he replied. "Are you going to tell me you interrupted potential customers and are considering leaving me because your foundation is rock-solid?"

"Sometimes I hate you so much."

Bell smiled. He reached into the leather bag affixed to the beaded leather belt that slung low over his hips, lower than the black leather trousers he wore.

There was so much leather in this circus that they could have been single-handedly responsible for the extinction of all the cows south of the Mason-Dixon line. At least, Valorie thought the skin was from cows. She *hoped* the skin was from cows.

He pulled out a thick, studded collar with a heavy metal ring in the front. Attached to it was a thin but strong leash, nothing delicate or decorative. It wouldn't break from a sudden jerk or anything short of a bolt cutter. If it could hold a large dog, it could hold a human.

There was no way that heavy-duty thing fit in his bag.

He then pulled out another collar — fierce-looking, with real metal spikes instead of studs. Both collars were of the same style as the cuffs he'd given Maya back when she'd decided the only way she could handle being in a demonic circus was by consenting to become Bell's slave, which didn't seem all that rewarding in Valorie's opinion. But Maya was still wearing the cuffs. And here Bell was handing her her own hardware.

"If you believe he should be shown no mercy, then show him none. I didn't hand him over to you just for the one night, my dear," Bell said, setting the collars and leash on the table in front of him. "I thought you could get quite some use out of him. And now I pass on responsibility over him from me to you. If he steps out of line, it is for you to see that he is punished by the Ringmaster and your duty to heal what needs to be healed. In the meantime, he is yours to discipline as you see fit, for your own pleasure or for his pain, as long as you stay within the rules of this circus."

"Like you do with Maya?" Valorie asked.

He nodded. "You've done quite well with him so far. He would have to consent to your punishment, to your ownership, but I believe he has made his wishes quite clear."

"Is that what this is?" Valorie asked, nudging the chain with one of her dusty feet. "A fulfillment of one of his wishes? Am I roped into another person's wish again, Bell?"

"Unspoken," he replied. "He continues to heed Kitty's warning. She does make sure that my circus runs more smoothly, without repercussions of wishes to contend with, but it also makes my life less entertaining. The wishes in this tent, Valorie... You cannot imagine how mundane. I need a challenge, my dear, a real challenge."

"Install a wishing well," Valorie said. "So you saw fit to fulfill his wish without him having to say it?"

"I fulfilled your spoken wish too," Bell said. "I could have compelled a wish from him, but I suspected you would value more his being bound to you of his own will rather than my magic. What do you think?"

Valorie's lips thinned, but she hooked the collars and the leash on her ankle and brought them to her hands. She glowered at them.

"I don't know whether this is enough," Valorie said. "And I'm not sure whether I want that creep. Shit on all that reformed rhetoric. I don't care if it's genuine. He hasn't proven himself to me."

"Then make him," Bell said, standing.

Her audience with him was over.

He slid his fingers around her wrist before she could leave, drawing her back toward him. He snaked an arm behind the small of her back.

"Bell..." she whispered. Having him so close brought everything back, desire that went so much deeper than lust. That was how it manifested only because that was all her body could process. It hurt like a whip to her heart to be this close, yet not to have him no matter how tightly she held him — not to have anyone. The wish Maya had made had taken away her jealousy, not her yearning. If Valorie had a wish left to spare, she would have wished her love away. It hurt too much and had made her far too vulnerable, far too unpredictable. It had changed her without her realizing it then left her out in that cold—all her changes for nothing.

She tried to back away but stepped closer at the first sign she would lose contact. God, she hated herself so much right now.

"He's not a consolation prize," Bell said. He traced her collarbone with the tips of his fingers then found the line of her cheekbone. "You aren't second best, and you aren't my leftovers fit only for the dogs. I don't like it when you think so little of me. You know that you could still have me."

"Not the way I want you," Valorie said. "Maya gets your heart, Bell. I know that. I accept it. But I can't have anything less than that. It's why I cut you loose. It's why I cut Lennon loose. I don't want a timeshare arrangement. If I can't have all your heart, I don't want the rest. Whether you want me to feel like tossed-out leftovers, that's how I feel, and I feel it most when you try to convince me that I'm not."

She stroked his cheek but forced herself to retreat, once again the loser in a battle Bell hadn't meant to start—but he'd done it anyway.

It was like ripping open an old wound over and over again. Lennon had been the consolation prize, not John. John was the consolation for the consolation prize—a poor bandage for such self-inflicted wounds. Bell needed to stop trying to be the man she'd fallen in love with. He needed to become her boss again. This needed to become more professional now, or else she wasn't going to be able to stay, not without the wound getting infected.

Perhaps with something worse than jealousy this time.

Valorie couldn't help but feel a little justified by the hurt in Bell's eyes. It was difficult to hurt jinn. Perhaps that meant she had some power left, although it was hardly the kind of power she'd signed up for.

"It was never my intention," Bell said.

"No, but it was the outcome you knew would happen," Valorie responded.

"Could happen. Until I became sure that it would happen," he said.

"You know that doesn't make any sense to us, Bell, and it's not helpful knowing you put me through this even when you knew what would definitely happen," Valorie said.

"I had to," Bell said. "Because it was going to happen."

She sighed and held up the hardware. "Thanks for the gifts. I'll think about using them."

"Valorie, you are still a queen here, as much as you ever were," Bell said. "What can I do to convince you to stay?"

A deposed queen was no longer a queen. His logic was faulty, or it wasn't human logic. Either way, it wasn't helpful.

"Just leave me alone."

"You came to me."

"I came to the boss. There is nothing *you* can do for me. Let me try to fix this on my own. And if I can't..." Valorie unhooked the tent flap to open it up for customers again. "Then I need you to let me go. You can't have everything you want, Bell. That's not how this works."

The inaccuracy of her saying he couldn't have what he wanted was tempered by the knowledge that Bell only took so much for himself. He was at his most ruthless when fulfilling wishes. The rest of the time, he would rather let his toys do the things they did without too much of his interference—as long as they didn't interfere with the progress of his circus.

In truth, Bell could have everything he wanted if he didn't have a soft spot for free will. Sometimes he indentured a will, but he'd always let it free after a time. 'Free', though, was a relative term.

Some part of Valorie would always be trapped in his clutches as long as she stayed.

All the more reason why she should probably leave.

So she'd decided. But she wouldn't leave all at once. Time to start looking for what she could do after she left, where she could go.

Until then, maybe she could have a little fun, the last bit of amazing sex she might ever have again. Valorie would make sure it was worth the short while.

Then John would have to go back to depending on his hand and impressing the boss into giving him some other kind of reprieve. And she would have to find a way to live outside this place, surrounded by people and the demons unseen, never quite fitting in even if she never flew her freak flag ever again. She'd never belong on the outside. She just didn't know whether she'd ever belong here either, and here hurt more.

* * * *

"Hey!" Valorie shouted in the middle of the crowd. "Fire hose!" she added, just in case the boy couldn't recognize the voice of his Queen.

John turned around from where he'd been cooking customer's raw sausages on a stick for them. People loved it when he did that. Whenever anyone thought to sic health inspectors on them, they always found that the sausages were cooked through. It was safer to eat anything here than just about anywhere else. Unless a person made the wrong wish, of course.

They were in the middle of Oddity Row, John in front of Christina's, Sandra's and Arnie's tents, which were down-curve from her own and meant she could sometimes see John and sometimes not when he was doing his usual stunts.

"Come here!" she called, pointing imperiously in front of her — at her feet.

He looked around, anxious about the crowd of now-curious onlookers. But when she directed him to her again, he slowly made his way through the crowd. It parted before him, just like it had when he'd done his candle walk.

"What are you doing?" John whispered.

Valorie cut him off with a hiss. "I didn't tell you to speak, did I?" she asked. "No. I'm telling you to kneel, pet."

"Here? Right now? Isn't that — ?"

She hissed again, snapping her fingers, and he stopped talking.

It was important that this be done. Here. Now. Where all could bear witness. That was the only way this was going to work for her. And it was John's final test before she declared him ready for duty or kicked him to the proverbial curb.

She wasn't going to jump him in front of everyone, but she could make him obey. The crowd would think it was only an act. Suggestive. Strange. But that's what Arcanium was.

"I want you to kneel. If you want to be my pet dragon, you will kneel before your Queen."

John visibly bristled. Public submission was very different from private—just a step up from public humiliation.

Valorie lifted her left hand, which had been holding the leash and studded collar against her thigh. Now she exposed it for what it was.

"If you want a queen, dragon, you have to be bound," she said. "It's your choice. Submit to me in all things and wear my collar, or you can have your freedom…and its price."

Smoke rose from his nostrils. He sniffed the heat in and shook his head, against the discomfort rather than in denial. There were murmurs around them at that.

"You said anything," Valorie reminded him quietly. "You promised you would do anything. I'm showing you what anything looks like."

John clenched his teeth, making the tendons at his temples twitch. But his knees buckled as though he'd given himself a mental kick.

And he fell to his knees before her.

She was still a little nauseated from her time with Bell, but damn, watching the man do that in front of everyone was *sweet.*

"Whatever I require. Nod."

He did so.

"Your subjugation. Your submission. Your humiliation. If I require it, you will give your life to me."

He nodded again.

"You will serve your Queen with everything you have, every weakness, every bit of power. If the dragon agrees, raise your head and set the air on fire," Valorie commanded him.

The exposed fine hairs on her arms crinkled at the dry heat that emitted from his parted lips. He blew the fire at her, and for a second, she thought she'd stepped over his line, that he would retaliate the same way any man like him would retaliate—with violence, extreme destruction. He could leave her as so much ash if he applied that power against her. Bell could probably resurrect the ash, but it would hurt like hell then become terrifying nothing before Bell could get to her.

The flames forked well before they hit her abdomen, instead surrounding her with a ring of fire.

She hoped he'd taken care not to get the fire close enough to scorch the leather. That would be unfortunate. Valorie would think it was humorous. Lady Sasha would be less inclined toward humor.

The audience that had gathered around them leaped back from the heat, but they weren't in danger either. Valorie could see from the glitter in his eyes how maintaining the fire ring pained him. She gave him an almost imperceptible nod. John drew the fire back in on the same paths he'd made for it, like a recording in reverse.

"Good boy," Valorie said, stepping forward to stroke the scarred side of his face.

She didn't think he'd intended to lean into her touch.

Valorie licked her lips. Her mouth was dry for reasons that had nothing to do with the way he'd burned away all the moisture from the air around her.

She stepped around him and straddled his calves. When she looked around at the crowd, she could pinpoint the people who understood what this was, that it wasn't just the circus version of a fairy tale about a beautiful but wicked queen and a dragon giving her his allegiance. There were a few people out there who recognized a collaring ceremony when they saw it. Valorie liked their shock that she was bold enough to do it in public, even if they didn't know whether it was real or not.

Valorie opened the leather collar. The insides were slightly padded for comfort. She adjusted his head with her knuckles against his chin to make fastening it easier. It was like tying a belt around his neck.

"You can remove this at night if you're not with me, before a shower or a rainstorm, or if I remove it from you. But when you wake up, you'll wear it so that everyone in Arcanium, cast and crowd, will know that you belong to me. The leash is mine."

It was already fastened to the collar ring and wrapped around her wrist. She unwound the chain so that it curved down from the ring, slithering against his skin. A link caught briefly on his nipple. He shuddered.

She walked back around him and spread her arms.

"If you would like, you may thank your Queen, pet," Valorie said.

John glanced up at her. *Fuck.* If she had to feel vulnerable, she could handle it so much better when someone else was more vulnerable than she. And he didn't stop looking at her like that as he crawled forward, dusting up the knees of his trousers. She wrapped the leash around her wrist again as he approached.

He hovered his hands on either side of her hips. She could practically see him consider cupping her ass, but he stayed teenager-appropriate with his warm hands on her hips, half on her skin over the low-cut leather. John blew gently against her navel, cool air then the light burn of a candle flame before he smothered it with a kiss. Blood rushed between her legs, swelling her folds and the inner walls of her pussy. If she were allowed to have him eat her out again, she'd have commanded him to open her pants and have at it. But she had to stay appropriate as well.

"Thank you," he murmured, velvet against her belly.

Valorie smiled, as cold and calculating as any monarch, although her insides had heated enough to thaw winter. She bent down to unclasp the leash from the collar.

"In thirty minutes, meet me in the back of my tent," she whispered in his ear. "Remove your leather and make yourself hard. Do I have to tell you not to come?"

He shook his head.

She kissed his bare scalp and stroked him like a puppy before stepping back.

"Rise, my dragon. Even though you are not leashed, you shall know that you are mine," Valorie said, backing away.

John stood up, made to step toward her, but she clicked her tongue and wagged her finger at him.

"I know," she murmured. "And just so you know who rules you..."

She bent over backward into a handstand, turned around on her hands as she spread her legs until she'd done a full rotation to wolf whistles from the crowd and John's avid attention.

When John tried to step forward again, Valorie stopped him with a foot to his leg. She'd be calling attention to his semi-erection, but that was well within the rules of Arcanium.

"Go, pet. Fly free now and fly home tonight. The Queen has her duties for the day, and so do you," she said.

And to the applause of the crowd, she back-handsprung all the way to her tent and did a flip onto the platform, landing on her hands so that she could seamlessly return to her routine, folding down the placard that said she was out in the circus and would be back. She left the leash unraveled on top of it, a reminder to those who had seen her with the fire-eater of what had occurred. She didn't mind it being a mystery to the rest. Was the chain for her, or could the contortionist not be chained, just like she couldn't be contained?

* * * *

Thirty minutes seemed to crawl, as time tended to do in the wake of anticipation. At the same time, once the thirty minutes were up, they seemed to have flown by. She put up her placard again and scurried, twisted and backward as though possessed, off-stage to laughter and applause.

A girl liked to know she was appreciated. She didn't like it when customers talked because they almost invariably said all the wrong things. However, when they didn't speak, they almost invariably said all the right things.

Speech was overrated.

Which was why, at the sight of John flogging his cock as though desperate to come—too desperate—she clicked her tongue.

He immediately jerked his hands behind his back.

She rose. Then she snapped her fingers and pointed at the ground. This time he knelt right at her command. The man acknowledged his commitment and honored it. Too bad she couldn't reward him. Not yet.

She snapped and pointed downward again. John fell forward so that he was on his hands and knees, his cock caught between being pulled down by its weight and drawn up by its stiffness. Its head was darkly flushed, the eye leaking its thick tears of pre-cum over the flesh.

"You're not just a one-off gift anymore, fire-eater," Valorie said. "He gave you to me. Or rather, he gave you the opportunity to give yourself to me. The vow still stands. You do whatever I ask, for whatever reason or no reason at all, and you'll have some relief for that cock. If you decide to terminate our arrangement, I can't stop you. But you won't get me anymore. Simple as that. Still interested in keeping that collar on, pet?"

John nodded. He opened his mouth. Hesitated.

"Permission to speak softly. We've still got a crowd outside," she said.

"I told the truth last night," he said. "And I gave my word today. I'll do anything for this circus. I've already given it my life, and when I give, I give a hundred percent."

"I ought to kiss you for not saying a hundred and ten percent," Valorie said.

He let his head hang as though his neck was tired, but he laughed. "I got a lot of clichés in me, like most people, I guess. But even I won't use that one anymore. Anyway, I have plenty to atone for. Whatever you think I deserve, I'll accept—as long as it isn't death or dismemberment, and I'm thinking you can't do that anyway."

"Do you realize what you've done?" she asked. "You've given me carte blanche to do terrible things to you—or let the demons do them to you. Bell's already given me that, but you...you know I'm a vindictive bitch, right?"

"You're my Queen," he said drily. "I'm your dragon, one of your subjects. Put me in a dungeon or cast your spell on me. I'm the one who put myself in your hands. I'll take it. I'm telling you I can take it. I've been burning myself every day for the last year and a half. Nothing can be worse than what I've gone through."

"You'd be wrong, of course," Valorie said. "I *am* somewhat limited in what I can do to you, but I'll do my best to absolve you, fire-eater, with all the tools in my arsenal. Believe me."

"I do," he murmured.

"Then I want you to spread your legs a little more. Just like that. Now stay still," she said. "I'll count."

He didn't ask what she'd be counting.

Valorie traced the line of his body, from the slight dip in his skull to the dry riverbed of his spine. He swayed in his position, his hips moving him forward against his will. But with his hands on the ground, he couldn't touch himself anymore, and he knew better than to change position without her say-so.

She stepped over him and sat down on the small of his back, facing those firm, round buttocks. The ass of a football player. Valorie bet he'd been devastating in football pants for all the ladies to ogle. Leather pants did him justice too, but a different kind of justice. In football pants, a girl could convince herself that she was admiring his athleticism.

Valorie straddled him as though riding a horse backward. This way she could knead each buttock like clay on a wheel, separating them to reveal his hole, pushing them together like a man plumping big breasts. When she leaned forward, she could glimpse the wrinkling at the back of his dangling scrotum. She pinched it between her nails. She giggled when he bucked like a horse, but he couldn't unsaddle her when she tightened her knees against his hips. Valorie softened the harshness of her pinches with firm, broad strokes over his balls. There wasn't much to handle in that regard, but he groaned, working to keep his shoulders up instead of buckling down. She kneaded the pliant flesh, brushing the base of his shaft here and there by accident.

She'd devoted so much of her gentler attention to his balls that the first slap to his left buttock took him by surprise, and he bucked again.

"Stay still," she ordered him, "and take your punishment."

Valorie beat him like a bass drum, though he sounded like a snare, and at one point she hit him so fast—one hand on each buttock—that he might as well have been one. She slapped him until the flesh started showing flushed handprints and grew even hotter than usual, like a fatal fever under her palms as she ran her hands over his ass again. She didn't bother actually counting. His punishment would take years, so counting was superfluous. She just beat him as long as she liked.

She could tell when fire came out of his mouth against his will in response to her choice of punishment. Not only did he get hotter under her own ass, but he coughed and the air suddenly became drier for a moment. He panted, each exhale a soft moan at how tender she'd made his ass. When she stroked him, he hissed at the sting, oil on a hot skillet.

She stopped at one point because her hands were stinging too, but she started up again once they'd calmed down. Sometimes the spanks were fast and lighter, but in this second series, she also took the time to outright wallop him. She wanted a shout, something for which she could punish him more, since he'd be drawing attention to them from the public.

But John was good. The juddering of his breathing underneath her told her he fought against the impulse to cry, but he managed to keep himself under control vocally. Valorie had underestimated the willpower of a man who'd had to hold back the pain of third-degree burns for months on end. He didn't complain. He didn't beg for her to stop. They hadn't established a safeword or anything. For now they didn't need one. If John said 'no' or 'stop', she'd have to. He had the power in that respect. But he respected the promise he'd made. He was trying to prove himself to her.

It was working. She admired a man in control of himself, even if that control was borne of torment. Here in Arcanium, every human underwent some kind of torture—some more than others. A person could make a case for whether psychological or physical torture was the worst. But control was something a person learned quickly here, whether it was to hold one's tongue and hide one's shame or embarrassment in front of the normals or whether it was to relearn how one's body worked after Bell had had his transformative way with a wish.

Valorie hadn't had to learn how to walk like Joanne and Jane, nor had she had to depend on other people to take care of her like Christina. But her body *had* changed after being taken into Arcanium, and she had been extremely resistant to the transition after being ripped from her old world, inconsiderate boss or not. Her professional life had been lacking at the time, but her personal life had just been starting to get good, and it had taken several escape attempts—each more painful than the last—and several sessions under the Ringmaster's whip before she'd finally given up.

Which was its own torture. Resignation. Resignation was when the spirit was finally broken. Like bones, sometimes what was there after healing was nowhere near what it had been. And there was no way to get what she'd been back. All a woman or a man in Arcanium could do was move forward, adapt, survive and come out the other side a fucking king or queen of his or her individual court.

So when she beat John like this, it wasn't because she lacked empathy.

Some people called this place hell. Valorie knew better. Arcanium was purgatory. The Ringmaster was the one taste of hell the cast ever had, even for most of the demons. The rest? The rest was of this world, pain and all.

After all, hell was unending. Arcanium could make torture feel like forever, but John's suffering would eventually end.

Even Valorie knew that this beating wasn't true suffering, not when she peeked between his thighs and couldn't see his cock, which meant it hadn't flagged an inch. Valorie had probably left bruises on his ass. She'd probably done the same to her hands too, she thought, shaking them. But a person didn't get turned on by a true beating. Not without magic that Valorie didn't have at her fingertips.

She kissed one reddened cheek, licked it, bit at the sweat-shining flesh.

"Ah...ah..." John cried, twitching but keeping himself as still as he could.

"You've been very good taking your medicine, pet," Valorie said. She kissed him again, the other cheek this time.

"I do what I can," he said breathlessly.

She patted his thigh. "Back up." She laughed a little as she rested her feet on his calves and he carried her closer to the ottoman. The floor in the back of the tents was carpeted with cheap rugs, but they looked decadent.

Valorie stood up on either side of him and walked backward on tiptoe so that she faced him after her leather-clad cunt brushed his skull. She lowered herself down, crossing and folding her legs until she sat in front of him with her hands in her lap. She inspected between his arms. More giggles spilled from her mouth when she saw that there was a line of pre-cum from the tip of his cock to the carpet.

It pleased her that the spanking had maintained rather than deflated his erection. That would make her time with him so much easier — for her, not for him.

"You know, I had the pleasure of meeting a man with diphallia while working here," Valorie said. "He no longer does — work here, I mean — although he sometimes joins us on the private circuit in winter if he has a yen to. When he first joined Arcanium — a few years before I did — one of the penises wasn't fully functional, although it would get a little hard. But with his wish and Bell's power, he ended up with two fully functional cocks."

"Is now really the moment for story time?" John asked, still panting, his hips moving in the air as though he was trying to will something to appear around his cock so he could fuck it.

Valorie grinned and began to undo her pants. "I've also had the pleasure of watching this same man show off his flexibility by sucking one of his own dicks. On one memorable occasion, he got both of them in his mouth. It was one of the hottest things I'd ever seen. Apparently he'd discovered his flexibility early in his masturbatory experimentation. Admit it. If you could suck your own cock, don't you think you'd do it all the time? It's like guys talking about how, if they spontaneously turned into girls, they'd play with their breasts all day. It's not as fun as they think, but still... I asked you a question, pet."

"Yeah, I probably would try it at least once if I could do it," John admitted, although he looked down at his hands to do so. "I wouldn't go around telling other people about it."

"It's not gay if there's only one of you," Valorie said cheerily. "After all, you're not gay for giving yourself a hand job, right? Why's a blow job any different? Anyway, after watching him go after himself like a man at a sausage-eating contest, I got inspired."

"God help me," John groaned as she pulled off her leather. She'd eschewed underwear for a long time. She'd wear a bustier or a costume corset—the boned corsets weren't good for contortion—and she'd wear bloomers under her skirts, although she didn't wear skirts much anymore. But when she removed her pants, she was just sitting bare in front of him with her legs bent and parted, hugging her knees as what she'd been saying sank in.

"If this man, imbued with natural flexibility, could tend to his own needs, well… I thought it was worth a shot to see if I, imbued with unnatural flexibility and naughty bits that are a little farther away from my mouth than his were, could do the same," Valorie said.

She grabbed her ankles and pulled herself almost completely into the splits, displaying herself to him.

"Now, the problem with oral sex on a woman has always been visibility. You're a virile young athlete. You're probably aware of the various issues in Internet porn. Visibility is one of the driving forces behind most technical aspects of pornography. Did you know that? That's why the anatomy is so exaggerated. When Eddie deep-throated himself—a skill that made him a lot more sympathetic with any female partners that gave him the same treatment—the placement of the cock made it easier to see from several angles. There aren't many good angles to watch a girl lick herself. It took me a while to find one so that my partner as well as myself could appreciate the position. Normal sitting was out. Then all anyone would see is my head. But if I do this..."

She rolled onto her back and hooked her arms over her thighs to hold herself open as well as to pull her torso forward. This was one of the few strains on her spine, the kind that made her feel the pull, but it never hurt, and Valorie was almost certain that it was impossible for her tendons and ligaments to tear or her bones to snap in the process of expressing her flexibility. Any damage she might do, though, Bell could rectify.

She was rewarded in her tenacity by the look on John's face, like a dog being denied a bone, when she rested her chin on her mound, not inches from her clit. She could see her folds, damp from the arousal stimulated from spanking him and listening to the sounds he made from it.

John didn't dare look away from her eyes, but they were conveniently right above the compelling parts of her anatomy as she snaked her tongue out and licked around her clit. Valorie's eyelids fluttered, and John made a choking noise and jerked his hips again. It had been a long time since she'd done this, given that most of the time she had a man happy to do it for her.

She alternated slow licks over her folds and darting her tongue into her pussy like a reptile. When she moved her mouth back to her clit, Valorie nearly lost her balance. She knew exactly the kind of pressure she wanted. It wasn't the same spontaneity she could get from a man doing it, but she could make herself moan, just like with the toys. Nothing beat a real, live tongue, though, even if it was her own.

"Fuck, please, my Queen. Let me help you. Let me do that for you," John begged. His eyes were still red from the side effects of the spanking, but his face was dry and his lips were wet. "You shouldn't have to work so hard."

"What you mean is that *you* shouldn't have to work so hard," Valorie said. "Just kneeling there, but oh so *hard*, pet... Look at you, you're dripping all over my nice carpet."

She slid two fingers into her aching pussy then gave her clit a few broad, firm licks that had her tightening around her own digits. She started losing track of her body, as though she'd truly tied herself into knots. The rush of her blood and the tingling of her limbs and her skin, the strain both of muscle and of her cunt, all these things conspired to twist her head into knots as much as her body.

"*Please*," he said hoarsely. He licked the scars that made up his lips. She knew what those scarred lips felt like on her cunt. They were strange in their smoothness, but as warm and dexterous as any man's.

Valorie relaxed, letting her body unravel itself because she couldn't immediately figure it out herself. She fell back, her legs still parted like a burlesque dancer's.

"Dinner time, my dragon. Eat until I'm satisfied," she said.

Now that John knew how good oral sex could be on a woman, he was thoroughly enthusiastic, as though he believed he would come by giving *her* an orgasm. He didn't touch her, didn't take his hands from the carpet. She would have let him, but she was irrationally pleased that he hadn't. It meant he wanted to obey, wanted to do what she told him so much that he wouldn't even test the boundaries. Such blind obedience wouldn't continue forever, but his service was new. In the future, he'd no doubt give her more reasons to punish him than the ones she already had.

Valorie stroked his head with both hands, smearing her essence over the unscarred skin and massaging the scalp. When he got her raising her hips against his mouth, she crooned her encouragement, let him know through her whimpers and cries that he was doing something right. When he sucked her clit between his teeth and pulsed his tongue against her, she shouted in spite of her command for him to keep quiet. And she didn't care if anyone on the outside heard, because he kept doing the same action, more intensely with each passing moment, until she clutched his shoulders and moaned her climax into her arm.

As soon as her cries faded, he dipped down to lick at the fresh draft of her juices, lapping as eagerly as a thirsty man—or a thirsty dragon with a dry mouth.

"Can I have more of you?" he asked between licks. "Please, can I have more of you? Can I touch you? You haven't let me, and I..."

"Yes. Cover me. Cover me and take me, pet."

Valorie unfastened the ties of her halter from behind her neck and at her abdomen, where the deep V plunged between her breasts. Lying on her back, she didn't have much more than her nipples, but that didn't seem to bother any of her partners. They loved the deep V, and they loved her nipples, as though because they were the only things there when she was on her back, her nipples got all the attention women like Maya or Kitty got for the whole of their breasts.

She hummed in pleasure and wrapped her arms around his beautiful body as he kissed up to the navel that he'd saluted earlier, stroking his palms over the tattoos that embellished her hips. He slid his hands under her shoulders to prop her up. The protruding buds of her nipples called him like they called others. Men just couldn't seem to keep their teeth off, tugging at the flesh before sucking almost all of her breast into their mouths. John was no exception. His cock smeared sticky pre-cum against her thighs as his body undulated over her.

He crawled up farther and marked her neck with his teeth. The roughness of his bites left her squirming underneath him. Arousal vibrated through her like electricity all the way to her fingertips. She liked it rough, had been screwing mostly demons for the last twenty years. If there was one thing she could give to Lennon, it was how good his sharp little demon teeth felt on her skin — not quite as much as she liked his tentacles in her cunt, but a close second. John wasn't the dragon that she called him, and Bell hadn't seen fit to follow that characterization to its logical conclusion — yet. But he did just fine, pressing harder when she didn't express any discomfort and instead scratched at his shoulders, curling her leg around his hip and bucking up as though her pussy begged for his cock after his thorough tongue.

"Can I kiss you?" he pleaded against her neck.

He'd learned at least some of his lesson about consent. Under other circumstances, she might have considered the constant questions for permission annoying, but she found them endearing, especially with his history. Better safe than sorry. And he'd probably lose some of that uncertainty about what she wanted around the same time he lost his obedience. At that point, the punishments would flow, but so would their comfort with each other, to the point where he would no longer have to ask. She'd almost miss it.

She guided him up by his chin and opened her mouth for him, this time letting him control the kiss. When she was on top, she wanted the control, but when she took the bottom, she wanted to be taken. He was frantic, fevered, driven by a rhythm that moved all the way through his body. His cock slid through her slick folds as he rutted but didn't take, not while he was kissing her. Not while he hadn't made sure that he could, even though she'd already given her order and her permission.

She smiled as she sucked at his tongue and lifted her hips to poise the head at her cunt. Her teeth raked along the length of his tongue as he entered her, the weight of his cock slipping him in before he was ready. Valorie exhaled sharply as he slumped against her, his belly flush with hers. He had almost single-handedly heated the whole back of her tent with his fevered body. She was sweating where their bodies met.

"Sorry," he whispered.

"Well, go on. Don't rest on the job," she said with a grin. She kicked his still-sensitive ass with her heel.

Her mouth fell open with a delighted gasp as he raised himself up again on his knees with her legs wrapped around him and kissed her again, even as the push of his cock inside her forced her hips to rise off the ground. He was so rigid, so thick, she thoroughly felt each unrelenting stroke as he pounded into her with the same rhythm that he kissed. The arousal in her head from his touch and from his mouth joined the purely physical arousal that he'd stoked between her legs. The intensity nearly had her screaming.

This time when she scratched her nails down his back, she definitely broke the skin. His hips jerked at the new pain, burying his cock even deeper at a new angle.

She broke away from his mouth to push him down to her neck so that she could breathe her encouragements into his ear again, her mouth so near his collar. "Yes, pet. Yes, yes, so strong, so big inside me. Skin's burning. You're gonna make me come so hard. Should I let them all hear what you're doing to me? You know they've been imagining it since they saw me own you. You know they've imagined you licking me, fucking me, sucking me. Everything you've been doing, just keep doing it, just...like...that..."

His shout got lost in her neck, but she let hers out as he snapped his hips and pushed his cock in as far as it would go at the ripple of her pussy around him. Valorie shoved her hand between them to stroke her mound and her folds around her clit — the little button too sensitive to take direct stimulation after her first orgasm. John considerately made a few more shallow thrusts to help her draw out her pleasure as he came hot inside her.

"That's my pet dragon," she said in reward, rubbing his neck under the collar.

She slithered out from under him to crawl over to the curtain that separated the back of the tent from the platform. Everyone kept towels under the platform for sweat. It would work just as well for other fluids, but she didn't want anyone on the other side of the platform to see the curtain open or her naked body.

Thank goodness for the fact that most patrons rarely lingered in front of a tent when an oddity wasn't there. A few die-hard fans sometimes came especially for one or two oddities or performances, but Valorie wasn't the sort to have as many fans as the more arcane oddities in the circus. Actually, that wasn't true. She had her share of male fans, but when they had Lady Sasha to gape at when Valorie wasn't around, they weren't likely to linger when they knew they could come back later.

"Here," she said, carefully closing the curtain behind her. She handed John one of the towels.

As he cleaned off his cock and the rest of him as best as he could with a small towel alone, Valorie checked his back. The places she'd scratched were a raw red, but where she'd drawn blood, it had already dried. She traced them and let her fingers trail down to his darkened ass. She liked it when he twitched.

"You do realize you'll have to go out with leather over this," Valorie said, smiling. "And the scratches on your back bare too."

"I guess I'll have to be careful not to sit down," John said evenly. "And if anyone asks, just act mysterious. They'll fill in the blanks. It doesn't matter if there are no blanks to fill in or not. They do it anyway."

"Normals are good at that," Valorie said. "Silence leaves room for so many lies."

"Speaking of silence, can I ask you a question?" John winced as he pulled on his leather trousers.

Valorie rested on her knees, sitting on her heels. She held her towel between her legs to catch his cum as it seeped out of her. She was comfortable staying naked. In a past life, she might have been concerned about the fact that anyone could come through the door in the back and anyone could come through the curtain behind her. It had taken her a while to realize that most people respected the borders set for them, even when there weren't locks.

However, she'd learned at the same time that she didn't usually need to care about the ones who crossed those borders. Arcanium had its own enforcement, and it could be much uglier than the kind on the outside. Valorie sometimes thought it was more just, though.

"Sure," Valorie replied. "I might not answer."

"You sound like him again," John said. "I just... Are you human?"

"What?"

Of all the questions she might have expected, that wasn't one of them.

John rubbed his hand over his scars. "Sorry, I don't mean to be an ignorant loser. I'm just confused. There are times when you talk about the demons as though they're not like you, and other times I...I wonder. As demons go, the ones here seem all right. They're not all whips and chains and hellfire, I mean. But I hear about a lot of you girls being with them, and you don't sound like you're afraid. You talk about Bell as though...as though you're not afraid of him either. Aside from your contortion tricks, though, you don't seem to be very demon-y. Your eyes and teeth are normal. Bell's eyes and teeth are normal too, though, so that's not—"

"You're rambling," Valorie interrupted.

"Yeah, I am. That's what I do when start chewing on my toes. Did I stick my foot in my mouth here or—"

"Was it my lovely disposition or the fact that Bell gave you to me to punish?" Valorie asked.

"Um. Both."

Valorie finished cleaning up between her legs, bunched the towel up and took care of the rest to try to hide how her body seemed to have gone light and weak. She wasn't even sure why. Or if she was, that part of her was hiding.

"They tell kids that Grandma or Auntie June become angels when they die," Valorie said. "It's bullshit. Angels are born angels. Jinn are born jinn. Nothing short of a wish would make me not human, and I've used all my wishes. Sometimes I think things would be easier if I *were* jinn, but I'm human as you. I've just been here longer."

"Kitty's been here a long time too. She looks stranger than you, but I never wondered if maybe she wasn't human," John said. He tried to appear casual, but there was tension in his face, shoulders and spine.

"Kitty was a voluntary from the very beginning," Valorie said. "And she's Kitty. I'm me. I ended up choosing this place, but I lost friends and family too. Choosing made it easier to handle when I decided to let them go. When I fell in with Bell. When I decided to become the best contortionist this circus has ever seen and leave my mark. The only thing that would have made it even easier would have been to lose my soul. I still got that one with me, even if you think I'm soulless."

"I didn't mean—"

"Yeah, you did. You might have heard the rumors that I can be worse than this. I can. Most of what you see and hear from me, it's illusion. We get good at illusion around here. I tell you that so you don't go thinking you really are a dragon or something."

"I don't think it's all as much of an illusion as you think it is," John said. "Believe me, you've got emotions. And I'm not the best at reading them in women, but you don't seem to be happy. The only other guy I see looking your kind of unhappy is Bale, when he's following Lady Sasha around. And he's demon. So I know demons have emotions. And pasts. I just didn't know a person could own another person around here. Like, I thought it might be against the rules, reserved for demons only. That's all."

"That's all," she muttered. She turned around to pull on her pants and start tying her halter back up. "I don't know where you got that I was a demon, I really don't. Did someone tell you that?"

"No one tells me anything," John replied. "I don't get close enough to eavesdrop—most of the time anyway. I just see what you do. You always hang around Bell and that tumbler demon guy, the one you're mad at. You talk about Ciàran and Moss..."

"Newsflash, wood-fire grill, most of us girls have had Ciàran and Moss. It's practically a rite of passage," Valorie said.

John literally stopped moving halfway to his feet. "Really?" he finally asked.

"Really. And Maya's Bell's lover, but I'll bet you think she's human."

"I see her talking with other humans," John said. "With Kitty. With the twins. Not you. You'll talk with them at breakfast because you eat at the same table, and you work with Victor, but what do you do when you're not hanging out with demons or playing with me or doing your contortion thing?"

"Sometimes I choreograph," Valorie said. "Equal opportunity services."

The obvious thing she wasn't saying was that she'd barely noticed that, aside from John, whose relationship with her now was decidedly unbalanced, she didn't much hang out with other souls in Arcanium. She'd been forced to live alongside Maya until Valorie had split with Bell. She got along with Kitty and was comfortable with her because of their shared longevity. She got along with the twins. She *got along* just fine. She'd been a social butterfly once, and she still used those skills in performance and instruction. But friends? Had she ever had friends?

The closest she thought she'd gotten to friendship was Troy. They'd talked while he'd inked, and their sex had been...friendly. He was a nice guy.

"I think it's time to not talk about this and go back to work," Valorie said.

"I'm sorry if I hit a nerve—"

The slap filled the close, warm air of the tent. It wasn't a hard hit, but a blow across the mouth got her message across just fine.

"This discussion is over. Go outside and do your job," she said. She tried not to snap. She tried to sound controlled. She thought she mostly succeeded.

John folded the towel and left it on the floor. He seemed to consider saying something, but wisely shut his mouth and ducked out before she could silence him again.

Chapter Six

November slipped into December. The golems had made everyone a Thanksgiving feast for the sake of tradition, and the costumes had shifted from an autumn palette to winter. It wasn't a dramatic change. Springs and summers saw brown leather, autumn and winter black. The colors that they took on now leaned cool instead of warm — purples, indigos, blues and greens. However, Arcanium always had room for red.

In addition, some of the costumes transitioned into cream or white. Lady Sasha appeared almost naked in her cream-colored leather bikini set if a person wasn't looking at her directly — which almost always caused a person to look at her directly for quite a while, just to make sure.

Most of the men stuck with black, the unimaginative morons, but Seth and Lars went adventurous in ivory leather that almost blended in with Seth's complexion and sharply contrasted with Lars'. Under their usual blue light during performances, the change was actually quite striking. It had been Valorie's suggestion years back, and the two men had learned to trust her judgment on what would make their performances shine.

Valorie embraced the white and cream tactic herself, but Kitty had edged it up with black lace, thread and other accents. She limited color to her face paint, makeup and hair. The face art still leaned toward the creepy, but less explicitly so. Fewer bleeding mouths and skeleton faces, more rhinestones.

John blushed at Valorie's request for him — tight red leather trousers and sometimes a red and brown leather jacket, less polished than the Ringmaster's regalia. For the patrons, he took on the persona of a wild dragon, tamed and bound to human form. Valorie made sure to walk him over the grounds every day for everyone to see him leashed to her. She'd command him to perform and gave her own performances on John's back whenever she made him get on his hands and knees for her. It was steadier than the nights she did her routine on Jason or Lily in their lion or tiger forms.

Bell approved of the direction, and although John still remained on the outskirts of the cast when the circus wasn't in session, at least some of the tension between the rest of the cast and John thawed as the weather turned colder. Seeing him regularly speak with Bell on circus matters may have had something to do with that.

Bell spread his magic across Arcanium. There had always been plenty of lights to illuminate the evening, but during the winter months, those lights multiplied across the booths and the tents, even the big top. Some of them were ordinary white or multicolored Christmas lights, but they were there merely to accent the bluish white icicle lights that were strung all through Arcanium. The circus wasn't a stranger to generators, but there would have been some real surprised outcries if someone were to follow the light cords to where they weren't plugged into anything.

The transition occurred seamlessly from one location to another. Valorie didn't even check where they were turning up anymore except to ask Kitty what the weather was going to be like so that she'd know what to wear outside the circus during the week. Rehearsals took up most of the weekdays until Friday, but voluntaries got to leave the grounds if they wanted to. Valorie mostly didn't. However, it was nice to get away from the cuckoo family now and then and eat at a restaurant by herself without people gaping at her. Kitty did most of the outside plugging for Arcanium because short of wearing the *niqab*, Kitty couldn't hide what she was. Valorie could blend in more, and although most of the voluntaries left in one vehicle, they usually spent their time alone — with the exception of Kitty and Maya, who seemed to take other people's nasty comments toward them as a personal challenge.

Valorie, on the other hand, didn't leave Arcanium only to let it follow her. Normal was overrated, but in moderation, it was nice not to be on all the time. Performing could be exhilarating, but it could also be exhausting, which was why she was glad that most of the time they only performed three times a week.

When she was out, she wore some of her leather and still wouldn't wear a bra, but she was more covered and included some cotton in the mix. The people around her thought she was maybe a tattoo artist or stylist on her lunch break. She was rarely recognized as part of the circus when she was alone on the outside.

When Valorie came back — and she always came back, since even the voluntaries had to come back by Friday morning at the latest — she joined the rest of the performers rehearsing in the big top tent. During the times she wasn't practicing her own routine, she consulted with the others to help them add new elements to old routines or develop whole new acts. Arcanium liked to keep its performances fresh. Not only did it keep the cast from getting too bored, but it gave people a reason to come back to Arcanium. Some even followed it around the country like groupies, just to see how they changed things up.

In this, the brave new world, Bell liked to keep ahead of the amateur videos that popped up on social media. Recordings weren't encouraged, but he didn't discourage them either. The accessibility of their performances pushed them to try new things constantly, and that distinguished Arcanium from other circuses of performers who actually had to learn the skills and risk life and limb to do their stunts.

When skill and risk weren't issues, Arcanium could move ahead of the pack, though it didn't try to compete with the scope of those other circuses. Arcanium was best as a relatively intimate venue that stayed under the radar from the wrong attention while still attracting all the right attention. Part circus, part freak show, part carnival, Arcanium was somehow a niche outfit with broad appeal. And Valorie helped him ensure that in the ring.

But Seth and Lars didn't need her much anymore. Occasionally Lord Mikhail and Lady Sasha requested that she choreograph an act for them when they wanted to work together. Those routines were more difficult for her, since she couldn't direct them through touch. Even gloves didn't save her from the impact of their power.

All Valorie really had to occupy her downtime now was teaching Victor, and since Lennon was still the star of that particular routine, he could take care of most of the direction until Victor decided he wanted to be something other than a launch pad. For now, he still seemed happy in the supporting role.

The rest of the cast didn't require choreography or did their own. For instance, the clowns had never asked Valorie for help with their raunchy, comedic pantomime. Carlo and Christina worked more with Lennon or as living props for the Ringmaster when he was dominating the big cats. Troy worked with Misha, whose skill set was beyond Valorie's knowledge. And Maya worked with Bell, whose vision was just as astute as Valorie's. He liked letting Valorie take over some of those tasks for him with other members of the cast, but not with Maya. Valorie had helped her with a few tightrope tricks. Otherwise, Bell handled it just fine.

She had much less to do during the week than she used to, even though she was doing solo performances again. If she thought staying away from Arcanium more would help her find some kind of outlet, she'd do it. But while Kitty and Victor got a galvanizing charge from interacting with the outside and spending some of their nights with new people, Valorie couldn't find it in her to do the same casual stranger sex thing. It wasn't pregnancy or disease she was worried about. Even if she caught something on the outside, it would wither and die inside her as soon as she stepped over the Arcanium threshold. It was just that she'd always had someone to come back to in the past.

John wasn't the same. Coming home to a pet couldn't beat coming home to a man, as far as she remembered, and she tried not to encourage him too much. Sex every night would have been entirely too much gravy. If she was going to teach him that his climaxes were completely at her disposal and dispensation, she had to deny him. Unfortunately, that meant denying herself, not that she was feeling up to it other than the usual physical imperative. And if Kitty could handle several weeks of such an imperative when she wasn't boning an outsider or the Ringmaster, Valorie could handle a few days here and there between the days the circus was open and the sex demons dialed their magic up to ten.

If it sounded like Valorie played the 'anything you can do, I can do better' game, it was because she did. Competition was one of the only things she had left. It might occasionally make her homicidal, but it also helped her make Arcanium and her place in it what it was today. She'd made her mark.

The question, she thought as she waited for another day, another crowd, to start, *is whether that's the only mark I'll ever make.*

The question is whether I'm over.

Valorie couldn't remember the last time she'd experienced this kind of discontent, and those who spent the most incidental time with her noticed, including John. They didn't comment because they had a good sense of self-preservation, and Bell had already decided to leave her to her conflict. But Valorie was acutely aware of their awareness.

She couldn't help but think that if she was this unhappy in Arcanium, it was truly time to leave. She had lovers instead of love, colleagues instead of friends and demons instead of humans. If she had at least one of those things she needed, perhaps the strands attaching her to the massive spiderweb that made up Arcanium could still keep her tied on.

She wanted Bell, but she couldn't have him. John wasn't the incentive she needed. He was weight holding her down, but he wasn't a tie, no matter how earnest he was. That was the magic and the guilt talking. Even free will couldn't be trusted sometimes.

He'd latched onto Valorie because someone had *let* him latch. Simple as that. He would have taken anyone.

Valorie had just been convenient because she'd been the one to open her legs. And John was just as convenient to her.

Not exactly the stuff ties that bind were made of.

* * * *

She had to admit, walking on her hands and rocking her body across booth partitions got some good reactions from circus-goers, but they responded even better when two cast members interacted with each other as well as the crowd.

In addition, when she was with John, the crowd was much less likely to touch her unsolicited.

Valorie sometimes extended a foot or a hand to tap someone on the shoulder, tousle their hair or play with a hat or sunglasses. People loved that. But when she was that close to other people, especially twisted up the way she was, she was also more likely to have to slap off someone else's hand. And when she was knotted, she couldn't always move in the right direction to do so. A few times, other patrons had a conscience and did it for her. But most of the time, she had to just deal with it and move away from them as soon as she could.

When she was with John, using him as a human platform and giving him instructions to stand or kneel so that she could move her act to his shoulders or even to his head, she was more protected — with a big, strong man right there with her.

It made her mad, but she couldn't voice that frustration to all the bastards around her who only kept their distance because she was visibly possessed by another man. Her tone was dominant, and she never released the leash with which she led him around Arcanium, but the fact he took the submissive role didn't seem to make a difference.

At one area, she might let the leash out and direct him to do some of his simpler routines, which usually consisted of a box of matches and his bare hands, sometimes torches that he juggled or thinner sticks that he deep-throated. At another part of the circus, she'd make him kneel so she could do a few of her simpler routines, improvising on the spot most of the time. The usual contortionist suspects were fixed in her muscle memory by now, as easy as walking. In some ways, Valorie knew her simple repertoire was more impressive than the usual contortionist because of her long-limbed frame. She should have looked more ungainly, even when flexible. Thank Bell for magical favors, she surpassed expectations.

They'd done this routine many times now, and it always garnered a good crowd. Looked like John was going to be popular in the winter months—like gathering around a campfire. Valorie also reaped those benefits, although Lady Sasha's leather kept heat in during winter as well as it breathed during the summer.

In white leather trousers and a black lace overlay on her cotton tube top, Valorie wasn't nearly as pure as Lady Sasha's dirt-resistant clothing suggested. She jerked John forward and led him around to face her.

"Kneel before your Queen, dragon," she declared loudly enough for the casual observers to hear— enough for them to become less casual in their observation. "Show whom you serve."

"I think you enjoy that a little too much," John muttered, but as he bowed his head, his scarred lips curved in a smile that most of the crowd wouldn't be able to see.

"Nothing wrong with a woman enjoying herself," she muttered back, resting her hands on his shoulders to urge him down onto his hands and knees.

John nuzzled her thigh, a mostly innocuous gesture to those around them, although she was sure it sparked the same arousal in a few others as it did in her. He did that to her when she was naked too, showed her thighs appreciation for leading him to her pussy.

Valorie stroked his head as though he had fur — or scales. Then she secured the leash around her wrist and cartwheeled into a handstand onto his back.

People holding cotton candy, cups of hot chocolate or hot coffee, cinnamon-roasted nuts and fresh funnel cakes gradually gathered around them.

There was a hierarchy to the crowd. Every crowd settled into it after a few minutes.

Children and shorter teens were ushered to the front. Sometimes parents lowered themselves to their children's level if there was a particularly large audience so that more people behind them could see. Shorter adults not afraid to elbow their way in would do so without too much resistance, although sometimes younger adults or groups of teenagers could either be oblivious or deliberately deny access. Others in the crowd compensated for the jerks. In the end, almost everyone in the circle for several rows was happy. And if they'd already seen the show, they were unlikely to stick around for a long time during the next one, so they wouldn't hog the real estate.

Such a hierarchy was one of those few small victories of humanity, as opposed to one of the myriad of ways that everyone on the planet needed to die in a fire.

Valorie had one foot on the small of John's back, both hands on his smooth skull, and her other leg slowly lifting behind her. Anticipation was the word. The more slowly she could raise her leg—each inch eliminating someone from the crowd who couldn't reach as far back—the more engaged the crowd was with her.

Her raised leg reached the eleven o'clock position, and she leaned her head back, preparing to bend her knee as she continued its trajectory. That was when she saw him.

He was older. Of course he was older. She didn't know why she'd expected him to be the way she'd left him. She wasn't sure whether he was taller than she remembered or whether she'd just shortened him in her memory. She had changed in a few ways, but height wasn't one of them.

There was gray in the close small knots of his hair and in his goatee and mustache. He hadn't changed the trim, which was part of the reason she was able to recognize him in spite of the spots on his face, the crow's feet and lines bracketing his nose, the rimless glasses. He didn't used to look like a professor, didn't used to look like a grown-up. When they'd parted, neither of them had felt like adults, but damn if they hadn't wanted everyone else to see them that way.

His parents had believed they'd been going into the engagement too quickly. Her parents had wondered why it had taken them so long, but they'd certainly not wanted their little girl to be living with him before they were married. He hadn't listened to his parents. Valorie hadn't listened to hers. As far as they'd been concerned, the wedding was a technicality. They'd already been husband and wife.

She knew that face and frame. His abdomen hadn't used to push against his waistband, and he hadn't needed a belt to hold up his trousers. She'd had to fight to get him in the dress shoes he was wearing at the moment, and for some reason, he'd seen fit to wear them to a circus that planted itself on grass, dirt and sawdust. He hadn't needed the glasses back then. Those threw her for a second.

But he was unmistakable.

The man with his hands on the shoulders of a little girl of around seven or eight years old, standing next to a mid-teenage boy and a woman with natural curls and a headband... This man had been her fiancé when Bell had stolen her away. This man was Charles Grable.

And the years had done nothing to lessen the love that swelled up like hot springs inside her.

She shook, her balance hit by the earthquake of past meeting present, as disorienting as déjà vu. John tensed underneath her. She literally couldn't fall by accident, but John was no fool. Valorie had been doing this long enough that her experience had finally coincided with the level of skill she'd been given by Bell to begin with. Valorie didn't wobble, especially not while in such a standard position. It wasn't like she was balanced on only one hand or one toe or one finger. She had solid footing.

She shouldn't have shaken.

Even worse, she shouldn't have stared.

An Arcanium cast member needed to perform for the whole audience. They could give personalized attention in little gestures, but they quickly learned that too much of a good thing led to unwanted attention in return. By staring, Valorie made herself noticed as a person rather than a performer. And damn, it meant that Charles started staring back.

Valorie continued with her routine, touching her toe to the top of her forehead. She tried to pretend that she hadn't been caught, but she also kept glancing over at the man in case she'd been wrong. She wanted to make sure. And every time she did it, he caught her doing it.

Somewhere between making a circle with her body on the small of John's back and planking with her arms holding herself up from John's body, recognition suffused his entire expression. With that recognition came shock — and horror.

She didn't blame him.

But she couldn't respond. She couldn't acknowledge what had occurred to him or the dread that had settled like one of the icicle lights turned real in her stomach. God, she needed to talk to Bell right the fuck now, but she couldn't hurry or else he'd know why.

She went through the rest of her routine, irrationally inclined to be demure instead of spreading her legs like a seaside whore, but she forced herself to do what she always did anyway. She angled it away from him and his family as best as she could, but it was hard to hide her body when she was in the middle of a crowd gathered to see it in a costume meant to display it.

Once she was finished, she vaulted off John and bowed with him before tugging him with her. The small crowd parted opposite of her ex-fiancé to let them through.

"What's going on?" John asked.

"Quiet," she whispered.

"Did I do something wrong?" John asked, stopping abruptly and pulling her up short. Valorie held the leash, but he was like a big dog with a little girl. If he didn't want to move, he could easily refuse.

Valorie could play the stubbornness game too, though. She jerked the leash toward her. He stumbled forward then dug his heels in.

"It's not all about you," she whispered, glaring up at him.

"No. It's all about you, isn't it?"

Damn it, she still couldn't tell whether he meant what he said when he talked like that.

"Yes, it is," Valorie said. "And when I tell you it's none of your business, you forget it ever happened. You forget you were ever curious in the first place."

She unlatched the leash from his collar. "Now go. Do your thing. I'm not going to need you again today, so you've got to fill the time by yourself."

Before she could leave, John grabbed her by the wrist. It was the first semi aggressive thing he'd done to her that she hadn't asked for. And while she relished his strength when she asked for it, a jolt of adrenaline forked through her, like mainlining espresso straight into the heart. It was all she could do not to slap him again, this time soundly across the cheeks. She couldn't do that in broad daylight among people who thought their act was just that—only an act.

He wasn't hurting her. She had no reason to lash out for everyone to see if he wasn't doing something grossly awful. And Bell handled things if someone on the inside did any real harm.

Valorie was the one seriously courting Bell's retribution right now, not John.

She hissed at him like a snake, baring her teeth. John literally reeled back and released her.

"I told you what you need to do, fire-eater," she said. The harshness of her whispered words attracted the attention of some of the patrons around her, if the hiss hadn't already done that. "The rest doesn't concern you."

"What's *wrong*?" John insisted.

"It. Doesn't. Concern. You." Valorie emphasized every word just in case he was having trouble with comprehension. She wrapped the leash around her wrist and latched the clasp to the handle. It had become a regular accessory lately. "Go. Away."

"But—"

"I swear, boy, it's like you're asking for a punishment that doesn't end happy."

John held his hands up, palms forward, as he took a step back. "I was just worried," he said softly. "I worry about you."

"I don't need your worry, your concern or your damn pity. I just need your obedience," Valorie said.

"You need it?"

"Figure of speech," she replied. When she turned on her heel and strode to her tent, he didn't come after her.

But she didn't stop at her tent. She doubled around Oddity Row and returned to the midway booths where she'd been performing. In spite of her better judgment, she surreptitiously searched for Charles, trying to get a direct look at him while he couldn't see her.

When she couldn't find him there, she crept on the outside of the midway, looking for his wife. His son. His daughter. Anyone that could lead her to him for confirmation. It just couldn't be. She'd seen what she'd wanted to see in the surprise of the moment. It wasn't *possible* that after all this time she'd cross paths with him, now or ever.

He hadn't wanted to go to the circus that day. He didn't like them, especially the freak shows. There was no reason for him to come to one now, twenty years later. He'd probably become more conservative rather than less, age and parenthood making him cautious and protective. He'd always been protective of her. Valorie had been more daring, the one who wanted him to take her places she'd never been, even though he'd have been content to staycation the rest of his life. Because she'd always come home to him, eager and loving, he'd never minded if she went off and did things on her own. He'd had his mini man cave — she'd had her mini road trips. Sometimes with her girlfriends. Sometimes by herself.

That had been one of the many things that had conspired to take her away from him. Her impulsiveness. Her curiosity. Her terrible boss. His introversion. Bell's will, his covetousness, his possessiveness.

She kept trying to find something to blame, be it her, him, Bell, fate, God. She'd never been able to pin the fault on any one thing except Bell — but who knew what Bell had been working for at the time? Chaos, justice, logic, God, the devil, himself, the rules of the wish…?

A person had to search for some kind of reason. Insanity was never finding the reason. Sometimes, if Valorie thought too hard, she believed she really had gone a little insane. Why else would she be stalking a customer through Arcanium, a man who couldn't possibly be who she thought he was, even though he'd been unmistakable when he'd first caught her eye? Why else would she have seen him at all, this cruel hallucination?

She didn't know exactly where Arcanium had put down its stakes, but she was pretty sure it wasn't anywhere near where she'd left him. What were the odds he'd be in Arcanium and *not* be where she left him? He was a homebody. He'd want to be close to family. It wasn't out of the realm of possibility that he'd moved, but put it all together with the rest, and it didn't add up.

Either he'd never been here, had never been Charles, or she coincidentally was always in the places in Arcanium that he wasn't at any given time, like phone tag played out real life.

Which is more likely — that he's never where you are or that he was never here at all? You're seeing things, woman. You're losing the thread.

She thought about going to Bell and asking whether she'd seen what she'd seen.

In the end, she decided not to. If she hadn't seen him, she was crazy. If she had seen him...

If she had seen him, she didn't want to know.

* * * *

Bell was avoiding her.

John was avoiding her too, but that was because she wouldn't let him get near her right now. His neediness didn't do anything for her at the moment except grate on her nerves like claws on a fucking chalkboard. He suffocated her when he tried to be solicitous, not least because he seemed desperate in his submission — as though if he tried hard enough, he'd still get his gold star and another month off his pain sentence.

Valorie hadn't quite thrown him to the curb last night and this morning, but she'd left him in the cold, and that had him panicking like a kicked puppy in the corner, stroking his collar as though to reassure himself it was still there. She hadn't withdrawn from the arrangement as long as he was still collared.

He could keep telling himself that.

She didn't mind John keeping his distance. She needed the space. But when Bell was avoiding her,

Valorie had to wonder. It didn't help her figure yesterday's events out, though. He could be avoiding her just as much to avoid her asking to leave as to avoid her asking about whether she'd seen Charles.

"You okay?" Kitty asked. "It's not like you eat as much Caroline—"

"Hey!" Caroline exclaimed. She threw a balled-up napkin at Kitty.

"Or Maya—" Kitty continued.

Maya threw her own balled-up napkin at Kitty too. This one caught in Kitty's beard. She'd recently started trimming it closer to her chin, in spite of the winter season. It made her look like a chestnut Viking. With litter in her beard. Valorie was startled into a giggle.

Kitty removed the napkin with as much dignity as a person could muster in such a situation.

"Or, say, Ciàran—"

Ciàran raised his head when he heard his name. He blinked his ink-black eyes like a docile cow. His thick, curved, sharp teeth jutted his mouth out as though he had the mother of all braces, so he wasn't much of a cow. But for a demon, he *was* relatively docile. In fact, he was kinder than about ninety percent of men in the world, as most of the women in Arcanium could attest.

Case in point, he didn't toss a napkin Kitty's way. He just went back to his sausage meal that looked like a plate of fresh intestines. Moss sat on the table next to him, stealing from his plate.

No one understood how Ciàran and Moss worked exactly, even Bell. They were one of Arcanium's few real mysteries.

"But you're picking at your plate," Kitty finished. "Don't you know there are starving people somewhere else who can no longer eat that food because you put your dirty fork all over it?"

"Send my regrets to the hungry," Valorie said, stirring the scramble over the picante-sauce-soaked tortilla for the hundredth time. "Not much of an appetite."

"John came up to my tent last night after the performance," Kitty said.

"For the love of *shit*..." Valorie swore.

"I don't think you thought that one through," Maya muttered.

"He didn't do anything," Kitty said.

"Except meddle."

"He said you nearly lost your balance yesterday."

Maya raised her head from where she'd been eating. She was more aware than John and even Kitty what a big deal that was.

"A girl's allowed to have one bad day. I made up for it during the evening performance," Valorie replied.

"That's not what this is about and you know it," Kitty said. "We don't have to discuss it here."

"We don't have to discuss it at all," Valorie said, lifting her plate and climbing over the bench. "There's nothing to discuss."

It was a bald-faced lie, of course, no pun intended. If it was nothing, she'd stay. Everyone knew that.

But they couldn't hound her about it if she finished her breakfast in the back of her tent before taking to Kitty's tent early to do up her face in blue harlequin, light blue rhinestones and black lips. Joanne and Jane came in as she was setting the lip color. She barely recognized herself the more makeup she put on, which was why she considered doing more tomorrow. The less she looked like herself, the less likely anyone would ever recognize her again.

She tied her hair into a loose single braid, still in keeping with Bell's wishes, although why she should give a damn anymore... At least this way, she wouldn't have to let Kitty tether her down by her hair and force the discussion on her. *Now, what should we talk about? The weather? The local sports team? That time you lost your balance when you never lose your balance?*

She left Joanne and Jane perched on their stool, back-to-back as always, without a word.

It was with some relief that she climbed into her suitcase and closed the top over her, enclosing herself in darkness. The only light came through the little air holes.

There had been a time in her life that she'd been a bit claustrophobic — the flip side to her wanderlust, she'd supposed. Now she accepted the close darkness as an embrace. Today was no exception. In fact, it was even more welcome. She thought about not coming out at all, except then Bell would threaten her with the glass box if she wanted to stay confined all day, and the glass box wasn't nearly as comfortable as the suitcase. The suitcase was lined. The glass box was just glass, and it had originally been created for a smaller contortionist. All those cramped, hard planes on all her bony protuberances... She'd done it on a few occasions when she'd wanted to turtle up, but she much preferred her suitcase.

As soon as she heard customers in Oddity Row, she pushed the small suitcase open and unwound herself, jerking her limbs like a wind-up doll whose springs were slowly being tightened.

She popped up her head to sit upright, with one leg and one arm still and stretched out above her.

Charles stood right in front of the platform, her first customer of the day, with a twenty-dollar bill that dropped into the clear tip bin. He'd been reading her placard with his glasses low on his nose. Now he pushed them back up and met her eyes.

"Do I know you?"

Chapter Seven

He kept his voice low, the musical baritone it had always been. He'd been so good singing in the choir, although he'd been shy singing solo.

Valorie hesitated, practically frozen.

"Please tell me I don't know you," he added. The whites of the eyes behind his glasses were red, as though he'd either not gotten any sleep or he'd given himself something to help him sleep.

If she were kind, she'd pretend she was confused. She'd tell him, 'Move along, mister. I don't know you and you're blocking the view.' If she were kind, she'd pretend he hadn't spoken, a hint to take a hike, Mike. Scram, Sam. Leave, Steve. Sorry, Charlie.

If she were kind. But no one had ever called Valorie kind.

She unfolded herself. "Hi, Charles."

He staggered back.

"That's...that's...that's i-impossible." Charles' hands clenched and loosened, searching for something to hold him up, but there was nothing. He managed to keep from falling.

"I'm going to need you to move along," Valorie said, standing. "I have work to do."

"But you...you're...you're still *young*. It's *impossible*."

"Charles, I need you to leave," she insisted, although she kept her volume low.

"I'm not going to—" Charles started.

"Good morning, sir," Bell said, coming around her tent as nonchalant as could be. All he needed was a pimp cane to complete the image. "Is there a problem?"

"That's my... That's my..."

Valorie didn't blame Charles for his inability to articulate. He couldn't possibly believe his eyes, but he also couldn't deny what he was seeing. Such was the dilemma of anyone who entered Arcanium. What they'd never know was that, yes, it was *all* real. That was Arcanium's biggest trick—convincing the public that their tricks were illusion and skill rather than magic and power. The horror happened when the veil lifted, the curtain closed and nothing changed— nothing except souls. But the magic never ended, and the reflections stayed the same. Could a person *really* grow when nothing changed?

"She's indeed a spectacular young woman," Bell said. "But she's working at the moment, sir, and I'm going to ask you to not take up her time."

"You don't understand," Charles protested.

"Oh, I do."

Charles stopped stammering, stumbling over his words, searching for a handhold in reality. Before him was a man solid and immovable as an idol. He carried his power quietly because he was certain at any given time that he was the most powerful being within the borders of his Arcanium. He didn't need to resort to puffing himself up and declaring his dominance. That was for men who were small, cowardly, lacking. For men who needed to compensate. Bell needed to compensate for nothing. The quietest predators were almost always the most deadly.

When Bell spoke, even when he lied, what he said had power. Charles didn't understand what was going on, but he visibly recoiled.

"We can discuss your trouble during her break. If you could come with me, sir, I have somewhere you can wait," Bell said. He smiled, placing a hand on Charles' shoulder, and swayed into a welcoming gesture that beckoned Charles to join him, as though they were old friends.

If his guidance was a little forced, only Valorie would be able to see it. The crowd would believe that Bell was taking care of a troublesome patron. Perhaps the professorial man was an admirer or a stalker. No matter the circumstance, the crowd either ignored the scene or paid it little mind. They had better things to look at.

Charles' confusion allowed him to be led, but he kept looking over his shoulder at her, twenty years of pain and bewilderment deepening the lines on his ashen face.

Bell raised two fingers while Charles' attention was on her. Then he led Charles beyond where she could see him.

The implication was clear — two hours of work. He wanted her to give him two hours of work. Valorie couldn't imagine why when the last thing on her mind was grace, poise and flexibility — especially when the latter was the reason for this fucking mess in the first place. It wasn't so he could have time to think. The bastard had obviously known this was coming.

For the first thirty minutes or so, Valorie's head filled with visions of what Bell could be doing with Charles while she was otherwise occupied. Maya was the only one who voluntarily took a front seat to Bell doing his work and granting his wishes. No one else had the stomach for it, and most of the human souls of Arcanium preferred not to think about anyone's wishes but their own. It was the only way to handle living with Bell, accepting his affection and even his love — and yes, he felt both, as varied and textured as the same emotions in humans. One might argue his ran deeper, like veins buried within a mountain from shifting lands over geologic time.

That didn't make him merciful, if mercy wasn't his whim. He could be feeding Charles to Lady Sasha right now, although Valorie hadn't felt a spike in the constant, low-level sexual tension of the circus. He could have invited the clowns into the big top ring and let them feast upon Charles' body, though they preferred younger meat. He could have granted a wish that left Charles bound to Arcanium like Valorie — leaving behind a wife and two children instead of a fiancé as she had. He could have granted a wish that doomed Charles in any of a hundred thousand ways. By silently demanding that she work, he could have ensured that Valorie stayed out of his way while he disposed of or dealt with the potential threat.

So why was she doing it? Why was she staying in her safe little tent and performing like a music box doll moving to the violins coming from her speakers? It certainly wasn't because she was obedient.

And she didn't want anything bad to happen to Charles.

Did she?

Had part of her done what she'd been told so that when she returned to Bell, there would hopefully be no trace left of her ex-fiancé? No trace, no man, no problem.

It made her sick to her stomach.

Somewhere around the thirty-minute line, though, those fears and anxieties faded.

The comfort of routine and the ordinary endorphins from exercise, even when that exercise was magically enhanced, put her into a sort of trance — the autopilot of normal. Normal for her, at least. She went from position to position, song to song. Time ceased to have meaning. The clenching of her stomach subsided. Her brain went delightfully blank.

When John walked through Oddity Row and raised his remaining eyebrow because she hadn't left her tent yet for one of their joint routines, she just kept dancing and contorting, the burn in her muscles one of continued effort and the early stirring of weariness. She didn't usually go a full two-hour stretch without at least taking a walking break.

What he was *really* curious about, she thought, was the fact she hadn't leashed him up and paraded him around like a damn dog, as though that was something to look forward to. She passed her gaze over John the same way she passed it over the rest of the customers.

Besides, she felt good. Correction, she felt nothing, which was good. She didn't want to disrupt all her work by bringing John into this. He'd look at her with those dark, puppy dog eyes and kicked puppy expression and puppyish eagerness for a walk, and she'd have to *feel* all these things she really didn't want to deal with right now.

Unlike Charles, John could take a hint. When she didn't do much more than blink at him before turning her attention to the small crowd gathered before her tent, he spun his fire fans in irritation and continued on his way. If there was a pang somewhere in her chest region, she dismissed it as quickly as it occurred, returning to the Zen of her routine.

* * * *

She overshot the two hours by about fifteen minutes. It took her stomach growling for her to realize that it was well past noon and she was allowed to take a break.

Nonsensically, the side of her head that had taken over during the performance to keep her calm and steady whispered, *I hope this doesn't take long. Breaks aren't supposed to last forever, and I have things I need to do.*

The less brainwashed side of her head took that other side to task effectively and efficiently. She could spare the time to meet with the man who was supposed to have been her husband. *Bell* could spare the time. And John could give her time off for one fucking day. She was the one in charge of him. He didn't yet have the right to demand a damn thing.

Valorie put up the placard explaining her absence and made a quick exit, maintaining her performance persona until the last minute. She kept her leather duster in the back these days in case she got cold. She pulled it on now. Some patrons walked the circus in costume, especially if Arcanium was attached to a Halloween park, a festival, a kink convention or a medieval faire of some kind, but they were doing a solo event this time, so there were fewer customers dressed up. Nevertheless, the more skin she covered, the less likely people would feel entitled to her.

The coat worked, as did her determined gait. Nothing beat looking like she knew exactly where she was going to dissuade people from getting in the way. Except maybe being a black girl in leather who looked like she'd take a one of Misha's blades to anyone who tried. People tended to avoid both freaks and black girls in leather, so she had those in her favor — if one could call that favor. At the moment, she did. She had no use for normals except the one with whom Bell was presently keeping company.

Valorie stopped outside the fortune teller tent. The flap was open. When she peeked in, she half expected to see it empty or with Charles' crisp white dress shirt soaked Christmas red, portions of him missing or slit open in a bloody murder scene that Bell had hidden from anyone else entering for a fortune.

Instead, Bell sat in his usual spot, with Charles in the short armchair that Maya usually inhabited. He looked uncomfortable, his long legs unsuited to something made for a much shorter woman. Naturally, Bell had kept him safe and unharmed — as far as she could see — but hadn't gone out of his way to make Charles comfortable. Had gone out of his way to ensure that Charles was mildly inconvenienced, in fact — the wait, the chair, the company, like a doctor's office.

"Come in," Bell said. He twirled his crystal ball on one finger as though it didn't cost hundreds of dollars. Then he rested it back on its pedestal next to the runner as Valorie entered.

Charles had to work to get up from so low to the ground.

"And here I thought Maya'd be sitting on his lap when I came in," Valorie said.

"I'd wanted such a tableau for you, my dear," Bell replied. "Maya thought you wouldn't appreciate the humor."

"You have many fine qualities," Valorie said drily. "Your humor isn't one of them."

"What the heck is going on?" Charles asked.

The tent flap fell and tied itself closed. Charles clutched the back of the chair, once again shaken. Valorie's stomach sank. Bell had shown his magic. She didn't know whether that was ever a good thing with an outsider.

Then again, his power had been revealed the moment Charles had recognized her, which wasn't any better.

"Have a seat, sir. You can sit with me now. I needed him in my sight but out of the way of the customers. I told them he had received some bad news and was taking some time to recover. Charles was kind enough to go along with my little falsehood. Maya has occupied herself elsewhere for now, so you needn't worry yourself that she has an eye to steal another man of yours."

"I didn't say anything," Valorie replied.

"You didn't have to," Bell said. "She did. Please, sir, join us. We have some things to discuss. It's why you came."

"I didn't come here to talk to you," Charles said, keeping his distance.

"No, but you'll have to speak to me because anything you discuss with her concerns me," Bell said, unshaken and unfailingly polite.

"Because you're the one holding her hostage. That's what this is, isn't it? Valorie wasn't a contortionist, of all things, when she disappeared. And that's what she did. She disappeared. They couldn't ever find her, not even a body. After a year and no trace, they told me they had to move on to other cases, especially since you were young and had a reputation for being impulsive," Charles said.

He edged toward the table, but not because Bell wanted him there. He kept coming closer to Valorie, as though he couldn't believe his eyes, not even now.

"You've done something to her. Torture, conditioning, threats, rape... You've *done* something to her. You're the reason I lost her."

"You're not entirely wrong, sir," Bell said.

Charles lunged at Bell.

Bell raised his hand, perhaps to make Charles freeze where he stood, maybe to do something more forceful. Valorie jumped from her chair and grabbed Charles first, holding him back by his shoulder.

"Stop," Valorie said quietly. "Just sit down, Charles, and maybe we can start to explain."

"*We*? What's this *we*? Tell me it wasn't what you wanted, Valorie. Tell me you didn't throw in with him from the beginning. Or that you haven't thrown in with him since, if he did take you away. Tell me." He struggled against her, not sure which of them to go after first, his fear turning to anger.

Valorie was well-versed in that particular transformation. She saw it in the circus' victims, yes, but she'd also experienced it in herself. Anger was her weapon as well as her shield. Charles had been a tempering influence, a pacifist to keep her tamed and give her perspective. But this wasn't an ordinary situation, and there had been twenty years since that idealistic young man had been her fiancé. This wasn't quite the same man. All she had to do was look at him.

To Valorie, he was the man she'd left and the man he was today. She could see them both at the same time, but she had trouble reconciling the two images, one before her and one in her mind—like watching a 3D movie without the glasses.

And she wasn't quite the same woman either.

"I didn't torture her to change her mind," Bell said. "She did nothing to be brought into my circus except say the wrong thing at the wrong time. I had no desire to hurt her, but the pain caused was inevitable once I brought her in."

"That's so much bullshit," Valorie said, wrestling Charles to the spindly chair next to hers. He collapsed into it, all of a sudden not strong enough to hold himself up in spite of the fight he'd had in him seconds ago.

Bell waited for her to elaborate, as though he didn't already know what she'd meant. He'd heard these arguments before, and he still insisted on spewing this kind of crap. If she didn't know better, she'd think he liked being called out.

"You didn't have to do it the way you did it," Valorie said. "You could have just made me flexible, and I would have figured it out at some yoga class or with some experimental sex position with my fucking husband—"

"Valorie!" Charles said, suddenly scandalized. But Valorie was so beyond scandal.

"You could have had my boss give me the flexibility I asked him for, either for the rest of my time at that company—which would have made my job much better—or just that day so that I could enjoy the circus like I'd wanted to. I remember that day so vividly it could have been yesterday," Valorie said. "There were literally hundreds of ways you could have handled the wish. You took my words and twisted them because you wanted me in your circus. Nothing more, nothing less. You saw something you wanted and you took it, because you don't know any other way. I've come to accept that part of you, as much as a person can, but *don't* pretend you're just a victim of circumstance like the rest of us."

She sat down at the conclusion of her rant, unafraid of any repercussions. She didn't know why he bothered to lie like this. Was it delusion, or was it his usual inability to understand himself as humans saw him, distanced as he was from being human? His mask was just another lie, but the question had always been whether he understood how much that mask was a lie or whether he'd fooled himself from all the times he'd looked into the mirror.

"I don't understand," Charles said. "Did he force you into this or didn't he?"

"He forced me in," Valorie replied. She set a hand on Charles' shoulder again so he wouldn't jerk right out of the chair again. "But after a while, he didn't force me to stay."

"They have a name for that," Charles said.

"*They* can shove a summer sausage up their rectum. They didn't have to go through what I had to go through or what any of us go through," Valorie said. "If there's a phrase that *they* might use, it only makes them feel better about themselves. I eventually decided to stay. It wasn't to make *him* happy. It was because *I* was happy with where I was, and going back would have caused more problems than it would have solved."

"What are you talking about? You would have been *home*," Charles began.

"Look at me!" Valorie shouted. She stood up and spread her arms. "It wasn't a trick of the light, Charles. It's not a really good makeup artist. A woman can look ten years younger to strangers or acquaintances, maybe, but to my family? The friends who knew me well? And now...I couldn't go back even if I wanted to. How can I turn up looking twenty years younger without someone wondering who I sacrificed my firstborn to?"

Charles flicked his gaze from Bell—who sat with his legs crossed and his hands clasped on his thigh as though bored at a business meeting—to Valorie. He squinted through his glasses. It wasn't his prescription that failed him. Even so, he removed his glasses and cleaned them on the edge of his jacket. Then he slipped them into the inside pocket.

He took her hand.

What he could deny with his own eyes, he couldn't deny to the touch. She could see signs of age in his hands, the more prominent veins, the way the fine geometric lines of his skin had become more pronounced, the gathering of flesh around the knuckles of each finger, the quality of his nails.

He traversed his thumb over the back of her hand, testing the texture, the undeniable smoothness, although the skin of her palms was tougher than it used to be, just as her body was a little sleeker. These were changes that were beneficial for her new profession, changes Bell had encouraged in her body.

Charles studied her nails as though they held the answer to immortality. Sure, she had the answer to that one. Make a wish in front of a jinni who happened to grant wishes and hope that he or she liked the idea of having the person around for a while.

Charles slowly drew her back down to her chair. He was tentative, unfamiliar with such familiarity after so long. Valorie tried not to shiver when he tucked the loose part of her hair behind her ears to get a better look at her face. He brushed the pad of a one finger over the paint, but he didn't smear it once he determined it wasn't intrinsic. Same with the rhinestones she'd attached near her eye makeup. He leaned close to see past the paint and color. With the brushes of his fingers and palms, Valorie had a simultaneous fear and longing that he would kiss her.

But that was unfair. To him. To her. To his wife.

It wasn't unfair to Bell. If it got him jealous, tough shit. This was his bed. He had to lie in it.

"How is this possible?" he asked, his breath warm on her lips.

"Magic," Valorie said.

"No, seriously."

"I wasn't being flippant, Charles. It's magic."

He jerked his hands away as though her skin burned him.

"The exact thing I said to my boss before I got pulled into this place was, '*I wish you'd give me a little more flexibility on this.*' That was the wording that Bell needed," Valorie said.

"What does the wording— You said 'wish'. You mean the wording of the wish? You can't be serious, Valorie. Stop fooling."

"Do I look like I'm fooling?" Valorie said. "Scratch that. Do I sound like I'm fooling?"

"No," Charles said. "But you also sound like when you're telling a good lie. I could never tell."

"You could always tell. I just had stories that seemed like they *should* be lies," Valorie replied.

"So you're...you're not lying now," Charles said slowly.

"No."

"It's magic."

"Yes," she said.

He processed that, his expression blank but his eyes bright. Then he turned toward Bell, more cautious than before. Trying to attack Bell had been uncharacteristic. This was the Charles she knew better. "It's you. You're the one with magic. And you forced her in here with magic—with her wish. So you're what, some kind of genie?"

"Yes," Bell replied. No adornments. No obfuscation. No lies. No more hiding.

"You expect me to believe that?" Charles said.

"I have no interest in convincing you of anything. The only way to know for sure is to wish and see if it comes true," Bell replied.

"*No*," Valorie interjected quickly. Was he trying to torture her now that she was thinking of leaving? Was that what this had been about the whole time? "No. We don't use the 'wish' word unless we mean it, and even then we shouldn't most of the time. Don't let him rope you into his games."

She glared at Bell. His demeanor remained unchanged. He really was infuriating sometimes, but he wasn't usually this infuriating with *her*, which made the conversation even more frustrating.

"I never said he should," Bell responded. "I merely said it would be the only way he could know for sure. People rarely believe in magic until it happens to them, especially in a place like this."

"I can't tell whether y'all are bats crazy, pulling my leg or telling the truth," Charles said. He leaned down to bury his head in his hands and rub them against his face. "I'm not sure which one I want to be true. I'm leaning toward crazy, because crazy can be fixed."

"Sorry. It's true. I wished for more flexibility. That's what I got. And Arcanium got a spanking new contortionist to add to Oddity Row and the evening set list. I was a prisoner then. Yes, Charles, I was kidnapped. I was held captive. I couldn't have contacted you if I tried, and I did try to run away—several times. There are things that happen to us when we try—"

"What? Do you get flogged or something?" Charles said.

"Well, yes, but that's not the only thing keeping us here. It's physically painful for us to leave when we're being kept," Valorie said. "I went through that enough before I gave up. I probably went through it more than a normal person would."

"Y-you do that to them? Whip them? Cause them pain?"

"My rules are few but very clear, my punishments effective. As a result, I rarely have to punish," Bell said.

"That's...that's..."

"I know what you think it is," Bell replied. "What you think is irrelevant. My enforcer is happy, and my people who test their boundaries learn what lines they cannot cross—for the safety of the circus as well as themselves. And it is *my* circus. *My* people."

"They don't *belong* to you," Charles said.

"And yet they are mine."

"It's not important," Valorie said, before Charles could get into a full-on slavery rant that Bell probably deserved. It wasn't the same. This wasn't a man enslaving another man. That damn mild-mannered alter ego fooled people every time.

"What do you mean '*it's not important*'?" Charles snapped.

"Can you stop him from doing it? No. Are you going to remember this conversation in thirty minutes? Who the fuck knows?" Valorie said. "You're here because you recognized me when you weren't supposed to ever see me again. And because you saw me, you recognized there were serious questions that needed to be answered. You have those answers. It's up to you to accept them. Now what?" She directed that last question to Bell. This was his court in the end, for good or ill.

"Now, I must silence him," Bell said. "I'm sorry, Valorie, but I cannot let him leave without some kind of assurance he will not sound the alarm on Arcanium."

"Sorry, my ass. Even if you didn't see him coming the first time, which I doubt, you *definitely* saw him coming the second time, and you could have changed my appearance or something to make me seem different enough. You've done it before."

"Wait, when you say 'silence' me, what exactly does that mean?" Charles asked, holding up his hand to interrupt Valorie and Bell's side of the conversation.

"It entails a number of possibilities," Bell replied.

"You are *not* killing him to punish me," Valorie said. "You're not going to do that to me, not after everything I've done for you, Bell. Not after what we had. You are *not* going to kill him because of *your* fucking mistake or something that *you* wanted to happen."

Charles stood up and backed away from the table, but there was nowhere to go. There were shelves of fortune teller trinkets, the armchair, rugs and pelts on the ground and a latched tent flap. Above, there was nothing to weaponize but beads, feathers and scarves. He could try to crawl under the tent canvas, but it was well staked and taut. Bell could stop him if he wanted to, or the clowns could be waiting for him, patrolling the exterior of the tent. All Bell had to do was say the word.

"If you were going to kill me, why didn't you do it earlier?" Charles asked.

"Because he wanted to see your reaction when you were told the truth," Valorie said.

"And this is the man you've thrown your lot in with?" Charles asked, gesturing emphatically at Bell as though he were the devil himself.

"He has his bad qualities," Valorie said.

When dealing with an outsider, it seemed a weak justification. But Charles hadn't been here for all these years. It took time and a treasure map to find the good, but once people did, it was no wonder many of them stayed in the sanctuary Arcanium could provide. She didn't know how she could explain that to Charles.

She could try. "You've got to understand, Charles, *he's not human*. Once that sinks in and you stop expecting him to be human, he starts making more sense."

"That doesn't mean anything," Charles argued. "Even the angels are subject to His will."

"Because the angels have no will," Bell said. "Your religious arguments amuse me. You think you can argue theology with someone who was there at the beginning of creation, before any of the creatures of the earth crawled from the dust?"

"Then you know right from wrong, and you know what you're doing is wrong," Charles insisted.

"I know my place in this universe, sir, better than you know your own," Bell said. "Perhaps you should consider this before accusing me of stepping out of my place. If I wanted to kill you, I'd be well within my boundaries. The laws of your people are not my laws, man. Not even the laws of your reality are mine. Remember that. But I don't have to kill you for your silence. Your former fiancée said that I could wipe your memory. The risk in that is that you could always come back and rediscover Valorie, and this entire headache would occur once more."

"It's *your* headache, Bell. I have zero sympathy," Valorie said. She crossed her arms over her chest to conceal how her abdomen had decided to twist itself into knots without her. "I gave you the simpler option. You chose complicated. Congratulations."

Aurelia T. Evans

"But then I would have never found you," Charles said. "I would have never known what happened to you. You still would have been missing. Do you know what that did to me?"

"Yeah, I noticed how choked up you still are about it when we met while you were with your lovely family," Valorie said.

"What was I supposed to do? Wait forever?" Charles asked, holding his hands out in supplication. "Janice is a good woman, and I love my kids."

"No, I didn't want you to wait. I wanted you to never find me...ever."

"I didn't know if you were flaky, in danger, in a desperate situation or whether you were dead," Charles said.

"How's knowing working for you? Because it sucks over here, Charles."

Charles abruptly closed his mouth. "How have you been, really?"

"Peachy."

"Valorie."

"Started out a little shaky, ended up transcendent for a majority of the time, recently turned shaky for different reasons. The contortion part doesn't suck, though. How about you?"

"Why can you never take things seriously?" Charles asked, deflating a little.

"What makes you think I'm not taking this seriously? I was summing up twenty years. What did you expect?" Valorie asked. "A bedtime story?"

He sank back into his seat. "Fine. I guess the sum of my life was covered by what you saw, then. Good catching up with you."

"You too." Being cold to him again hurt like ice picks stabbing her all over. But making him regret ever

174

seeing her might be the only thing that could save him. A girl had to do her part.

"Do you have to kill me if I just try to…forget? Assume she left me for another man and go with that? My wife doesn't know I'm here. I told her I had to go back in to work. She had no reason not to believe me. I can just leave, go to work, go home and pretend this never happened. You don't have to do anything to me. I won't tell a soul. Who would believe me if I did?" Charles laughed a little. "I'm not sure whether I believe it myself, even now."

"If you believed it, I would be less worried," Bell said. "Those who do not doubt me don't cross me. But I can hear the truth in your words. I see the truth in your mind. You will not tell your wife. You will not tell your pastor. You will not tell the police. You will keep these memories for a while. Then they will fade by your choice. I can accept this end."

He stood. With Charles sitting, this was one of those few times that Bell would be taller than him in his human form, but perhaps Charles got a flicker of what Bell carried inside him, a glimpse of the intensity barely contained in the man who he walked around as — a power that was effortlessly charismatic, a power not to be reckoned with. And all in the way that he carried himself when he looked down upon the two humans in the small room.

"But only this end," Bell emphasized. "If you speak of the real Arcanium to anyone — if you *think* of speaking of the real Arcanium — I will be there. My power is not limited to this circus. I can punish you here, and I can punish you in your home. I assure you, you do not want me to punish you in your own home, sir. Your family would be quite upset."

"Don't you dare threaten my family. It's bad enough you did what you did to Valorie. And I'm still not sure whether you did something her mind too or not. But don't go near my family," Charles said.

Now he stood again. If he'd hoped his height would faze Bell, he was disappointed.

"I won't threaten or harm your family if you give your word that you won't threaten or harm Arcanium and the people in it," Bell replied.

Charles glanced down at Valorie as though expecting her to protest in some way, interfere on his behalf. But what Bell was offering was a risk, a bigger risk than Bell usually made when it came to his precious circus. Valorie kept her suspicions to herself, however. She didn't want to get in the way of Bell's generosity.

"It's a good deal, Charles. Believe me," Valorie said. She bent one leg against her chest and wrapped her arm around it. "You should take it. Take it. Run. And don't come back."

"But…" Charles tried to continue, but sound didn't come out of his mouth.

"No. Don't come back. Don't make this more complicated than it already is. Forget about it. Forget about me," Valorie said.

"Is that how you handled it? You forgot about me?" Charles asked. He fussed with his jacket and finally shoved his hands in his pockets like the young man he had been with her. It was funny how a person regressed like that when confronted with their past.

"I didn't forget," Valorie said. "I just…put you aside. There was nothing I could do then, and there's nothing you can do now except protect yourself and your family. And let's face it, Charles, we were *almost* family. We weren't family."

"Doesn't mean I didn't lose something just as precious to me," Charles said quietly. "You'll never know what it was like when you disappeared."

"Neither will you," Valorie replied.

Charles looked down where he toed at the rug with his dress shoe. His throat worked as he fought to swallow.

"I'll take the deal," Charles said. "I give you my word, but I won't like it. I don't like any of this. It stinks to high heaven, Valorie. If you can find a way out of here, I suggest you take it."

"It's my business now, Charles," she said. "Not yours. That ended a long time ago. It wasn't what I wanted, but it's just the way things are."

He nodded, still not looking at her. "Can I leave now?" he asked Bell. His gaze landed on Bell for a bare second before flitting away. It seemed like scared or sullen behavior, but Valorie recognized it as another sign that he was mulling on something.

The tent flap unlatched.

"You're free to leave. Would you like your ticket for today refunded?" Bell asked, back to the consummate professional.

"You'd do that?" Charles asked, glancing up again.

"Of course, sir," Bell said, pulling a twenty-dollar bill from his leather bag. "You didn't come for the circus. You came for a personal visit. And I kept you here in my tent so that you couldn't avail yourself of our attractions even if you'd wanted to enjoy them. It would be unacceptably dishonest of me to not refund your ticket."

"'Unacceptably dishonest'," Charles said drily. "That's a unique bit of wordsmithing."

"Well, the carnival booths use a certain amount of trickery," Bell replied. "And we lie by pretending truth is illusion. It's what the customers expect. It's what they want. Many professions involve such acceptable dishonesty, as you should be aware."

Charles gave a side-nod of concession. He accepted the money that Bell gave him.

"So now I just forget. Somehow," he said. The glance he gave her took a few more seconds, as though committing the woman he now *knew* was her to memory.

"It'll get easier with time," Valorie said.

She got up and enveloped him in her arms, although she was careful not to press her cheek against his chest. The makeup would smear on his jacket or his pristine white shirt. That would be a trick to explain to Janice. At first, he stiffened. Then he relaxed and embraced her as well, although he tried to keep it detached. It was a fool's errand, but Valorie appreciated that he'd tried.

"It'll get easier?" he whispered in her ear.

"I promise," Valorie answered, curling her fingers into the cheap material of his jacket. "Eventually, it'll all seem like a dream. Best to think of it like that."

Charles stepped out of her arms. He took a deep breath. "Okay. I'm going."

"Have a good day, sir," Bell called after him before Charles ducked under the tent flap.

Valorie clutched the back of her chair. "Are you proud of yourself?" she snapped at Bell. "What the ever-loving *fuck*, Bell?"

Bell walked around his small table. "I don't know what you mean. I made this all work out perfectly. Better than I could have. You understand that more than most."

"You're playing a game, and I'm going to figure out what it is," Valorie said.

"There's nothing to figure out," Bell said. He kissed her lips warmly. He wouldn't smear her face paint like Charles would have.

Valorie jerked her lips away and stepped out of his arms. "You're lying. If you hurt him, Bell, I'm out. I'm so out of here you won't even get two weeks' notice. And I know you'll tell me if you hurt him, because otherwise you wouldn't get the satisfaction of my broken-hearted meltdown. Besides, what does it matter if you drive me away? There are a lot more where I came from, aren't there?"

She stalked out of the tent before Bell could say anything more or placate her with his charms. The Zen from the morning was gone, but a contortionist's work was never done. She still had to give the rest of the day to Arcanium. And if she had to curse Bell's name the whole time in order to get through it, she'd do that.

Somehow, she got through it. She always did.

Chapter Eight

Valorie jolted awake when she heard someone inside her RV. Without thinking, she went for the knife under her pillow, holding it in front of her as she sat up.

"You keep a knife in your bed?" John asked, holding up his hands.

He'd turned on a light in the living area. His body was a nothing but a dark silhouette, but one she recognized.

"I used to keep demons," Valorie said. "Once they went away, you bet your ass I kept a knife. What do you want? It's —" She checked her digital clock. "Okay, it's only two o'clock in the morning. Not as late as I thought it was, but I just got to sleep, man."

"I'm a night person. It didn't occur to me that you weren't, after some of our evenings," John said. "Sorry for waking you. I guess it was the light."

"And your big, skulking body creaking the vehicle. What are you doing here?"

"It's been half a week, and —"

"You're pissed off that I haven't given you the amount of sexing you think you're supposed to get from me. Is that it?" Valorie said, but she let her knife hand fall to the sheets.

"Would you stop putting words in my mouth? No. It's not about what kind of sex I'm getting. I mean, it's inconvenient that I'm not getting any when I kind of expected I'd be getting more, but that's my problem, not yours. I get it. What pisses me off is that you keep thinking the worst of me when I told you I've changed. And I've done things to prove I've changed," John said.

"There's where you're wrong," Valorie said. "A few weeks doesn't prove anything. You're relieved you're getting sex, and that makes you more inclined to be obedient. But if you don't feel entitled to it now, you'll feel entitled to it after maybe a few more months. A person doesn't change that fast, not when you've been a douchebag for *years*."

"No," he insisted. "You put enough pressure on something, it'll change fast. We saw it all the time at church, people turning their lives around. It happens. And this place…this place makes a man want to change. It's like I died a little and had a vision of hell, Valorie. I've experienced what happens to guys like me. I'm a different man than I was. You've got to believe me."

"I'm not convinced," Valorie said. "You take the humiliation and commands like a good boy, but I'm not convinced you're a completely changed man, fire-eater. It's going to be a long time before that happens. Now, did you come here to argue your redemption? Because I'm so not the one for you to be having this conversation with, and I want to go back to sleep."

"You haven't used my collar in days," John said.

"The circus hasn't been open," Valorie replied, flopping back down on her pillows. She didn't let go of the knife.

"I didn't know the collar was for the crowd. I thought it was for us, and you just happened to make it public."

"Us? There is no *us*," Valorie said. "I told you that at the beginning."

"Mistress and pet is still an *us*. That's all I'm saying," John said, sitting at the foot of the bed. But he didn't sit anywhere near where her feet were. Smart man.

"The collar wasn't a wedding ring. I'm not required to give it up when I'm tired just because you need a fuck," Valorie said. She turned over under the covers and closed her eyes.

"How many times do I have to tell you I don't need sex from you?" John said.

Even with her eyes closed, she could raise a skeptical eyebrow just fine.

"Okay, maybe I do need sex. Maybe I am uncomfortable. But I'm not here for sex right now. That's not the only reason I want to be with you, Valorie," he said. "Can't I just...help? Whatever's bothering you, can I help?"

"No," she murmured.

"Can I stay?" he asked quietly. "No sex. No expectations. Can I stay and help you relax?"

Valorie opened one eye to peer up at him. There were those damn puppy dog eyes again. Valorie wasn't one to be swayed by scars like some of the girls who came through Arcanium. She barely saw them, actually. But his expressions were somehow enhanced rather than masked by those scars. The way his collar framed the lower half of his face didn't help her either.

She sighed and closed her eyes again.

"Fine," she said, kicking off the sheets and tucking the knife back under her pillow. She was wearing a gray T-shirt and boy shorts only because it was cold. In the summer, she slept naked. "Do whatever you like. But we're not having sex, and I'm going back to sleep. I don't care how blue your balls get."

The incubus had been sending out signals as strongly as usual, but it turned out that his magic wasn't infallible. Valorie was aroused, but God if she didn't have a single fuck to give for sex right now. Let her nethers tingle all they wanted, her pussy ache, her nipples press against her rehearsal T-shirts. Seriously. No fucks to give. Even if Bell, Lennon and John were to join forces and request a Valorie-focused foursome, she'd have walked out of Arcanium just to get some alone time.

She knew what was wrong. There was no mystery to her mood. She wasn't interested in sharing her feelings with anyone else, though. Not Bell, who had caused this strife in the first place. Not Lennon, who hadn't mourned her absence, as though glad she'd cut him off so he could give all his attention to his new mermaid. Not John. A person confided in pets only because they couldn't understand, and John would be able to understand her all too well.

"Thank you," John said. The burning man actually sounded sincere, thanking her for not being allowed to shove himself up her ass, even though she'd seen him in profile, and the man needed relief.

He turned her onto her stomach.

"If I take off my pants, are you going to stab me?" John asked.

"As long as you keep your dick to yourself, no. I don't want it touching me," Valorie said. "One thing leads to another. You'd only make it worse for yourself."

"I get it," he said. "Believe me."

"Make me believe you," Valorie muttered, burying her face in the crook of her elbow on the pillow.

She heard the zip and the whisper of skin on skin as he removed his trousers. He unsettled the bed when he sat back down again.

John lifted her right foot and rested the instep on his warm thigh. He brought both hands to her sole to rub his firm fingers into the muscles.

Valorie fought not to groan as he massaged her feet, first one then the other. There was a place in her arches that, when he pushed just right, sent electrical shocks of pleasure throbbing to her clit. She wasn't a stranger to those areas of her feet, but it had been a long time since they'd been stimulated. If John knew what he was doing to her — and she had every reason to believe that he did, since he devoted an awful lot of time to her feet — he didn't comment. Nor did he press the matter. Just her soles. Even though her feet rested on his thigh, he didn't so much as brush his cock against them, either by accident or accidentally on purpose, which meant he was making the effort not to.

She gave him silent points for that.

Sexual surges aside, the rest of her melted under his massage, especially when he moved away from her feet and up her legs. He parted them so that he could kneel between her ankles, but the touch remained sensual without turning suggestive. He dug his fingers so far into her muscle that it sometimes hurt, but then he'd withdraw and it would all be roses again. Her breathing was even, her eyes closed. She drifted between sleeping and waking, drawn down by the sweetness of the massage but held back by the changing reality of his touch.

True to his word, although he slipped his fingers over the edge of her panties, he didn't get near her cunt. He straddled her hips when he was finished with her legs so that he could start in on her back over her shirt, but he didn't let his ass rest against her thighs. She wished she could turn over and check whether he was still hard. She wanted to see what he was sacrificing for her. But that would require her to move and acknowledge that she was still awake, and she'd rather stay right where she was than stop him from doing what he was doing.

"You talk mean, Valorie," he murmured. "Lots and lots of talking mean. Maybe it's what I deserve or maybe that's just you. But I knew when Bell handed me over to you that I won the lottery. Whether we have sex or not, it's insane that I'm able to do this. I don't know what those demons were thinking. I want to tell you this when you're not asleep, except then you'd either laugh or throw me out or tell me how bad a man I am. And I guess I am. I have a lot to make up for. But I promised I'd do it all for you. I'll keep my word. I'd do anything just to be close to someone like you, viper tongue and all. I'll take it. I'll take it all and like it. Maybe one day you'll believe that."

Sometime when he started to massage her neck and scalp, her hair loose over her shoulders, she finally untethered and slipped off into sleep, mulling on whether he'd known she was awake or not and not knowing what to do about it either way except pretend it had never happened. There was a lot of that going on lately, self-delusion. But there wasn't much else she could do without her chest hurting so much it made her heart skip.

Sleep was better. Sleep was where she could forget without trying. And what John was doing felt so good that forgetting was that much easier when he made it hard to think at all.

* * * *

When she woke up again, John had spooned up behind her — possibly in his sleep. He'd remembered to put her sheets back over her, so she was pleasantly heated by his body and enveloped in his arms, but his skin wasn't touching hers except where he had his fingers on her arm.

There was, however, an undeniable erection pressed against her ass through the sheets and her thin clothing. Morning erection or continued from last night, it was impossible to tell, nor was it relevant.

He'd done what she'd told him he was allowed to do and no more.

She didn't feel bad about how she'd treated him, but she acknowledged the step forward that John had made. And she'd woken up in a much better state of mind than when she'd gone to sleep.

Valorie turned around in his arms and guided him onto his back. He didn't protest. She kept her sheets around her body, but she brought her arms out from under them to have full access to his long, lean, strong torso. It wasn't a massage like the one he'd given her, but she moved her hands over his abdomen with the same sensual, firm strokes. She didn't dig in, however, and he didn't wake up yet. He sighed, his eyelids fluttering as she circled his dark nipples with the pads of her thumbs.

When he was asleep, she didn't have to control him, didn't have to ensure that he was doing exactly what she told him to do, didn't have to think about what kind of man he was or what his motives might be. When he was asleep, he was all innocence. Even his cock, darkening the sheets with blots of his pre-cum, was innocent. It didn't rear up at the promise of power or subjugation. It just wanted someone to touch it and help it come. That was all. Simple. Innocent.

Valorie liked the way his lips parted in a sigh when she trailed her fingers down to his navel, brushing through the dark hairs just above the insistent head of his cock. The way his hips moved upward when she traced the lines of the V almost to the base of the shaft. The way he turned his head against his arm, stretched up over the pillows, when she caressed his inner thigh, knuckles brushing his scrotum. The way he moaned when she ghosted her palm a hair's breadth from his erection's feverish flesh. It seemed to strain beneath her hand, as though if it thickened just a bit more, it could touch her.

God, he was beautiful like this. Vulnerability from waking up after a spectacular massage with the amazing specimen of manflesh before her was the only reason she could think of for why she bent down and ran her tongue from base to head of his cock — slow, torturous, wanting her tongue to caress every contour that it could reach, sparing no nerve ending on her way up.

His sighs turned into light moans. He tossed his head on the pillow, his eyelids shut tight, but he still appeared asleep. She thought he'd be more controlled if he wasn't. And he'd be watching. He'd definitely be watching.

Valorie flicked her tongue along the ridge of the glans, tasting the drips of his pre-cum and swallowing them down as she adjusted her position next to him. She stroked his inner thigh with her thumb as she ever-so-slowly took the head into her mouth, all lips and tongue, practically worshiping him. She'd never gone down on Lennon — he'd been far more interested in going down on her — but she found that she'd missed it since Bell. And as big as Bell had been, his magic helping her accommodate him, John felt more substantial in her mouth. The stretch of her lips and the solidness against her tongue, it was all real, nothing to spread her lips wider or make her throat relax for him. She'd have to draw on muscle memory, because just dealing with the head wouldn't be enough for her, she could already tell.

"Oh..." he murmured, tossing slightly. "Don't. She won't let me." He threaded his fingers through her hair, although he didn't seem to know whether to push her away or pull her closer.

Valorie sank down over his erection then pressed her tongue against the underside as she swept back up. "Shhh," she whispered with her lips against the head. She pressed a kiss to the treasure trail leading down from his navel. She was absurdly amused by the fact that he was telling her no because even in his sleep, he was trying to obey her. "Yes, she will. She's telling you yes. Just enjoy it."

"No, I...Valorie. Oh fuck, Valorie..."

She took him in again, the lifting of his hips pushing him into her mouth smooth as honey. She moaned into his cock. He tossed again from the vibrations, muffling his own groans into his forearm. She bobbed over him, shallow movements, then relished his loud cry when she twisted her head down, taking in as much as she could before pulling off him with a gasp. She brought her hand away from his thigh to wrap around the hot, throbbing shaft, pumping him while she caught her breath and took in the unfettered expression of blissful agony on his face.

"Wake up, sleepyhead," she said quietly. "Mistress is feeling like less of a bitch, and pet tastes *good* this morning."

When he still didn't wake up beyond a few more indecipherable murmurs, she held the base of his cock and sank down over him again, going even farther when he bucked up against the back of her throat. She swallowed frantically to keep from gagging. Her breath came harshly through her nose, but she was gratified when her lips touched thumb and forefinger where they held and stroked the base.

His eyes flew open, the whole top half of his body coming off the bed. His arousal throbbed through the cock in her mouth.

"Oh my God," he panted, disoriented by sudden consciousness as well as overwhelming pleasure. "Oh fuck, is this really happening? Ahhhh…"

She swirled her tongue against the underside as she made her way back up to the head, where she applied such intense suction that he cried out again, jerking his hips up.

"It's happening, pet. Now just lay back down and let it happen some more. Your Queen has things she wants to do to you," Valorie said.

"Fuck, I always wanted to wake up like this…" His voice got amusingly high near the end of it. Now that he was awake, Valorie didn't mind letting him feel her teeth.

She wouldn't bite down, though, not unless he became more like his old self. Valorie still didn't believe he'd changed as much as he thought he had, but he *had* changed some. She could give him that.

It was too early in the morning for anything complicated. Still, she didn't think John would complain about a simple blow job — stretching her mouth around him until the head nudged her soft palate, stroking the base where it was harder for her to reach, smearing his pre-cum over her tongue like syrup, thrilling in the sounds that he made and the way he had to hold himself back, because she'd caught him at a vulnerable time too. The ache in her cunt turned deliciously keen, but the sheets were twisted around her, and she had her hands full. Valorie pressed her thighs together, poor substitute for real pressure.

"I'm gonna come," he gasped, with that adorable push-pulling of her hair, telling her to leave if she didn't want him to ejaculate in her mouth and at the same time begging her to stay. "I'm going to come."

Valorie moaned as she took him in halfway down. She undulated her tongue over him and sucked his climax into her. He grasped fistfuls of her sheets to hold his hips down while his cock pulsed inside her mouth, hot fluid hitting her throat with each pulse. She swallowed again and stroked the exposed shaft to coax more of his cum into her, thick, salty, each spurt as satisfying to her as a finger through her folds.

Finally he slumped, shoulders and abdomen relaxed. His panting breaths slowed down. He rested his hand on the back of her head, idly stroking her hair as she eased off him. His cock fell from her mouth and listed to the side, glistening. A thin thread of cum attached to her lip before she licked it away.

"I thought you weren't wanting sex," John said, looking down at her where she rested her chin on his hip. It was an awkward angle, but he obviously preferred to stay lying against the pillows, not ready to get up for the day after what she'd done for him. "I thought I was still the wrong kind of bad boy and you didn't want me anymore."

"I wanted to reward you for last night. Encourage good behavior," Valorie said. She rolled over and opened the top drawer of her nightstand before pulling out her trusty bullet vibe. She brought her hand under her sheets. She didn't even bother going underneath her panties.

"I can help with that," John said, covering her hand over the sheets. His warmth seeped through like liquid. "You know I can."

"No," Valorie said. With her free hand, she took his away from where she'd turned on the vibrator against her mound, working it down to her clit in tight circles. She interlaced her fingers with his. "Just stay here a while."

She let her instincts lead her into an easy orgasm, quick and unadorned, attending to her needs rather than her desires without fuss or frills. She still wasn't up to sex, in spite of her arousal, because every time she thought of John's hands on her, Valorie couldn't help but remember being in bed with Charles.

Valorie had told him to forget. Now she was trying to do the same, and it was so much harder than she'd thought.

Was it going to take her years, like it had when she'd first been taken? God, she hoped she could get over this more quickly than before. She couldn't imagine having to go through the five fucking stages of grief all over again.

Valorie tucked her cheek against John's arm as she turned off her vibe and just lay there. It was a rehearsal day, so she was in no hurry to get up, no schedule to adhere to that she couldn't change, and she'd had trouble getting out of bed for the last few days as it was.

If John was surprised at the gesture, he didn't comment. He just stayed still, stayed with her like she'd asked, his breathing sometimes aligning with hers, sometimes a counterpoint. He didn't even hold her. He just gave her something with which to ground herself, an anchor to the present against the current of the past.

She didn't know if he was strong enough for it. But right now, he was all she had.

* * * *

She still didn't let John have sex with her, no matter how their joint routines worked him up or worked her up. It occurred to her with some disquiet that part of the reason she kept refusing John was because it wouldn't be fair to him. Since when did she care about what was fair to John? Since when *should* she care?

Either way, she wasn't interested, although she sometimes brought the vibe out and held his hand. Sometimes she rubbed him off. Sometimes he rubbed himself off while holding her hand as well.

John was allowed to spend the night, though, if he came to her RV. On the long, cold winter's nights, he was a good heater to have. She ascribed the lack of flame bursts during these sleepovers to Bell not wanting his contortionist burned to a crisp by accident — or ticked off as hell because her wardrobe had been charred in the night. All the more reason for John to want to stay overnight with her. All the more reason for Valorie to let him, since he wasn't going to destroy anything, and she got a warm body to sleep with. Lennon used to kick in his sleep, since having a diurnal schedule wreaked havoc with his nocturnal demonic sleep cycle. John was much calmer.

He never pushed her for more. The closest he came was asking. He accepted her answer when she said no, accepted her hand when she offered it, accepted what contact she gave him when she didn't.

Over the course of a week, Valorie gradually allowed herself to be pulled back into her usual life, or something close to it.

Yet if she had to be honest, she wasn't surprised when she stepped out of the back of her exhibition tent after a morning's work to have Charles standing there, waiting. She wasn't surprised when he took her hands, stepped forward and kissed her.

She wasn't surprised at all.

Chapter Nine

After twenty years, the kiss should have been the most awkward, uncomfortable thing in the world. Their tastes and tendencies should have changed, their tricks altered, their desires evolved. But he stepped forward to kiss her without preamble, without hesitation, and the action of her exiting the tent and him taking her into his arms carried the same smooth motion of a perfect machine—as though they'd been made for this moment and none of the twenty years had separated them.

He wrapped his arms around her waist. She wrapped hers around his neck. She barely had to stand on tiptoe and he barely had to dip. They angled their heads and their mouths met with instant familiarity.

No, she wasn't surprised. She hadn't put on lipstick or face paint this morning. Instead, she wore a purple lip stain that wouldn't smear on his mouth as he kissed her so thoroughly her knees almost couldn't support her. His lips still felt like his, moved like his. His mouth still tasted like him. Old memories took the fore, because she could swear he'd kissed her almost exactly like this after he'd proposed and she'd said yes. He'd known then how to make a woman melt. That hadn't changed a bit.

He does this to her *now,* she thought weakly. *He makes her feel this way. Or was this only ever calibrated to me?*

The things a person thought in the midst of a maelstrom. The weather was uncharacteristically warm, actually, with a light breeze, yet Valorie felt swept up in the moment as though she'd been blown into his arms, neither of them with any choice in the matter.

The lust that exploded from his kiss and his body against hers fed off both of them until Valorie nearly tore his jacket off. His erection wasn't confined at all by his trousers, which gave him room to grow, no room to hide. It pressed against her hip as he tasted her.

Charles moaned into her mouth like an alcoholic twenty years sober taking his first illicit sip. He raised a hand to grasp the back of her head, as though afraid if he loosened his hold she would run — or disappear.

He was the one who broke the kiss, though, gasping as he leaned his forehead against hers.

"I tried," he murmured. "I told myself all the reasons why I shouldn't come back. They were good reasons. If I made a list, there would be far many more reasons why I should be home instead of here. But I couldn't stay away, Valorie. I couldn't let you go without…"

He brushed her lower lip with the fingers that had clutched at her head.

"They declared you dead," Charles said. "I never stopped hoping. I never visited your grave because I knew you weren't in it. Even if the longer you were gone and alive, the more likely you were in a bad place, I never stopped hoping. This is a kind of bad place, though, isn't it? That's what you said, that it started bad before you…"

"So you hoped I was in a bad place, as long as I was alive?" Valorie asked.

"I know. It's selfish, isn't it? I'm not such a good man after all. If you'd been dead, you'd have been in heaven. But I would've rather you feel like you were in hell, just for one chance to see you again on this earth. I tried to let you go, babe. I even thought I had until I saw you again," he said. "I shouldn't be here. I lied to my wife again. I had to break a promise to my daughter. I didn't think I was this kind of man. I love Janice. I love Kendra and Elian. I love my family. I made a life for myself. But the two of us… You were The One first. I can't help but think it all should have been ours. Our house. Our kids. Our life. Our love. Because it wasn't our fault that it got destroyed. I was mad at God for a while. I guess I should have been mad at the devil."

"He's not the devil," Valorie said. "He's just different."

"I've been through the freak show. I've seen what he does to people. He's the devil, Valorie," Charles said.

"Some of them aren't human either. And some of them were already like that before they came here," Valorie explained.

"But not you."

"No."

"So others were also made into what they are for your boss's freak show?"

"Yes."

"Then I call him the devil," Charles said.

"He could be a lot worse," Valorie said softly. She thought of some of the wishes he'd granted, inside and outside the circus, and shivered. "Believe me, the people you see…that's him being restrained."

"I don't want to talk about him," Charles said, pulling her back in to kiss her again, his hold on her arms bruising. His facial hair rasped against the sensitive skin of her palms.

This time, she took control of the kiss and brought her hips tightly against his until he grunted, swaying away from her to contain himself. His scent, emanating from his skin and suffused in his clothes, surrounded her with the heart's pang of nostalgia. But she couldn't help but think that he hadn't had those glasses the last time, and his body had been slightly different against hers — his muscle tone firmer in his youth, his clothes more fitted...all the little things that had changed and that she needed to be the same to make this kiss less guilt-ridden.

The man she was kissing wasn't hers, and she knew it. She'd be a hypocrite if she let this continue, and it was bad enough she was a bitch.

Yet Valorie couldn't let him go. Every time she broke away, he would follow her and she would let him. They stumbled against the stiff canvas of her tent, the hum of people talking so close, with the occasional outburst of shouting or laughter. Anyone could have seen them if they'd walked halfway around the tent or bent over one of the closer souvenir tables.

The cast was allowed to engage in certain kinds of encounters with customers if the mood struck them, but not in public. Not where they could be seen, not least because circuses already had the same reputation as ballet and theater of prostituting lovely young women to wealthy patrons. Charles wasn't wealthy, if his off-the-rack suit was any indication, but Arcanium didn't need a potential customer getting disgruntled when a cast member said no after the customer had clearly seen an instance where they'd said yes.

Yet Valorie couldn't stop.

"You're married," she finally gasped between their kisses.

"It was supposed to be with you," he replied.

"But it's not." She wound her arms around him under his jacket, traversing the contours of his back. "Come on. You're the grown-up here." Valorie gave a soft cry when he dragged his tongue along her jawline then began kissing her neck, just like when they'd been young and leaving hickeys had made them laugh. He'd had twenty years to perfect the technique, and he hadn't been anywhere near bad to begin with. "You need to stop this."

"If anything, I was cheating on you with her. You were there first, Valorie, and you were taken from me against your will," Charles said against her neck before biting at the base and sucking on her skin, running his tongue over the sensitized flesh and coaxing blood to the surface with his heat. "I wish—"

Valorie's eyes flew open.

And as she feared, Bell leaned against the big top not twenty feet from them, casual as the devil Charles believed him to be, his arms crossed as he took in his contortionist and her ex-fiancé wrapped around each other after he'd told Charles to stay away. Charles had promised, and though what he was doing wasn't intrinsically damaging—he wasn't telling anyone about Arcanium, for instance—Bell might take offense to the broken word.

Bell was here for the wish. He'd known that Charles would make it. He'd gone out of his way to be near them for it. This was bad. This was very, very bad.

"I wish this had never happened to you, that we could go back to how it was before you ever came to this circus and got trapped, that it could have been how it was supposed to be," Charles murmured into her ear, the turmoil of twenty years thick in his voice.

"No," Valorie whispered, but it was too late. She pushed Charles from her, as though she could take back the wish by pretending the last few minutes hadn't happened — the way he had wished away the last twenty years. "No, Bell, whatever you're thinking, don't. Don't do this to me. Please. Don't do this to me."

"You don't even know what I'm going to do yet," Bell said. He pushed off the big top canvas with his shoulder and approached them.

Charles whirled around when he heard Bell, struck with a bolt of horror. His expression was almost comical, masklike in its exaggeration. But Valorie knew that any fear associated with Arcanium was far from exaggeration. If it appeared exaggerated, it meant that the person understood perfectly what he was in for.

Then Charles froze — and not from fear.

The world around them went quiet, not so much as a breath of wind.

Valorie turned from side to side, breathing deeply because it seemed like whatever she took had to struggle to get into her. There was the golem manning the souvenir table. And when she turned to her right, another pang of the guilt she hated sliced through her.

John stood a few tents down. It looked like he'd been heading for her tent when he'd seen her with Charles. From what she could tell, he'd been caught between continuing toward her as though it didn't matter — when it clearly did, judging by the shine in his pretty eyes — or staying put and forcing himself to witness Valorie with another man.

But the golem and John were just as frozen as Charles.

"What did you do?" Valorie asked, whipping her head back toward Bell. Her hair, free today, swept over her shoulders.

"I took a moment," Bell replied. "You might get lightheaded, but you can breathe, my dear. I recommend you do so."

"You were lying in wait," Valorie said. She stepped away from Charles and met Bell in the middle. "I'm tired of your games, Bell. You've always played them, but I hate it when you play me like you have been lately. You did it with me and Maya too, and we were *not* amused."

"I already show my favorites their special bit of favor," Bell said. "It would truly be unfair of me to spare you from *everything*. Besides, you weren't the one to make a wish."

"I *can't* make another wish," Valorie said.

"So I obviously couldn't grant yours," he replied.

Sometimes she could just throttle him.

"The wish is made," Bell continued.

"What are you going to do about it? What are you going to do to *us*?" Valorie asked.

"What would you like for me to do for you?" he asked back.

"It's annoying when therapists turn questions back. It's twice as annoying when you do it," Valorie said. "Especially when I know what's at stake if you...if you twist it somehow."

"Do you really think I'd hurt you just because you're no longer in my bed, Valorie?" Bell asked. He flipped a lock of hair away from her face like peering through a curtain. "My favor isn't only for my lovers, as you're well aware."

"Anything you do to hurt him will hurt me," Valorie said.

"I know."

"Then what are you going to do?" she demanded again.

"What do you want me to do?" Bell repeated.

Valorie tried to slap him. He caught her wrist before she could connect with his cheek, and she hadn't been pulling any punches. She would have walloped him a good one if he hadn't seen it coming.

His smile was frightening and attractive at the same time. The Ringmaster was his whip, his demonic enforcer, but Bell was ever the real ringmaster in the shadows of Arcanium. Valorie tried to remember that at all times. Bell always seemed tame as a trained lion. It was so easy to settle back into when she'd been the queen at his side, not having to worry about the whims of the king.

He wasn't tame.

It was times like this, gazing into those eyes that could hold whole worlds if she peered deeply enough, that Valorie wondered for the millionth time whether he'd driven her mad and she just couldn't tell. She should fear him more than she did, even now.

Old love died hard. With three of her four most significant lovers in the tent alley between Oddity Row and the big top, this was all too apparent.

"I thought your little pet might be what you needed to stay here with me a little longer," Bell said, "but we wouldn't be here now if he was truly enough. This is your chance to leave. Do you want to go back as though it had never happened? As though you'd never entered my circus at all?"

"Is that possible?" Valorie asked, too stunned by what he was saying to process it.

"It's difficult. There are threads in the tapestry of time that must be altered in order to keep the outcome of the present as close as possible to what it is now. You can go back if that is what *you* wish. You could have been called into work before arriving at Arcanium for the first time. That part is simple."

"You'd do that?" she asked weakly. The weight of time lifted, making her dizzy. "You'd do that to me?"

"For you," Bell said. "I'd do it for you. It's your ticket out of here, if you want it. Or I could alter Charles' age. The both of you could start over together as though your wishes had never happened, simply in the present rather than the past."

"You'd take him from his family," Valorie said.

"Just as I took you from yours."

"He'd hate me." The exhilaration of finding her would fade. Valorie had resented Bell for a long time, but she'd eventually let that resentment go because it didn't faze him, only her. However, Charles' resentment would hurt both of them. Valorie knew this as if she'd already lived it.

"It's still your choice, my dear," Bell said.

Valorie glanced over her shoulder at where Charles stood stock-still, a most realistic waxwork.

"I can't do that to him," she muttered.

But he'd made the wish. He'd made the wish and now Bell had to grant it, whether he wanted to or not — and he always wanted to.

Her plans to leave had been nebulous at best. She hadn't pinned down when, where and how, and now the choice was before her. Valorie might not get another perfect chance like this to leave and have someone to go with her.

Then there was the what-if, the classic question of what her life would have been like if she had never entered Arcanium.

She turned to Bell, her lover of over seventeen years. She might as well have been married to him and amicably divorced.

She turned to John in the background, her little dragon puppy pet, her firebrand, her fire-eater.

"I don't know," she said. "I don't know what I want."

"That's okay," Bell said, caressing her chin affectionately, that half-dark smile still curving his lips. "How about I give you time to think where you won't be disturbed?"

He blinked. The world around them started up again.

Charles stumbled around when he saw that Valorie had disappeared from in front of him, stammered in confusion at where she'd ended up in what seemed to him like no time at all.

Bell gently led Valorie over to him.

"I can give you what you ask for, sir," Bell said. Charles flinched when Bell touched his shoulder. "I can give her to you for as long as you stay in that tent. But as soon as you leave…"

He stared at Valorie. The gold in his hazel eyes almost glowed with the magic he was using to grant the wish, little more than a glint like sun on mica, but Valorie would recognize it anywhere. He didn't have to speak in her head for her to understand.

A moment. A moment to see what things could have been.

And whether they could be that again. Because she still had a choice ahead of her.

"I don't understand," Charles said quietly as she took his hand and guided him to her tent.

Valorie met John's eyes across the distance then lowered them, a quiet acknowledgment and maybe an apology. She didn't want to think about John right now, not when Charles was here. Not when his hand was warm in hers and the branding of his kiss still on her lips and neck. She craved more. She craved him as though years of lonely nights missing him had returned to her all at once, with the strength of a wife whose soldier husband had returned from war, even though she was the one who felt like she'd been strung out through the battlefield. She hadn't realized how much until Charles had seen her like this—in the den of the devil and wearing the costume of her enslavement, so thoroughly integrated that she didn't even realize she was a slave anymore.

Had she hit rock bottom and just grown used to the view, as Charles had implied? Or had she ascended long ago, thrown off the shackles for the invisible crown she pretended she wore?

Where they were going, did it matter, as long as it was something she chose and a choice that she owned?

"Come with me," Valorie said, lifting the flap to her tent. "You'll understand soon."

Revelation dawned. "Oh God, I said it," Charles said. "I said the W-word. You warned me, and I—"

"Don't worry, Charles," Valorie said. "This won't hurt at all."

The last thing she saw of the outside world was Bell's smile. Valorie let down the tent flap, latched it and turned around to face Charles' wish.

She couldn't help her gasp. She brought a hand to her mouth in a belated attempt to muffle it.

The doubling of Charles, the Charles of her vision and the Charles of her memory, suddenly snapped into a single man—the one she'd left behind that summer day, when he'd wanted to stay home and she'd wanted to go out and she'd eventually gone on her own, as she often had.

They were in an apartment, the same apartment where they'd been living together while they'd searched for a house before the wedding. The front door was a tent flap, but that was the only indication they hadn't really stepped back in time.

It was a small place, sparsely furnished, sparsely decorated—although Valorie had added her little touches here and there, plus a few coats of paint. Small, but cozy—it had been home. Valorie hadn't needed much more than that. They'd only been in the market for a house because they'd wanted to expand as a family after the wedding. She'd been looking forward to the point when she could stop taking her birth control.

Valorie wondered if the pills would be in the right bathroom drawer where she'd left them.

"Is this real? Is this happening?" Charles asked.

"Look at yourself," Valorie said. She struggled against the tears that threatened to pour over the edge of her lower lids.

His reaction helped. Now she fought against laughter when Charles did a double take at himself and ran out of the living room into the single bathroom. He was wearing a pair of jeans that had been cool in the nineties, although now it showed itself for the relic that it was. His shirt, though, was a classic plaid, nothing to be alarmed about. The grooves in his face had smoothed out, the salt in his hair had darkened and his close buzz had grown out about an inch of dense curls.

Valorie checked herself while he was out. She was wearing the same T-shirt she'd left in. It stopped short of the waistband of her tight high-rise jeans. Her giggles sounded giddy to her. She was pretty sure she was close to hysterical, but she was too distracted to be alarmed.

Her hair no longer brushed her shoulders, smooth and straight. When she touched her head, she could feel the permed curls that she'd tucked into a ponytail higher on her head than she could do these days without being ironic. Her arms, chest and hips were unadorned, not a single tattoo in sight.

And when she bent down to untie her sneakers, she realized that she couldn't just bend from the waist to reach them. She had to bend her knees.

The contortion flexibility was gone.

Her laughter cut off all at once, as though she'd slammed the switch down.

"Are you okay? Aside from some atrocious wardrobe choices I made in my youth, I think I'm doing all right, but you look like you've seen a ghost," Charles said, coming out from the bathroom, his face painted with all the wonder and awe Arcanium tried to inspire. Not often it happened in a place as normal as this.

"Maybe I have," Valorie said. She managed to keep her voice from shaking.

"Tell me about it," Charles replied. He wasn't wearing shoes. He was near silent as he approached her in bare feet and took her in, the Valorie he remembered—impeccably her from head to toe, without anything sparkly or colorful to get in the way.

Yet in his eyes, she could see the man he'd become, not the man he had been. She thought he saw the same in her. This place, this illusion-reality, it was *like* Valorie hadn't been stolen into the circus, but it was simply an elaborate masquerade. A fantasy. One that seemed real in every way but the years that they carried in their minds.

"I thought you were going to the circus today," Charles said.

It took Valorie a second to figure out what Charles meant.

"I was," she replied slowly. "But I decided that if I had to go alone, I didn't want to go at all. That kind of place isn't a solo scene. And if I can't share it with you, then I'd rather do something together that we *can* share."

"I didn't think I'd ever hear anything so sweet from you, little sister," Charles said, hooking a finger in one of her belt loops.

"You've been rubbing off on me," Valorie said. She grinned as he tugged her toward him.

"Not yet," he said huskily. "But I will. 'Cause I can think of a few things we can be sharing right now instead of that circus. How about you?"

They were both laughing when his mouth met hers, kissing through their grins. Charles turned them around, and they stumbled toward the bedroom. It had been a long time since they'd had to find their way blind through their apartment. He knew every inch of her body and she his, but he'd forgotten that chair was there.

She tumbled into it, still giggling madly. She gave a cry when he swept his arms under her and picked her up. Valorie was all flailing, coltish limbs. Her sisters had called her too skinny, bony in the hips instead of curvy, no boobs until she was eighteen and finally filled out her small bra cups, but Charles had always said that made it easier to hold all of her at once instead of piece by piece. He had pillows for softness, he'd used to say, and her for sexy. His gaze had strayed when a curvy girl had walked by, but he'd still made Valorie feel like the prettiest girl in the world.

Now was no exception. He carried her to the bedroom, kicked the door open then kicked it closed again behind them. He was less rough with her. He lowered her to the unmade bed as though she was delicate, precious.

When he climbed over her to lie down next to her, something in her belly shivered. For such a long time, all she'd had of him were memories. She'd remembered the way he'd made her feel when he was above her, as though she were some adult Little Red Riding Hood meeting a wolf with a different kind of appetite. But it had faded, as memories did, the edges blurry and the feelings like words on a page instead of experienced. Reliving them…it was like getting hit with waves on the beach, toppled back each time with the unexpected strength.

"Charles, are you sure about this?" Valorie asked, breaking the role play.

"Yes," he said with vehement conviction. "I wasn't before, to tell you the truth. I had shame all the way down in my soul for coming here and kissing you. But when I walked in here, it all went away. I'm not married here. Look." He raised his left hand. No golden band on his finger. "The man in this bed is your fiancé. God may smite me down for having sex with you before marriage — and I was never a hundred percent sure on that, as you know — but he's not going to smite me for cheating on a wife I wouldn't have had. I'm confident in that. I don't know why, because it's all being orchestrated by a devil man, but I am. So as far as I'm concerned, my conscience is mostly clear. Clear enough to be with you in this moment. Because this is all there is, isn't it? We're not going to disturb the neighbors or your circus' customers or run out of cheese in the fridge, are we?"

Valorie stroked the brush of his hair, solidifying more memories.

"I think it's just us. As the song says, we're all alone," she said. "When we're here, it's twenty years ago. And we're going to get married in less than a year. Planning is driving me crazy."

"It's your mother driving you crazy," Charles corrected with a broad, boyish grin.

"It's my mother driving me crazy." Valorie rolled toward him to kiss his bottom lip as he smiled. "But as far as we're concerned, the people in the apartments all around us are on vacation and we have a grocery gnome."

"How long do we have?" Charles asked, tentatively sliding his hand over her hip to the bottom of her shirt. He seemed unsure whether he was allowed to touch her skin after so long.

"However long we need. Two hours, two days, two weeks, two hundred years," Valorie said. She covered his hand and urged him upward. "He's very powerful. But don't think about that. Just feel. Touch me, Charles. You haven't touched me in what feels like forever."

She tugged his shirt over his head. There was that bookish but well-taken-care-of boy she'd fallen in love with, his shoulders and chest not quite filled out yet. He had been a late bloomer, like her. She regretted that she hadn't been there for his blooming the way he'd been there for hers.

He hissed and panted as she ran her hands over his chest, teasing his nipples between her fingers. He chuckled a little at her querying glance.

"Turns out there's another part of me that went back to being twenty-one. Threw me for a loop. I'd give you the full older-man endurance treatment if I could, babe," Charles said.

"Hey, I've still got my twenty-three-year-old libido too. That never left, actually," Valorie said.

"Oh yeah, I remember us going at it like wolves in heat. I'm surprised our neighbors *didn't* complain," Charles said. He eased his hands under her shirt and stroked up to her cotton bra, cupping her breasts. He pushed her shirt over them before pulling the cotton to the side to take one nipple into his mouth.

Valorie bit a knuckle, but she didn't have to hold back her moan or her whine when he teased the peak with his teeth, biting until it was flushed and erect. He nudged it back and forth with his tongue as he played with the other nipple between two fingers, twisting, tweaking. She writhed underneath him.

Her nipples had driven him as crazy as breasts did to other men. He'd been relatively modest for a man his age, but he'd talked about her getting nipple rings for him after they were married, and they'd played with clothespins. His adoration translated seamlessly into her arousal, as it almost always had. Now that it had been so long since the last time — and no time at all — she experienced it as new, as though it was their first time having good sex. Their literal first time hadn't been all that great. The third time had been the charm. This was like that, magnified by experience.

As he played with her tits, sending spiral after spiral of pleasure through her like charges through electrical coils, Valorie worked her jeans open and shoved them down her hips then fumbled with Charles'. She had to reach to get at the fastenings, but once she'd finished, he was more than happy to kick them off. They got trapped at his knees. He buried his face against her belly, laughing helplessly. Pre-cum had made a wet spot on his boxer shorts. She could feel it where it brushed her leg.

They each divested themselves of their own jeans. Valorie felt like she had the biggest, stupidest smile on her face, but that was all right because Charles did too. He looked happier than she'd ever seen him, like a little boy on Christmas Day. Before he could get his pants down off his ankles, she tackled him onto his back, straddling his hips, wearing her shirt over her tits and her bra askew, her panties practical cotton, yet his cock peeked out from the opening in his boxer shorts and strained up toward her as though she were magnetized. He was mesmerized by her, unable to take his eyes off her as she lowered her pussy down to frot over his partially covered cock. She bit her lip through a grin as his eyes rolled back and he grabbed her arms at the elbows.

"God, it's been forever," he muttered. He canted his hips up to meet hers. "Want to see you, Valorie. Want to see all of you. I have the memories. Heck, I have the pictures of you I keep in that box. But I want to see it with my own eyes, right in front of me, not on some piece of photo paper. Take your clothes off, babe. I don't want to come until you're naked."

"I want to make you come before you're inside," Valorie said, still rubbing her pussy against his erection. She didn't know which of them was making her panties wetter.

"And you know that I'll give back what you give me," Charles said.

"It's only polite."

"Tit for tat," Charles said, pinching both her nipples as her breasts quivered above him. Valorie cried out with abandon, throwing her head back.

A modest boy, yes, but he could get nasty, almost shocking, in the bedroom. This wasn't even close to what he could be like. And he'd always loved that she went along for the ride instead of getting offended or telling him he was going to hell with that mouth. She had been his dirty girl. He'd been her nasty boy. No wonder they'd fit so well together.

Does he call her filthy names too? Does she like it like I did?

But his wife of the present had no place in this small pocket of the past. Besides, she wasn't going to ask him what his wife was like in bed. They had their private life, just as she and Charles had had theirs, and she hoped Charles hadn't shared any of those confidences. She doubted he had. A person didn't usually dwell on the ex sex life with the present partner.

"Quickly, babe, I'm…" Charles winced, holding his breath.

Valorie climbed back between his legs to shove his jeans the rest of the way off and pull off her panties. That was all Charles needed to shuck his boxers and wrestle her down beneath him this time, her shirt off but her bra still uselessly clasped around her chest. He unfastened it while he pinned her down with his body. His gaze bore into her and stole her breath away. His hips made little bucking movements he couldn't control, but otherwise he was methodical and deliberate removing her bra so that she was naked and he was naked, and now he didn't have anything in the way of his orgasm. He dragged his cock through her wet folds, which clung to him as though they'd missed his cock too.

"Ah yeah…ah yeah, babe… You liking this as much as before?" Charles groaned.

She nodded, unable to speak. As he passed his cock through her labia, the head would bump against her clit, not enough pressure or sensation to give her what she needed. It tantalized her with the promise of more, drawing out anticipation to a frustrating point as Charles took his pleasure from her. She grasped the sides of his head in encouragement and so that she could watch as he came undone.

He gasped his moans out in time with his cum hitting her abdomen in thin ropes. It smeared against her belly and his as he continued to move his cock over her.

He reached down to stroke the rest of it out of him. Whitish fluid spilled over the shiny, bulbous head.

"Give it to me," Valorie said. "I want to clean you off, boy."

Charles scrambled up to straddle her shoulders. She gripped his thighs and strained up to lick the rest of his cum up his shaft. Then she took in the whole head in her eagerness to taste, to take, to touch every part of him that had once belonged to her.

She cleaned him, keeping her tongue and her suction light until he started to get hard again. Then he pulled himself out of her mouth.

"I gotta say, the quick draw isn't so much fun, but you want to know what is?" Charles said. He scrambled back down her body to kneel between her legs. "No cracks. No stiffness. A person forgets what it's like being able to move like a teenager. More than makes up for coming too early, but damn if you didn't wake it right back up again."

"Thank God for a young body, reason number three, right?" Valorie said. She made to find something to wipe the semen off from her stomach, but Charles pinned her arms down.

"You can say that again," Charles said. "Now, you cleaned up some of my mess, but you know I prefer to clean up my own."

He brought her arms to her sides, still pressed into the sheets as he bent down and lapped at his cum, leaving no spot untended. He licked at her as though he'd covered her with chocolate syrup, smacking his lips at the taste of her body, with his own enhancements.

Valorie hummed as his chin rubbed against her mound while he cleaned her up. He was mere inches away from her clit, which silently screamed for his attention.

Charles didn't make it wait long.

As soon as there wasn't a trace of his semen left on her skin, he moved down and applied himself with the same fervor to feast upon her other fine attributes.

There was always something about the sight of a man going down on her... It felt good, of course. It felt fucking amazing. But the sight of it. And the sounds.

When they'd been living together, this was one of those things that Charles had done to her where Valorie would have to practically smother herself with a pillow to keep from making too much noise through the thin walls. Now she had no such restriction. She arched up against his mouth, moaning as loudly as she wanted and more. Charles released her arms to hold down her hips instead. Valorie wanted to grab hold of his ears and force him closer to her, but she didn't want to discourage his fine work. As good as it had been back then, he'd actually improved, which made her glad she didn't have to walk any time soon, because her legs weren't going to be working for a while.

Instead, she brought her arms up above her, clawing at the pillow before reaching the headboard and holding on for dear life.

"Yes, yes, Charles, God, *yes!*" she chanted, thrusting up against his mouth as he worked his way back up from lapping at her cunt while stroking her clit with his fingers. She outright shouted when he swirled her juices around her clit then sank his mouth, warm, wet, intense, around the flesh. It was as though there was a direct thread between her clit and her vocal cords. Each suck and broad press of his tongue made her scream, the sound wrenching from her throat.

His laughter rippled through her with her climax.

"I always loved it when you could be a screamer," Charles said, rubbing his mouth against her thigh. His facial hair chafed. She didn't give a damn when he could do shit like that to make her feel good.

"I always loved it when you could make me scream," she replied.

He lifted her legs as he moved back up her body, folding her almost in half, but not as far as he would have able to if she'd had her abilities. Charles didn't notice. She could do what she'd always been able to do with him. If her contortions had intrigued him before, he'd forgotten them by now or else they weren't important.

He took the time to kiss her nipples again, ever appreciative, before meeting her mouth. She could smell herself, taste herself. Strangely, she thought it was a little different from the way she experienced herself now. She wondered whether there was a hormone or pheromone-altering quality to Arcanium. Or maybe it was just her diet. It was only a peripheral thought, especially when he was kissing her as thoroughly as he'd eaten her out—as though it didn't matter where he applied his attention as long as it involved her.

Valorie lifted her hips, and he slipped into her, as easily as they'd kissed outside her tent. He bit her lip when she gasped. Even when they'd been at their best, she didn't think it had ever been this perfect, which reminded her where she was. Bell had taken them out of reality, but not completely. The only way it could be this good was with the incubus and succubus plying their trade. Charles had been an excellent lover, but this... It wasn't supposed to be like this. Was it?

They fit together the way a hand slid into a satin glove. They didn't even have to give it a few tries. Charles entered into her like that moment that he'd carried Valorie over the threshold of their apartment for the first time—new yet achingly familiar. Comfortable. Right.

When he moved in her, she tightened her fingers against his shoulder blades, digging in the nails against the tremble that vibrated through her with each thrust—a tremble that made her feel like she was cracking apart, and not just from arousal.

"Charles," she whispered against his cheek as he broke the kiss, out of breath not from effort but from being as overwhelmed as she was. "God, I missed you so much."

"I missed you too," he murmured back. He kissed her lightly now on the lips, rolling his hips as he ground into her at the end of every stroke, the way she liked it because of the way it pressed him against her clit.

She embraced him, sometimes kissing his collarbone or biting the base of his neck, but mostly just holding on, holding him over her. She relished his weight. His muscles flexed deliciously under her palms as he pumped into her more quickly. Her legs felt the strain of being held over his arms, her knees in the crook of his elbows, and she relished that as well. It had been a long time since her body had been normal. It was almost a relief to know that her body could still experience physical stress like this—as though she was more real in this unreal world.

Aside from how far up he pushed her legs, her knees almost at her shoulders, this wasn't one of Charles' more elaborate encounters. She didn't need it to be.

Arcanium was elaborate. All she wanted right now was him, and that's what she got—his body around her and inside her, reminding her of all the other times he'd had her in this bed, in her old apartment, in his old apartment, in their cars, and that one time in a mall janitor's closet... The doors to those memories swung open all at once in a flood of experience that tipped her over the edge.

Valorie screwed her eyes closed, latched her arms around him in spite of the strain on her legs and canted her hips up as he continued to take her, his cock moving quickly and strongly inside through her orgasm.

And her climax just kept going, clenching and releasing around his pounding cock, as tears leaked down her temples and her body seized underneath him.

Charles reached up to grab the headboard so that he could rock into her with even more leverage, his breath harsh in his nose and expelling in a groan every time.

"Love you so much, Valorie," he whispered.

Valorie shook her head on the pillow as the orgasm climbed higher, fueled by the pain in her chest and the rapid pulse of her heart that sent blood racing to join the rest of her arousal.

He stopped her from shaking her head by kissing her as he came, still thrusting in to stretch out her third orgasm. She kissed him back like gasping for air. Even when he'd stopped moving, letting her legs down from over his shoulders and settling his weight over her, she kept kissing him until he pushed himself up and peered down at her with youthful wonder and less youthful sadness.

"Love you too," she finally said.

Chapter Ten

"If you love me too, why'd you go and scratch the hell out of my back?" Charles asked. "What am I going to say to people? That I was mauled by a mountain lion?"

He had always known just what she needed when the rivers flowed too deep. Laughter broke up the pain in her chest, and if her eyelashes were wet, he didn't mention them. She wiped her face with the sheets as he settled next to her, using his discarded shirt to clean himself off. She was less concerned about mess. It wasn't like they were having house guests, and they could always change sheets.

She didn't think they were going to be in here for two hundred years. Now that the sexual chemistry had been dealt with, Charles had his 'we need to talk' face on.

"You want me to see what's in the fridge, or do you want to start the serious stuff on an empty stomach?" Valorie asked.

"Good point," Charles said. Then he grinned shyly. "Do you know how long it's been since I ate in bed?"

"I know, I know. Crumbs aren't conducive to sleeping," Valorie replied, standing up and grabbing the dirty towels and clothes as she went. She used one of them to catch the trickle of spunk down her thigh, but otherwise she didn't concern herself with her naked state. When she glanced over her shoulder at him, Charles was enjoying the view, still with that heartbreaking mixture of excitement and sadness.

Valorie supposed she should have known how this was going to go.

She came back with pizza that had been chilling in the refrigerator. She'd warmed it up first. Charles liked cold pizza, but Valorie didn't hold for that kind of blasphemy in her house. She also brought two beers and a prepopped bag of popcorn. Not as good as the poppable kind, but it was all she could find in the pantry.

"Definitely brings back memories," Charles said, sitting up in bed and covering his waist with the sheets to protect his bits from the hot plate.

"A lot of that going on," Valorie replied.

They were quiet as they ate. They just sat there, side by side, enjoying each other's company. Usually they'd turn on the television or put in a movie while eating in bed, but they didn't want to waste the time.

"What's on your mind, Charles?" Valorie asked finally.

"Confusion. A lot of confusion. What did that devil guy mean when he led us in here? I got the feeling you understood it better than me," Charles said. "I didn't come here to wish, Valorie. I want you to know that."

"I know," Valorie said. "If you had, it would have been a better-worded wish or nothing at all."

"Gee, thanks."

"Bell thrives on spontaneous wishes, because he can see them coming," Valorie explained.

"The more I learn about this guy, the less I understand why you defend him," Charles said.

"He was as good as my husband for over seventeen years, Charles."

Charles put the piece of pizza he was eating back on his plate, failing to swallow back a shocked sourness.

"Your teenage son suggests you moved forward with your life pretty quickly too," Valorie pointed out.

"But *him*?" Charles asked.

"Do you realize that the only reason this wish ended up so well and reasonable was because he still likes me quite a lot?" Valorie said.

"How else could it have ended up?" Charles asked. "It was spontaneous and everything, but I was also pretty specific about what I wanted, all things considered."

"Easy. We go back to the way things were twenty years ago, but our relationship gets really bad. Maybe I cheat, maybe you do. Hell, maybe I cheat with Bell anyway and end up joining voluntarily, leaving you penniless, alone and probably never in the situation to meet your future wife," Valorie said. "And Bell still gets what he wants."

Charles stared at her. "You would do that?"

"I'd be manipulated into doing it. He can change who people are," Valorie said. "Or he can call on our capacity to do bad things."

"So *he'd* really do that?"

"Charles, I know him better than you do, and I don't want to talk about him right now," Valorie said.

"You said *was*. He *was* like your husband," Charles said, slowly picking up his pizza again, though judging from the reluctant way he ate it, his appetite hadn't yet returned.

"He loved me, but not as much as he loves Maya," Valorie replied. "It sucks donkey balls, but that's what it is. Now, I'm not inclined to be much more charitable to your wife as you are to Bell, but I would have wanted you to move on. The good part of me anyway."

"And the less good part of you would have wanted me to die miserable and alone because I wasn't with you?" Charles said with a wry smile.

"I'd be lying if I pretended to be a better person than that."

"We all have a little bad in us," Charles said. "After all, I would have rather you be turning tricks while strung out on heroin than for you to be dead."

"I guess you still hold on to the adage that 'where there's life, there's hope'."

"Yes."

"Yeah, I don't believe in that," Valorie said. "But I'll take the sentiment as it was meant."

"And I'll take your dislike of my wife as a compliment to me," Charles responded. "She's a good woman, Valorie."

"You wouldn't love her if she wasn't."

"She doesn't remind me a thing of you," Charles said. "I don't think I could have handled it if she'd had anything in common. We're a good match, you and I. My wife and I are a different good match."

"You said *are*."

"That's why I asked about the wish," he replied.

Valorie lowered her head and sighed. "As long as we're in here, we'll be like we were before I got wished into Arcanium. We can stay in here as long as we need. When we leave, though, it's up to me whether we're really taken all the way back to start over again or whether...this is it."

"But it was my wish," Charles said.

"Your wish. Bell's rules," Valorie said. "He's been concerned for me lately."

"Why? What's wrong?" he asked, sitting up a little straighter.

"Ennui," Valorie said. She patted his thigh. "It's just an existential crisis, so you can relax. No one's beaten me in years."

"I'm never going to get used to what you went through, am I?" Charles asked. "I mean, if you could hear how you sound..."

"I know how I sound. I also know what I've lived. So believe me when I tell you it's not as bad as it seems. No worse than the real world, although I wouldn't say it was better either," Valorie said. "You're not condemning me to a lifetime of morale-improving whippings and drudgery if I stay, Charles. So don't let's start over just so I don't have to be in Arcanium, all right? There are other ways out of the circus. Bell offered me this one for now. That's all. And I don't want to force you to start over with me if the wish you made was more wishful than real. I wouldn't do that to you. You have a life. You have a woman you love. You have two children you love."

"And occasionally want to strangle, but yes. Elian hit his rebellious years, and I swear, that boy's not going to make it to eighteen if he doesn't get his nose on straight," Charles said, shaking his head as he finished his slice.

"What about your daughter?" Valorie asked. It wasn't as hard to talk about his kids as she'd suspected. She and Charles had both been in enthusiastic favor of children prior to their engagement.

But in Arcanium, no one had children. Period. Arcanium wasn't a family circus in more ways than one.

"She either hasn't hit her rebellious phase or we're going to have to push her into one for her own good," Charles replied. "Kendra's an angel. I wish Janice and I could take credit for it, but both of us are dull, indecent and downright cruel in comparison to her. I swear, the Catholic Church is going to make her a saint if she keeps things up."

"How do you push someone into a rebellious phase?" Valorie asked.

"We're not sure yet. Mix some rum into her smoothies? Give her some magic brownies? We'll think of something," Charles said.

"Thank God I can tell when you're kidding."

"They're good kids," Charles murmured. He gazed at his empty plate with unfocused eyes.

"You wouldn't lose them for the world," Valorie finished for him. "And I'm not the world."

"You were once," he said, setting his plate aside. He slipped his hand into hers.

There was an arrowhead in her throat when she swallowed.

If Bell had just, poof, granted the wish, Charles wouldn't have known what he had lost. And Valorie wouldn't have known what she'd taken. This way, Valorie would know at least until the wish was granted, and so would Charles. And maybe somehow they'd know even when they were taken back. Maybe the circumstances of their staying together would feel off. Maybe not, but the possibilities were enough to give a woman pause before taking what wasn't hers anymore.

Charles, like this, in his twenties, in their apartment—this Charles was hers. But as soon as they stepped out of the tent and Valorie had to make her decision, Charles wouldn't be hers anymore. The last thing she wanted to do was steal another woman's man away, just so she could experience the life she'd thought she should've had. If she'd been meant to have it, she wouldn't have come to Arcanium, she wouldn't have made the wish and she wouldn't have stayed in Arcanium all this time.

"But you moved on," Valorie said. "And so did I," she added before Charles could respond with anything like an apology.

"This..." Charles gestured to the replication of their apartment bedroom. "All this. You. I came here because I couldn't get you out of my head, Valorie, and that's because I never let you out of my heart. Once I saw you, once I saw that you were alive and amazing and just as beautiful a person as you were when you left—"

"More amazing, less beautiful a person, but I guess there has to be a balance," Valorie said with a shrug and a self-deprecating smile. "Just as much alive."

"I never got to say goodbye," Charles said. He tightened his grip on her hand. "I know that most people who have their family or their lover ripped from them never get to say goodbye either. We got more of a goodbye than most. We literally said it to each other before you left for the circus. And we said *I love you*. But the two of us—the organism of our relationship—we never got..."

"Closure. Is that what we were having, from the time you kissed me to now? Closure sex?"

Charles rested his head against the headboard.

"I'm being blunt, Charles. I'm not accusing you of anything," Valorie said. "That's what it felt like to me too."

"I missed you. I loved you. I still do." He turned back to her and brought her hand to his mouth, saluting it with a kiss. "The love didn't die just because I moved on. I can't help but think it's still not fair to you, coming back, putting you in this position where you have to make the decision, putting you in the situation where you might have been pulled into the past against your own wishes."

"My, that's mighty mature of you, sir," Valorie said.

"Yeah, that happened without me noticing," Charles said, laughing. "I think around the time we started teaching our son basic boundaries and ethics."

"Before he knew how to say those things, I'm sure. I don't think I got mature," she said, closing her eyes. "I got older in my head, but I don't think I ever got mature. It's like the way that seasons change but they still follow a pattern year after year. Things moved forward for you. I moved on, but I don't know whether it's really possible to move forward in Arcanium."

"Maybe that's your ennui right there," Charles said. "You're ready to move forward, but this circus place doesn't let you."

Maybe, she thought. But while the statement sounded rational, it didn't ring true.

"So are you done with me now?" Valorie asked. "Or do you think we could have a little longer?"

"I could take a rest," Charles said. "Hold you like we used to spoon in the night. But, Valorie, I'll never be *done* with you. God, it hurts hearing you say those things. Did that demon tell you that?"

"Not that demon, no," Valorie replied. "*I* ended the relationship with Bell. And I ended the second one with the second demon. He as good as told me that, but our arrangement was temporary from the start."

"That could be your problem right there," he said, drawing her down under the sheets.

She put her plate on the nightstand and snuggled back against him. "What?"

"You keep attaching yourself to demons."

"Charles…"

"No, bear with me. Speaking off the cuff, completely open-minded. No judgment on this place. No religious commentary on whether or not you *should* be with demons. But you're trying to make a go of it with demons, and you said yourself that they're not like us. Fundamentally, not just culturally."

Charles' breath was warm against the back of her neck, fluttering against the wisps of hair there. He wasn't as warm as John. Only a demon could be, and only if they were doing it on purpose.

"You might be looking for meaning—love—in the wrong place. I'm no theologian. I'm just a humble guidance counselor," he said, stroking the line of her collarbone as he spoke. "But it seems fruitless to look to demons to help you grow or get anywhere you want to go. Isn't their aim to be an obstacle?"

"Bell's not a demon," Valorie said.

"Okay, he's not if you say he's not. If you say he loved you, just not the right way, then he did. But the second one was a demon. Were you going to turn to another demon to try to move forward?"

"No," she said slowly.

"Did you find yourself a man? A real man, not someone who kind of looks like one and has the, um, equipment."

"He's not exactly a boyfriend, Charles," Valorie said. "And he's supposed to be temporary too."

"Supposed to be?" Charles asked.

"I can't bring him with me if I leave. He's still got time to serve, and I mean that how it sounded," Valorie said.

Charles huffed his laughter against her vertebrae. "A genie, a demon and a criminal? How did I end up the most normal of your men?"

"There was Kasmir."

"Oh yeah, forgot about him. Perfectly normal."

Valorie slapped his upper arm. Bad breakup.

"You *are* really normal," Valorie murmured, running her fingertips over his arm much like he stroked her collarbone, to touch him, to feel the silkiness of his arm hair against her skin, to remind herself that he was really there—although now the trouble was remembering that what she was feeling wasn't real. "Completely normal, from head to toe. You're unique, but you're normal. Not that there's anything wrong with that."

"*You're* just not normal anymore," Charles finished for her this time. "Not that there's anything wrong with *that*."

They were finishing each other's sentences. It should have been right, she thought as she tried again to swallow.

But the synchronicity now was artificial. It was only because they were their young selves again—their physically young selves. Their respective soul beats would be out of sync the second they walked out.

"Sleep with me, Charles," Valorie whispered. She twisted around in his arms to embrace him face to face, tucking a leg between his. "A few more hours. Please."

"There's so much I want to do for you," he whispered, holding her even more tightly, "but I know I can't do it because we can't go back. I mean, we *can*, but we can't, not after all this time and what we've put into these last twenty years. I love you, Valorie."

"I love you too, Charles," Valorie replied.

"And this, I can do."

She rested on his arm and closed her eyes. She didn't want to, because it meant she'd lose precious hours with him.

But she was exhausted, and so was he.

* * * *

When they woke up, they hadn't moved, but Charles was hard again, as tended to happen even after rigorous sex. Almost without thinking, Charles moved onto his back, Valorie slid her leg out from between his and straddled him. She shifted until the head pressed against her entrance. Then she wriggled back to sink herself around him.

They weren't fucking. It was too slow, too sleepy. They weren't even making love. This was their bodies meeting, connecting, feeling, experiencing, the postscript to their previous session. They enveloped each other until it was as though they were one entity, their arousal climbing at the same pace, the quickening of their pulse and breathing matching up until Valorie pressed her face against his chest and whimpered, the orgasm like shattering glass in slow motion. They froze when Charles stiffened around and inside her, following her climax with his own, eyes tight shut.

But they had to wake up eventually.

"What time is it?" Charles asked.

Valorie propped herself up and glanced at the clock. "Ten o'clock. Holy crap. I don't know whether it's right because... But if it is..."

"Then I need to go home," Charles said. He sighed, rubbing his eyes then letting his hands hit the pillow in resignation.

And she needed to let him go. Charles had been the one to make the wish, but she was the one who'd wanted it more than him. Because he'd made a life for himself, and she...

She unwound herself from him and crawled off the bed to find something to put on, even though they'd probably walk out in the same things they'd gone in wearing.

It was also possible that this little pocket of artificial reality was on a separate timeline from the world outside it. They could walk out to Bell standing outside the tent, John in the distance, as though no meaningful time had passed, no mark of their final consummation on the world, only in their minds.

Valorie could live with that.

They got dressed in silence. Valorie fought against the impulse to request more time. Hell, a movie. They'd spent all these hours sleeping. They'd at least be awake for a movie. But it didn't matter how many things they did together. Just like their lives before hadn't been enough, nothing here would be enough. It would still have to end. *If* she was a decent human being. She wasn't, in a lot of ways, but she was decent enough for this. For him.

They stood in front of the tent flap that had taken the place of their front door, dressed as though they were going out somewhere casual. Normal. Someplace a future young married couple would go to together on a Saturday night.

Charles held his hand out. Valorie took it.

Together, they stepped out into the circus. The false world fell away behind them like a gust of wind. When Valorie looked behind, all she saw was the interior of her own tent.

They wore what they went in with. Charles was his real self again. Now she saw that doubling even more, with the image of his younger self fresher in her mind. She looked up at the night sky to fight the disorientation.

"Valorie."

She lowered her eyes to Charles'. He kissed her forehead with such tenderness.

"Goodbye," he whispered, still with his lips against her skin.

"Bye, Charles," she said. She slipped her arms under his jacket to hug him, but she wasn't clinging anymore.

"Mom!" someone yelled. A voice that hadn't fully dropped yet. "Mom, I found him!"

"I *knew* it."

Charles jerked away from Valorie and stumbled around. Janice was standing where John had been. Two tents closer, Elian pointed at his father. He clenched his jaw so hard that Valorie could see his cheekbones twitching in the dark.

Elian was furious, but Janice... Tears that must have burned her fiery eyes poured down her cheeks.

"You son of a bitch." Janice spoke quietly, but Valorie could hear her fine.

Charles looked like he was going to be sick and faint at the same time "This isn't—" he stammered.

And it wasn't. To her bones, Valorie agreed with him. The first kisses had edged the line, but they hadn't cheated. "I told myself it couldn't be. I told myself the father of my children and the man who sleeps in my bed could never stray, not if he wanted to be right with God," Janice said. "Elian was more suspicious. Said you were looking at this...this woman too closely. Said you had paint on your shirt last week, when you told me you were going in to work. I told him it couldn't be, but when you said you were going to work today too, I called Patrick. Guess who said he hadn't seen you today or last week?"

"I can explain," Charles said.

Valorie would have loved to hear the explanation he came up with. She'd already come up with one herself — she was her own daughter, the lovechild from the long-ago engagement. Conceivable. Understandable. Forgivable.

"No!" Janice shouted, slicing her hand through the air, baring her teeth against the sobs that wracked her body. "I'll kill you for doing this to us."

That was when Valorie heard the trill of the clowns.

The evening performance was over.

"You need to leave," Valorie said, trying to make herself heard without catching the clowns' attention. "Now."

Both Janice and Elian were where they weren't supposed to be — and Elian was underage.

"Shut your whore mouth," Janice snapped, her voice thick with emotion.

Whatever the reason Charles had married Janice, it seemed she had more in common with Valorie than Charles had thought.

"I'll take care of her," Elian said. He swung the large branch he'd been carrying up like a club.

"Really?" Valorie tried not to smile at the absurdity of the whole awful situation. A smile wouldn't set the right tone, not that Valorie was accustomed to the right tone. "You're not allowed here. You're going to get in dangerous trouble, both of you. You need to leave right the fuck *now*."

"Please, Janice, we can talk about this after we go," Charles said, alarmed by Valorie's urgency. She wouldn't be afraid of anything in Arcanium without a damn good reason, and he knew it. "It's *really* not what you think." He started toward his wife.

"Don't talk to me about what I think. Don't *touch* me. Don't come *near* me. I don't know what you got from her."

Now this was getting insulting.

"You're trespassing. You're going to die if you don't leave," Valorie hissed. She strained her ears, listening for the clowns again.

"You don't get to talk to us either, you fucking slut," Elian shouted. He brandished his branch as he advanced with all the rashness of a teenager in the throes of deep betrayal.

Valorie felt for him. She really did. But she was going to knock him unconscious if he tried to hurt her with that poor amputated piece of tree.

"You...you...you..." Janice tried to speak, but she shook her head and balled her hands into trembling fists—fists that could do serious harm, especially since Charles wouldn't want to fight back. Couldn't fight back. He'd never believed in using violence, especially not against women.

The clown trills came closer.

"You need to *run!*" Valorie shouted, abandoning stealth at this point.

"There's nowhere *to* run."

Valorie whirled around, stomach turning to ice.

Lady Sasha leaned against Lord Mikhail, running her long, clawlike nails down his bare chest. The incubus' and succubus' gazes landed squarely on Janice and Charles.

"He's with me," Valorie said quickly to Lady Sasha. Charles was closer to the succubus. And Elian was too young, although not by much. "Bell gave him to me."

All their years together meant Lady Sasha believed her, disappointment drawing her perfect dark eyebrows down slightly.

She also believed Valorie because Valorie hadn't taken ownership of the other two trespassers. She couldn't lie, not to the demons who protected Arcanium. There'd be hell to pay if she did. Everyone had had a front-row seat to Caroline defying the clowns and what the Ringmaster did to a person foolish enough to keep doing it.

There was no point in her trying. Janice and Elian couldn't hope to escape, even if Janice gave a flying fuck what came out of Valorie's mouth.

Because here came the clowns down the back alley of Oddity Row.

They were surrounded, and no Bell in sight.

Chapter Eleven

The clowns were the best in the circus at face painting. They'd mastered the terrifying, toothy illusion grins that extended from nose to throat. But that was because they needed face paint. They needed it to look normal. When Arcanium closed and trespassers made themselves a meal for the circus' guard dogs, the clowns showed their true faces.

Even most of the demons didn't go near the clowns.

Where a human's eyes would be white, theirs were black as ink. Where a demon's irises would also be black, theirs glowed bright yellow. Along the middle of their monster face paint, their faces split into a scarecrow grins that stretched from ear to ear — no lips, just the ripped seam of their mouths. Their tongues were long, thinner than human, and pointed. Behind their relatively normal faces when their mouths were closed were rows and rows of curved, conical, razorblade teeth.

She'd mentioned the clowns to Charles, but perhaps that hadn't prepared him for the crackling sound like thousands of breaking bones as the clowns revealed themselves, drooling over the elaborate art on their faces. They chittered their excitement at such a feast provided for them in the form of Elian—young meat, their favorite.

"Janice, come here!" Charles waved frantically to his wife, caught between running toward her and staying away from the clowns as they stalked closer. Under different circumstances, it might have been amusing, watching him run forward then stumble back again.

"If you think for one second I'll do anything you tell me, you cheating bas—"

"They're going to kill your son, you stupid cow," Valorie said, running toward the boy who wanted to murder her—or at least beat her into a coma.

"Valorie!" Charles really must have been in shock, to be annoyed that she'd called his wife a name instead of helping her get Janice away.

"And that man behind me is going to kill you," Valorie said to Janice before returning her attention to Charles. "So unless you want to watch her cheat on *you* with an incubus, you'll knock her out and carry her away like a goddamn caveman if that's the only option you have left."

"I knew it!" Janice said, pointing at Valorie, still with the tunnel vision.

"You don't know a *thing*!" Valorie shouted back.

Janice stopped crying in temporary surprise.

"You need to leave *now*," Valorie said. "Marriage counseling is still better than death. Go!"

"You're crazy," Elian said from behind her. "Whatever trick you're playing, it's not going to work."

Valorie ducked the branch that Elian swung at her and leveled a kick at his stomach. "I don't want to incapacitate you. I can't drag you to the gates. Dude, look behind you, kid."

"I'm not gonna fall for that," Elian snarled.

The boy had focus, and he loved his mother. But damn, he was dense.

Valorie had flexibility but not a lot of brute strength — certainly no natural defenses against demon clowns. The only reason they hadn't outright attacked was because Valorie hadn't stepped away, and they were visibly confused that she was interfering. They were used to Caroline being the idiot hero. Valorie had stayed out of their way all the years she'd been a part of the circus. Valorie knew the drill. So the fact that she wasn't giving them room to eat was the only slim chance that Janice and Elian had, and it wasn't going to last for much longer.

"You want to protect your mama? You go over there right now and get her out of here," Valorie said, pointing at Janice, who was now struggling with Charles.

He was trying to get her to leave, and she slapped at his hands, yelling unintelligibly, the fire of domestic homicide getting brighter in her eyes the more Charles tried to calm her down. Valorie could sympathize, but her stomach sank with each second that Janice kept backing away toward the clowns, who fortunately weren't in any hurry.

"Your father is protected," Valorie told Elian, "but you're not supposed to be here."

"You don't even get to point at her, you bitch," Elian snarled.

"Why are you doing this, Valorie?" Lady Sasha asked. She sounded genuinely curious, not upset.

Janice jerked her head over to the succubus and blinked, as though this was the first time she realized it wasn't just her family and Valorie here.

"You know there's no way they're getting out. It's too far, and we're too fast," Lady Sasha said. "You can't save them, and the boy you fight would have your head. They're so passionate when they're young."

Lady Sasha patted Lord Mikhail's shoulder, encouraging him forward.

"They're ours now," Lady Sasha said.

Valorie spun out of the way of Lord Mikhail's approach with the footwork she'd gained as a dancer. She slung her arm around Elian's neck and throttled him back, trying to pull him between the tents into Oddity Row.

"Get your hands off my son!" Janice shouted after her.

"Really?" Valorie muttered again. Then she shouted back like a fourth grader, "Come and make me!"

Now! Valorie screamed in her head, because Lord Mikhail was getting closer, ramping up his magnetism to high. He didn't have to hold back with trespassers who were promised to him. If Janice didn't feel it yet, it was only because she was distracted by her son and her sense of betrayal. But if Lord Mikhail got any closer, his influence would be undeniable, irresistible. And if Charles fought the incubus, Lady Sasha might get involved anyway in the interest of protecting her companion.

Elian stomped his booted foot on her bare one. Pain, bright and hot like a grenade blast, burst through her. She collapsed to her knees, releasing the boy.

Fuck, I think he broke my toes.

If this was any other circus than Arcanium, the injury would have been devastating for months. As it was, it was just painful—so painful, her body locked up. Her mouth dropped open, but not enough of her brain worked for her to say anything.

At first, she thought the glowing amber light was part of her pain.

Then she realized it was fire. Flamethrower fire billowing at Elian and making him stagger back.

Valorie raised her head from the ground.

It looked like the whole top half of John's body was on fire. He wore a mantle of his flames up his arms and over his shoulders. Even his head was ablaze.

She'd never seen John this alight. He was normally very controlled with his fires, scared of losing his grip on the magic, and for good reason. His scars and scorched trailer were constant reminders of what would happen if he let go.

Yet here he was, flaming from hand to hand and walking toward Elian.

"Are you okay?" he rasped as he reached her.

Valorie shook her head, still unable to speak, but she kept leaning her head toward Charles, Janice and Elian, desperately trying to tell John what she needed him to do. But she feared she was telling him to do something else.

Please save them, she begged in her head as she gasped for breath against the shocking pain from her feet. She was a good twenty or thirty seconds from being able to talk.

John suddenly ran at Elian, who shouted and fell back. He twitched like a crab on the dusty ground, his fear moving him faster than his limbs were capable of.

But John ran past the boy and into the back alley of the Row. He spread his arms, sending his flames out to create a barrier between Janice and Charles and the demons on the other side that were trying to kill them. Then he cast a line of fire through the dirt to surround Elian in a circle of flames.

The clowns were in Valorie's line of sight. They reeled away from the fire, trilling in alarm and more confusion that yet another cast member was keeping them from their prey.

Lord Mikhail continued after Janice, his dark brown hair slicked back tight in a ponytail at the base of his neck. He cocked his head at John, square jaw tight but not showing anger. Lord Mikhail wasn't a fighter, in spite of his massive stature and musculature. All of that was mostly for show, although he *could* fight if he needed to. He was an incubus — the only thing he really needed was his magic and his touch against most, a single fist against the rest. He wasn't fazed by John the way the clowns were.

Valorie's stomach sank to her knees underneath her.

"Do you think fire can stop me, brother?" Lord Mikhail asked. He stretched his hand out to clasp John's shoulder.

He wasn't allowed to touch the cast, even the ones unaffected by his magic, and unlike Lady Sasha, he'd been punished several times before for doing exactly that. However, John wasn't supposed to be protecting free game either. The woman was marked for his use by her trespass. There wasn't a single demon who didn't take their chances when given. The Ringmaster rejoiced at every back he could shred. The clowns devoured whatever they caught, although they preferred more tender meat. And when Lady Sasha and Lord Mikhail didn't have to leave the circus to feast upon their preferred prey, it made their evenings much easier.

The fire mantle licked through and over Lord Mikhail's fingers, but it didn't burn.

"I was forged from fire, fire-eater," Lord Mikhail said. He was twice his John's size. It required little effort for him to grab and jerk John away. "You cannot keep me from what is mine. Protect your woman and leave the trespassers to us."

"No!" Charles shouted as Janice stepped out from behind him. The fury was gone from her eyes, the fire turned to the glitter of arousal. "Janice, what are you doing?"

"Come to me, dear," Lord Mikhail said, beckoning to her. "If your husband interferes, Lady Sasha will take care of him. He won't touch you again. You won't have to think of any touch but mine."

"Lord Mikhail, please," Valorie called, finally getting control of her body enough to limp to her feet. She couldn't put her weight on her toes, not without another flare of pain. Almost definitely broken. "They're not here to hurt the circus. They were here because Charles was, on my invitation."

"They threatened you," Lord Mikhail replied, gathering Janice against his chiseled, muscular body. Janice looked as though she'd been happily hit with a thousand bricks. "If they had come in peace, perhaps Bell would have arranged for their swift exit. But you are injured, and violence was their intent. I have my own violent intent that you will find much more pleasurable, my beautiful dark rose." He caressed Janice's tear-streaked face. "New tears will you shed. Tears of joy before your welcome end."

"Valorie!" Charles cried.

"Then let's wait for Bell," Valorie said. "Let's wait for him to get here. He was supposed to be here. He needed an answer from me, one that might change the present circumstances. An answer to a wish."

Both Lord Mikhail and the clowns hesitated. Valorie had never been sure how much English the clowns understood. They kept their own company, and their mouths and throats weren't configured for speech. But apparently they understood the importance of the word 'wish'.

"Then why isn't he here, *cherie*?" Lady Sasha asked. "Hey, boy, come to me now. If the clowns can't figure out how to get to you, I'll provide a distraction until they get their heads together."

Why *wasn't* he here? Was this his grand solution – if Valorie hadn't chosen to ride the wish into the past, give Charles no one left but his daughter and Valorie to start a new life in the present?

What if Bell *hadn't* given her a choice to leave? What if this was his way of kicking her out? One more disgruntled employee taken care of.

Elian gaped at Lady Sasha, who wore her leather bikini and nothing more in spite of the chill in the early winter night. He was sixteen years old. He didn't have a chance against a woman who represented the fantasy of so many men. He staggered toward her like a zombie, his mouth parted, as infatuated as his mother was with the incubus.

Valorie noticed he wasn't getting murderous with his mother drooling over an incredibly attractive man who wasn't his father. Sure, there was magic involved, but Valorie still thought there was a teensy bit of double standard in that.

Even so, Valorie limped toward the boy to grab him away from Lady Sasha's clutches. Elian whipped around and flung a punch at Valorie that connected with her shoulder. He didn't stick around to do any more damage, though. Any murderous inclinations had been subsumed by his libido.

Valorie didn't fall. He couldn't knock her off-balance, even with broken toes. In this case, the magic that kept her upright was a blessing, but it didn't mean she recovered from his blow fast enough.

John threw a large fireball at Lady Sasha's feet. Smart guy. If Lord Mikhail wasn't affected by fire, Lady Sasha wouldn't be either. But he could make the fire too high and dangerous for Elian to cross.

Lord Mikhail, still clinging to Janice, backhanded John across his cheek with a sharp crack of his knuckles against the cheekbone. John literally flew through the air and landed on one of his lines of fire. Partially unconscious, the fire started to get out of his control. He screamed, writhing in his own flames as the unpleasant smell of cooked flesh rose around them.

"Bell, wherever you are, get here right the fuck now!" Valorie yelled.

"No need to shout," Bell said. He held his hands behind his back as he walked around Valorie's tent. "Do you have an answer for me?"

"Is this your—"

"No. It's the trespassers' doing," Bell said. "No more, no less. It's unfortunate, but I didn't manipulate it into happening. If Charles had stayed away as promised, his family would have been safe. It is their doing."

So it was Bell's doing by his inaction. But he wouldn't agree with that, and she didn't have the time to argue a human's understanding of cause and effect with Bell.

"They're not a threat to the circus," Valorie said. "Please let them go. Let them all go. Make them forget. I'd wish if I could."

"Do you have an answer for me, or do you want me to go get you some potion for that foot?" Bell said mildly.

Valorie turned back to the wife she should have been and the husband and son she should have had.

"I'll make it worth your while, Sasha!" Valorie called to her. "I swear it. Please, just give me a minute."

John coughed, trembling as though an electrical current was going through his body as he called the fire back in, swallowing some of it into his gasping mouth. The blazes around him calmed before they could reach people or the canvas tents. That left Elian open for the clowns until John staggered to his hands and knees in front of the boy.

Lady Sasha took Elian's wrist, but she touched her tongue to her right eyetooth as she considered Valorie's oath. A person didn't make a promise to jinn or demons lightly. The word of a souled being, even if spoken shallowly, went much deeper. That was why Bell could do so much with an idle wish.

"Take your time," Lady Sasha decided, addressing Lord Mikhail, who had tilted Janice's chin up to kiss her.

"With pleasure," Lord Mikhail said. He lowered his mouth to Charles' wife, who of course welcomed him in, clinging to his massive shoulders.

"Thank you," Valorie mouthed to the succubus. She struggled to ignore the burst of sexual tension low in her abdomen as Lord Mikhail's invisible magic swirled out from him in a storm of lust.

"Janice, no!" Charles shouted again. "Get off her, demon! In His name—"

Lord Mikhail hit him across the face without effort, as he had with John. There were worse things to do than go against a circus strongman, but not many.

"Charles!" Valorie glared at Bell and limped to her ex-fiancé, resting a hand on John's head in breathless gratitude before moving on.

She fell to her knees in front of Charles, who struggled to focus.

"You're going to lose them," Valorie said quickly, as Bell surveyed the scene with dispassionate interest. He didn't seem proud of himself, which meant he had another end game than senseless destruction, and that was the only reason she still fought to fix this instead of going straight to scratching Bell's eyes out. *"We're going to lose them. I don't want to go back, but I'll do it for you if you want to save her."*

"No," Charles said. His eyelids fluttered as his eyes rolled back in his head. Mikhail must have seriously rattled his brains. "Can't lose them. If we go back, Elian and Kendra…"

"Then you need to make another wish, Charles. No, don't poop out on me now," Valorie said, slapping his face. "You need to wish that you never came here, never saw me and never want to come to Arcanium again. That's the only way the demons won't seek retaliation. The only way you can have your family, Charles, is if you never found me. Charles!"

"But I did," Charles murmured. He was still losing consciousness. "We got our closure. Where am I…?"

"No, no, no, no, no," Valorie whispered as she slapped his face more forcefully, shook him by the shoulders, but all she got out of him was a groan and intelligible mutters. Lord Mikhail had officially knocked him out. The man had a concussion, a bad one.

Valorie looked up. The clowns were getting too agitated for John to keep them away for long. Lady Sasha held Elian from behind, her cheek against his shoulder as the succubus waited for Valorie to figure out what to do. Elian looked more than happy with this arrangement.

Lord Mikhail was still thoroughly engaged with Charles' wife, as tender yet insistent as he always was, surprisingly tender for his size.

John's burns healed before Valorie's eyes, but the wounds were shiny and black, and he continued to shudder in pain. He didn't look like he was in much of a state to take on the clowns if they decided to go through him to get to Elian.

"Bell, help them, please," Valorie begged, holding Charles' head in her lap. "He'd wish if he could. I can't. They won't."

"I have my obligations. You know this," Bell said. "*All* trespassers and those who would harm my people, no matter their good intentions or personal vendetta, belong to the demons. I cannot stop this from happening. Only you can."

"I'm not taking his children away from him," Valorie responded.

"Then it seems you have a very difficult choice," Bell said.

"God damn you!" Valorie screamed, pounding the dust with her fists. "Even when I wanted to leave, I was loyal. I've been loyal all along. Why are you doing this to me?"

"I'm not doing this to *you*, Valorie," Bell said.

The clowns darted forward, running around John to test whether he would send out his fire. He didn't.

"I wish that the man in Valorie's lap had never come to Arcanium and never will," John grated through his burned throat. "And that they, he and Valorie, still have whatever they needed from him being here. I'll do it. I'll wish it."

"You... That's your second wish," Valorie said, stunned. The terrible things going on around her seemed to fall away, and not because of magic this time. "You can't—"

"I just did," John said, his arms and legs buckling. The clowns had already passed him. He couldn't defend

Elian. Only Lady Sasha holding the boy protected him now, and she looked somewhere between pissed off and understanding. Lady Sasha and Valorie had always had a cordial relationship. It occurred to her that if the wish went through, Valorie should still fulfill her promise—if she remembered it.

"You don't even know why I need to save them," Valorie said.

"It doesn't matter," John whispered. "What matters is that you need to. And you don't have any wishes left."

"John, I… I can't let you do that."

"Too late," Bell said. He'd approached slowly and quietly, unnoticed until he chose to be. "And for the loyalty that you so aptly pointed out, my dear, I will grant you the full memory of what never happened. You, John and I will be the only ones who carry this timeline. It'll be easier to correct than twenty years." He stroked Valorie's tousled hair away from her face. "I knew you weren't ready to leave me."

"Don't make me watch his family die," Valorie said, although all demand had dissipated from her voice in relief and the release of her fear—because it didn't matter how hard Lord Mikhail had hit Charles or whether he or the clowns ate their fill from Charles' family. It would all be undone.

"I wasn't planning on it. Your second wish, fire-eater, is granted."

* * * *

In the blink of an eye, everyone but Valorie and John disappeared from Oddity Row.

Valorie spread her fingers in her lap where she'd been holding Charles' head. He was gone. He'd never been there.

She'd said her official goodbyes, but she hadn't had time to watch him leave. She hadn't been able to tell him everything would be okay. She hadn't been able to say her last goodbyes. He'd never know how close he'd been to losing everything.

He'd just had to lose her, even the memory. He wouldn't miss her — only as much as he'd missed her these last twenty years. The wish had given him the closure they'd found, what he'd needed to let her go.

But he'd been ripped from *her* this time. All at once, it wasn't enough closure for *her*.

She sat down hard on the ground and bent her legs up so that she could bury her face against her thighs. Hot tears like acid poured from her eyes before she could stop them. There was nothing she hated more than crying except crying where someone — anyone, human or demon — could see, but she couldn't stop.

John's burns hadn't disappeared when Bell had granted his wish, but they'd healed into new scars. He crawled over to her, his hands and knees whispering in the dust. When he touched her bare shoulder, she wrenched away. But as he smoothed his hand over her skin and wrapped his strong, warm arm around her, Valorie found herself leaning into him, her head against his chest, her face still against her legs, embraced in fetal position and crying as though she were a normal, heartbroken woman.

He didn't do anything but hold her while she shook and shivered, ruining her leather pants, not to mention anyone's perception of her if they happened by. Although no one had reason to be in Oddity Row, she never looked up, just in case she had to see someone's surprise at the contortionist showing the softer, leakier side of herself she'd rather die than admit she still had inside her.

Charles finding her had changed everything, brought all that dead detritus back to the surface. Now it poisoned her, because Charles was gone. Forever. And so was she. She'd been a fool to think she could leave Arcanium. A fool to believe she had any place in a happy ending outside the circus.

Eventually Valorie ran out of tears and energy. She sniffed the rest of it in, but otherwise, she didn't move. She didn't want to move.

Her throat was thick and moist. She heard it in her voice when she finally spoke, a little over a whisper.

"I'll never forget," Valorie said. "I'll never forget what you did, John."

"I don't know who he was. I don't know what you were doing with him. I don't care," John said. "I'm yours. My fire doesn't char the collar. I'll give you my third wish if that's what you ask of me."

"I believe you," she replied, this time barely a breath.

"Do you want me to take you home?" he asked.

She nodded, her throat too obstructed again to speak again.

John tucked his arms under her fetal body and lifted her up. Valorie pressed her wet face against his bare, scarred chest. She hated that she needed his comfort, but she accepted what he was willing to give.

Bell stood next to her RV, waiting for them, but he didn't stay. As soon as Valorie saw him, he nodded, arms crossed, and walked around the vehicle, disappearing from view.

"Not the bed," Valorie muttered as John carried her inside. "Can we just…on the couch?"

"Of course," John said. "Do you need water? Are you hungry?"

"Stay with me," Valorie said, resisting his attempt to leave her on the couch. She'd already shown herself to be pathetic and needy. No need to pretend anymore.

"I'm not going anywhere," he said. He lowered himself down with her.

They held each other much as they had before, except somewhere more comfortable than the ground.

"He would have been my husband," Valorie said into the silence, "before I was brought into Arcanium. We could have gone back. The option was there. But I don't think either of us would have taken it. We just needed —"

"Closure," John finished for her.

She nodded.

"I thought you were leaving," John said. "I was sure of it when I saw the way you looked at each other."

"I still may. But not soon," Valorie said. "And not with him. You'll have to endure me for a lot longer, fire-eater."

"I can live with that," he replied gently, stroking her shoulder with his smooth, scarred palms.

Valorie wound her arms around his waist and listened to his healthy, young, strong heart beating under her ear.

"I won't forget what you did, pet," she repeated in a whisper.

Chapter Twelve

"I want you to sit down here and put your hands behind the back of the chair. I'm going to have to cuff you," Valorie said, after leading him into the big top by his collar. It was a rehearsal day, so he wore thick cotton pants and a soft T-shirt instead of his leather. As commanded, though, he kept his collar on full-time.

John took in the empty ring, furrowing his brown in suspicion as he considered the plain wooden chair that she'd placed there earlier.

"What's this about?" John asked. But he did what he was told, in spite of his reluctance.

Valorie waited until she'd put the leather handcuffs on his wrists. They were the same style as his collar. She'd requested them from Bell, and he'd been more than happy to provide.

"This is your punishment," she said.

"Punishment? What did I do? Why didn't you tell me I'd done something wrong?" John asked, straining to look at her behind him.

"I'm telling you now." She ran her hand over the new scorch scars on his neck leading under the collar of his shirt. "I've been thinking about the wish that you made. It occurs to me you might not have been as unselfish as you tried to convince me you were. Yes, it was the wish I wanted Charles to make, and you repeated it the way I said it. But by making the wish, you conveniently got to keep me here, which was what you really wanted, wasn't it? You stood to gain so much that it hardly compared to the loss of a single wish. Turned out awfully well for you, didn't it, pet?"

"No!" John protested. "I mean, yes, but no. I made the wish because your guy couldn't, and I knew you'd be devastated. Yeah, it kept you here a while longer, but I wasn't thinking about you staying. I was just trying to give you what you wanted. I swear, Valorie. I didn't do this for me. If you'd told him to wish the two of you out and his family safe and happy, I would have wished that and accepted being unhappy. I *swear*."

"John, John, John," Valorie said, patting his shoulder and bending over it to look in his pretty eyes. She smiled. "I know."

"You...know. So this is... Oh. This is one of *those* punishments."

She kissed his cheek playfully. Then she returned to her position behind him, her knees against his handcuffed hands. He flexed his fingers to stroke her leather-clad legs with his knuckles.

"Lady Sasha, you can come in," Valorie called.

"What?" John said incredulously.

Lady Sasha, wearing a red leather bikini in honor of the season, stepped out from between the curtains with a knowing smirk.

A rumbling chuckle drew John's gaze up into the bleachers. For such a big man, Lord Mikhail could hide quite well until he wanted to be seen.

Lady Sasha slowly came into the ring toward where John was sitting, stroking herself over the leather.

"Wait. What's going on?" John asked.

"I think a delinquent such as yourself is acquainted with the rules of handling an exotic dancer, right?" Valorie said. "Lap dances? Stripteases?"

"Oh, fuck me."

"No, that's not allowed," Lady Sasha said, her trademark husky voice like liquid dark chocolate when she purred it just right. "*I* can touch, although you can't touch me. But I certainly can't fuck you, fire-eater. That would kill you, and your Mistress and Bell would be very displeased."

"I asked Bell," Valorie said, "and struck a deal with Lady Sasha. See, she's not supposed to touch a man in Arcanium, period. Nor a woman, for that matter, in case there's a trace of attraction. But that's because a touch often leads to more, especially at the man's insistence. It's hard for her to resist too, you know. But I owed her."

"Valorie tells me I did something for her that I can't remember because of Bell's wish-granting. Who am I to pass up a favor?" Lady Sasha asked, sliding her hands up to her breasts and squeezing them for John's enjoyment. She was probably more familiar with her own breasts than any human woman who had ever walked the earth, yet she handled them as though she'd never experienced their joys before, as though she were experiencing them the same way John would…if he were touching them.

That was the thing about incubi and succubi—they were like good escorts. They always made their sex partner feel like the first, the best, the only. Valorie guessed the demons themselves felt the same way, since they couldn't get enough of sex. Bell had told her once that as much of it as they got, they were still sex-starved in comparison to the ones who roamed free outside Arcanium.

"And I especially appreciate that your Mistress honored a promise she made to me that she didn't have to honor," Lady Sasha said. She traced the leather strings of the bikini top to the halter tie under her voluminous hair. "It inspires me to make this truly special for the both of you."

"Is that what h-he's doing here?" John had to swallow as Lady Sasha let her top fall. The leather clung to her skin, but gravity eventually won out, exposing Lady Sasha's glorious breasts. The only rival to them in Arcanium were Maya's, and Maya didn't have Lady Sasha's magic.

"My Lord Mikhail?" Lady Sasha said. "Yes. I imagine I'll have some sexual tension of my own to work out. You should also enjoy the indirect benefits when my lord and I enjoy each other within this ring, while your Mistress attends to any of your needs that might…arise."

John suddenly arched as she said *arise* in that particular way. And no wonder. The slight bulge Lady Sasha's entrance and the sight of her breasts had given him became more than slight, practically pitching a tent in his trousers.

"Oh my God," he gasped.

Valorie rested her hands on his shoulders, massaging the muscles there. She licked her lips.

Perhaps punishment wasn't the best description for this exercise. It would be such exquisite torture, really, to know that he couldn't have what Lady Sasha was offering. But he would get from the succubus what Valorie had never gotten from the incubus — touch. With his wrists bound, there was very little he could do back to Lady Sasha. The cuffs would be as fireproof as the collar.

"Now, since you're not going to be able to touch, I'm just going to have to do most of it for you," Lady Sasha said. She insinuated her long leg between John's, kicking them apart so that she could get as close as possible without climbing into his lap. Then she lifted her breasts and licked a line from one nipple, into the valley of her cleavage, over to the other before sucking it into her mouth with obvious relish.

"That's...uh...that's..." John struggled to speak, but the poor boy was losing blood flow to his brain fast.

"Delicious," Lady Sasha said, keeping her teeth tight on the nipple before letting it flick away. The flesh of her breast rippled. "You wouldn't be the first man to want to smother yourself between these breasts. I bet you've imagined me on my knees, haven't you, fire-eater, these breasts pushed together and surrounding your cock?"

The succubus rested her hands on his thighs. Her lacquered fingernails that sometimes looked clawlike from the right angle tapped mere inches from his prominent erection. The way she bent over him meant he got a front-row seat to her breasts at their fullest and heaviest. He panted heavily, helplessly.

"You can relax, fire-eater," Lady Sasha whispered in his ear, her hair brushing against his face, his mouth, his neck. "It doesn't matter how turned on you become. I can keep you from coming, and it is my delight to do so. You'll come inside your Mistress only once you have satisfied her. It doesn't matter how strong your desire is as it passes through your veins. It is only ever as much as I choose to give you. It will not be enough until I hear your Mistress scream."

"No pressure," Valorie said in his other ear.

"I'm just one man," he murmured as Lady Sasha stroked his chest over the T-shirt and Valorie teased his earlobe with her teeth, tongue and lips.

"A fine young man. Strong. I like strength," Lady Sasha said.

"Which surprises no one," Valorie said, glancing over at Lord Mikhail.

"Remember, boy, you can't come," Lady Sasha repeated. She drew her hands down his abdomen, closer and closer to his erection, which had left a damp spot in the gray material of his pants.

Then she encircled his cock with both her hands, one tightening the cotton over the head by wrapping around the shaft, the other closing over the damp head.

John shouted as though Lady Sasha had put his thumbs in screws. The tendons of his neck stood out under his collar as he threw his head back. Valorie was there for him when Lady Sasha began to twist her hands, gently wringing the cotton over his erection. Valorie stroked his scar-ridden, lovely cheekbones. It was a good thing only the people and demons of Arcanium could hear him. They knew that if they hadn't been invited to a beating, anything going on inside the tent likely felt a lot better than a whip, no matter how he sounded.

"Oh God, Valorie, God, God..." John gasped, trying once again — and failing — to get ahold of himself.

"Intense?" Valorie asked. Understatement.

"It's just her hands, and I know that. I can see it. But it's as good as five blowjobs all at once, and I... fuck... fuck... I feel like I'm going to come right now. Five times. At once. *Shit.*"

Lady Sasha had earned the smugness in her smile as she moved her hands away from his cock, gripping the soft material of his shirt as she climbed over his legs and straddled his hips. She'd kept her bikini bottoms on, but the leather was so thin that a person could see the delta outline of her folds when she leaned back. She braced her hands on his knees as she rubbed her pussy against his damp, clothed cock. Her breasts, almost unreal in their firmness, nevertheless shook as she rocked her hips. She tossed her head back with a whimper.

"Do you know what I would give to be able to take your cock in me without killing you?" Lady Sasha breathed.

"Why don't you wish it?" Valorie asked. *She* was still in control of herself. She liked being calm while John lost what little cool had been left in him.

"Because I don't need it," Lady Sasha said. "Our restrictions are acceptable for now. Bale would have it otherwise, but I'm not yet ready to ask to be something other than what I am. That's a dangerous road to open for Bell."

"How can you...speak...right now?" John panted, wrenching against the handcuffs as he jerked his hips up to meet Lady Sasha's. "How can you *think*?"

"It's doubtful that he can form words, Lady Sasha," Valorie told her in a stern voice.

"I do apologize for the oversight. I was distracted," Lady Sasha replied with a dazzling, yet somehow sultry, smile.

Valorie had to pull her hands away quickly as Lady Sasha reached for John's shoulders to draw herself upright again.

The succubus pressed her breasts against John's chest, her mouth inches from his. Every time he strained forward to kiss her, she deftly avoided him with a gleeful giggle. When they weren't the perfect escorts, sex demons were the perfect teases. Both Lord

Mikhail and Lady Sasha had made a circus career of the latter. Evasion and avoidance of physical contact was their bread and butter.

Then Lady Sasha let him catch her. John groaned, again sounding like he was in terrible, terrible pain. But he angled his mouth and deepened the kiss, getting as close to her as he could with his wrists still bound. Valorie traced the bulging muscles of his struggling arms as she watched her pet kiss the succubus. She thought she should be a little jealous, especially given how she'd felt about her previous partners. However, no matter how deeply his tongue reached, this had all been orchestrated by Valorie, and it was going to end with her as well. With enough sex magic in him to down an elephant, Valorie would still be the one to give him what he needed, not Lady Sasha.

John broke the kiss, gasping as though Lady Sasha had been sucking the air out of him. "I can't. I can't. I can't. I can't hold back anymore."

"Darling, we have only begun," Lady Sasha whispered against his cheek. She lifted herself up to press her tits against the lower half of his face. A strangled, high-pitched whimper wrenched from his throat. He screwed his eyes tightly shut, shaking his head.

She wasn't lying. Lady Sasha took her sweet time. Sometimes she stood with her legs on either side of his lap to rub her breasts over his face, teasing his mouth but slapping him lightly when he tried to kiss or taste them the way he'd tasted her kiss. When she was standing, Valorie could see how much John stood as well. He could hold up a piano with that wood.

Valorie's mouth watered. Her hands craved more than just her grip on his arms.

She thought John was going to completely break when Lady Sasha lifted up his shirt over his head to settle awkwardly behind his neck, with the handcuffs in the way of taking it off. However, that was the least of John's concerns when Lady Sasha's bare skin touched him, her belly against his as she simulated sex through their clothes, her tits sticking to the sweat on his chest. She kissed him in little flutters like moth wings, not letting him have her mouth again, but still driving him crazy over his jawline, his neck, his shoulder, his forehead, his ears.

When the first knifelike stab of arousal hit Valorie, too intense to be her own, she withdrew from John and pulled off her own rehearsal day attire until she was naked, her tight nipples and goosefleshed skin exposed in the cool air.

Lord Mikhail, too, had entered the ring, his gaze fixed upon Lady Sasha's writhing body. Valorie was more drawn to John's cries. He'd long since abandoned holding back. As strong as he was, he was no match for a succubus.

Valorie was there for John when Lord Mikhail, his trousers unbuttoned and his thick monster of a demon cock visible through the tight leather still holding him in, yanked Lady Sasha off John. He turned her around in his arms and mashed her against him. Lady Sasha thrashed as Lord Mikhail untied her bikini bottoms and ripped them down.

Valorie gritted her teeth, tightening her grip on John's shoulder the second Lord Mikhail's cock found its way into Lady Sasha's cunt. It was as though Valorie had been hit with a shock wave, and like an earthquake, the shock was exponentially more powerful near its origin. The incubus and succubus didn't usually do their nasty so close to the other cast. Valorie understood why when she nearly fainted from the pleasure that suffused her entire body, from cunt to fingertips.

John was wild when Valorie climbed-slash-collapsed onto him. He yanked against his bindings, made the chair groan, creak and crack. He calmed down some when Valorie took his face in her hands and kissed him, but he became frantic again when Valorie shoved down his cotton trousers and lifted herself up. She'd never felt him so rigid or so hot at her entrance. Sliding over him was like taking freshly poured metal into her cunt, except the heat didn't burn—at least not in the traditional sense. She moaned into his mouth, yielding to him as she took his cock into her. No. As she let his cock take her.

She was the one moving her hips, riding him, choosing the angle, yet it was his cock pounding places in her that were never usually this sensitive, even during the most violent of sex magic storms. Amazing what proximity could do.

The incubus and succubus behind her added to the soundtrack of moans and groans from the two humans making frantic love in the chair.

Valorie vaguely wondered how high Bell could hike the ticket prices if the four of them did this every evening performance.

She closed her hands on the sides of John's neck, his collar nestled into her palms, and stared into his eyes as the sparks of impending orgasm became more frequent.

"You belong to me," she whispered.

"Always," he gasped. He winced and jerked up, pounding his cock into her as Valorie let out a long cry to the catwalk heavens, but he was still in the grip of Lady Sasha's magical restraint.

Valorie knew the moment Lady Sasha let her own leash snap. John yelled like a growling roar, almost bucking her off. Valorie laughed with the giddiness of post-orgasmic bliss and held on to him as though it was a game as he came inside her.

It was a game, of course. But it also wasn't.

He slumped in the chair, leaking moans with every exhalation as he came down from the succubus's influence.

"Do I amuse you?" John asked. She was still giggling.

"Very much so," Valorie replied.

"Ah!" John shouted when she rose off of him. "John's very delicate right now, and you should try not to break him. Didn't your mama ever tell you to be kind to your toys?"

"I was also taught to put my pets through their paces," Valorie said. She patted his cheek as she dismounted then crouched down to unstrap the cuffs. "It's good for you."

"I think my heart's going to give out or my cock is going to explode — or both."

"But it felt good?" she asked.

"Well, *yeah*. Too fucking good."

"You'd be surprised what the human body can endure," Lady Sasha said.

She was clothed once again — if her costumes could be considered clothes — and too put together for having had crazed demon sex with two men, one of whom was demon himself. If she'd broken a sweat, there was nothing on her anymore. Valorie felt the same magic that cleansed the demons gust over her in a dry breeze.

"Thanks," Valorie said.

"No. Thank you," Lady Sasha replied. "Feel free anytime to repay me for other favors of which I have no memory."

Lady Sasha and Lord Mikhail exited through the red curtain.

"Ready for dinner?" Valorie asked.

John pulled his T-shirt back over his head and nodded. She started toward the curtain as well, drawing John along with his leash once more.

"Wait, they're *all* on the other side of the curtain?" John asked. "Have they been there the whole time?"

"You knew what time it was," Valorie said, poking his side. "What? Did you think they'd postpone dinner prep and eating just because we were using the ring?"

"I'm blushing, aren't I?" John said. "My throat isn't burning, but I feel like I'm going to burst into flames."

His scar tissue was better than his unaffected skin at showing a blush. Some of the scarring was almost black, but other parts had gone pearl, and that was where the blood flow became apparent.

"They're used to it," Valorie said.

When they entered the backstage, a few cast members gave them knowing stares, and a few others squirmed in their seats from their share of the sex demons' power, unresolved.

However, no one commented, although Bale glared at John with his crocodile eyes. Lady Sasha murmured something in his ear to convince him to return to his meal.

Bell stopped Valorie and John before they could get their dinner.

"Valorie has given you her gratitude, fire-eater," Bell said. "I'm obligated to show my own. It's not what you want. You still have suffering to pay."

"I know," John said, lowering his head not in shame but deference. Acceptance.

"However, you showed Arcanium great favor by protecting my contortionist. Your trespass against the clowns and the incubus and succubus can be excused because they have no memory of it, but I carry the memory of your loyalty to your Mistress."

Bell touched John's cheek with cold tenderness. John forced himself to stay still.

"I cannot yet remove your scars, nor can I take away the burn. But I can accelerate the healing, and you shouldn't get scars as extensive as this again. Perhaps in future years, with the right incentive, I can give you the relief you seek."

"Thank you, sir," John said. "I know it'll take time. But when I'm with Valorie, the flames are quenched. I appreciate that you don't let me put her in danger."

"I couldn't have that," Bell said, his gaze falling on her now. He leaned forward and pressed his lips to her cheek.

Everything had played out nicely for him, and as usual, he'd let things become complicated for everyone else for the sake of reaping his wishes. He had quite a ways to woo her if he wanted the intimacy he'd once had. She allowed the contact, but she didn't give him anything more than that.

"No, I couldn't," Bell murmured. "Have a good evening, children."

After Valorie and John served themselves, John started to walk to his usual table with Shawn and Marcus.

Valorie didn't let go of the leash. He pulled up short.

"What—" John started.

"Where do you think you're going?" Valorie asked. "Follow me."

John raised his eyebrows. His Adam's apple bobbed, but he gave the leash slack again as he followed Valorie to her usual table. Maya and Kitty watched them, intrigued, although Bell appeared unsurprised by the turn of events.

"At my feet, pet," Valorie said as she slipped onto the bench. "Dragons don't sit at the table, but they do get a place."

John couldn't hide his smile as he lowered himself to the dusty ground and crossed his legs to eat.

Valorie caressed the skin near his ear, occasionally brushing the collar that claimed him. He leaned against her leg, resting his head against her thigh when he'd finished. Eventually, she drew him in closer with her foot and curled her leg around his chest in a contortionist's embrace.

About the Author

Aurelia T. Evans is an up-and-coming erotica author with a penchant for horror and the supernatural.

She's the twisted mind behind the werewolf/shifter Sanctuary trilogy, demonic circus series Arcanium, and vampire serial Bloodbound. She's also had short stories featured in various erotic anthologies.

Aurelia presently lives in Dallas, Texas (although she doesn't ride horses or wear hats). She loves cats and enjoys baking as much as she dislikes cooking. She's a walker, not a runner, and she writes outside as often as possible.

Aurelia T. Evans loves to hear from readers. You can find her contact information, website and author biography at http://www.totallybound.com.

TOTALLY
BOUND

Home of Erotic Romance